IT'S ON
AND
POPPIN'

IT'S ON AND POPPIN'

A novel by

ALASTAIR J. HATTER

Q-Boro Books
WWW.QBOROBOOKS.COM

An Urban Entertainment Company

Published by Q-Boro Books
Copyright © 2006, 2007 by Alastair J. Hatter; Reprint
edition

ISBN-13: 978-1-933967-15-8
ISBN-10: 1-933967-15-3
LCCN: 2006936052

Reprint Edition May 2007
Printed in the United States of America

10 9 8 7 6 5 4 3

Cover Copyright © 2006 by Q-BORO BOOKS all rights
reserved.
Cover Photo by JLove (models Donald Carmichael,
Essence, and Jason Hurt)
Male model clothing provided by Tayion Clothing
(www.tayionclothing.com)

Q-BORO BOOKS
Jamaica, Queens NY 11434
WWW.QBOROBOOKS.COM

Dedication

When I initially wrote out my dedication it was to my parents, kids, and a mother and son who showed me love to the extreme, but now I feel a more sincere calling to dedicate this book to. So people forgive me, because y'all will have the dedication next time.

This book is dedicated to all the people that where affected by Hurricane Katrina. I know that your lives has been altered in a way that no one really can understand, and you may feel that you have lost your home for good, but know that the rainbow does not stop shining in the sky because there's a storm brewing and know that God does not stop showing his love and compassion for us because he takes something or someone away from us. I am from Galveston Island, Texas, and I know what it's like to endure hurricane after hurricane, having water flood your houses, cover your automobiles, and go without lights, water, and food. My grandparents were on the Island when the 1900 storm came through and destroyed Galveston, which was the biggest city in Texas at that time. The storm killed a reported 6,000 people, but guest what? Galveston's citizens rebuilt it just like Louisiana,

Mississippi, and Alabama will do for the cities and towns that were destroyed. People, if you were affected by Hurricane Katrina directly or indirectly, then my prayers go out to you and your family. I wish I could do more, so much more that I could give everyone a brand new house and car, but God's Angels already told me that he gots y'all. To the Katrina survivors, keep your heads up! Love y'all; 2005 is a good year because you're still alive. God Bless!

Chapter One

*D*ee Dee was just getting out the tub when the phone started ringing. On the first ring she was standing up in the tub. On the second ring she stepped one leg outta the tub and placed her dripping leg onto the bathroom rug. On the third ring she cursed something serious at the caller. "Damn! Mothafuckas act like people don't take baths around here." Whoever the caller was had caught her at the wrong time.

Dee Dee yanked the big beach towel off the rack and headed for her room. The phone was still ringing when she reached her room, so she figured the caller wanted one of three people who lived there very badly. The possibility that her mother could be the caller was slim, 'cause they weren't really on speaking terms. Ever since Dee Dee decided to pack her shit and move out, then move in with her two brothers, who were involved in the drug world, their relationship deteriorated. Her mother wanted the Christian life for her daughter, but Dee Dee felt that her mother's ways were choking her freedom.

She couldn't stay out past eleven, she couldn't have boys call the house, and she couldn't play R&B or rap music in the house. She loved her mother, but not enough to stay under her strict ol' ass rules that she would dish out. The calls from her mother came on a constant the first year after she moved out after high school graduation, but they slowed down drastically over the next two years. Then, during the last two years, the calls only came once in a blue moon just so she could say, "Mamma loves ya'll."

Dee Dee finally reached the phone and snatched the cordless off its base. She pounced her firm butt onto her soft, queen-sized bed and pushed the red "talk" button on her green phone.

"It's the one and only Dee Dee, so go 'head and say what's on your mind," she said as she dried her legs.

"Hey girl, what you doing?" a female voice said on the other end of the phone.

Dee Dee made the left side of her face twist up 'cause she didn't really care for Mieka. Mieka was her brother James's girl, but Dee Dee she could see Mieka wasn't nothing but a gold digger, not to mention a high-priced ho after Jay's money. Now her brother Bret's girl was more to Dee Dee's liking. She was a straight ghetto princess. Ronshay was cute as could be and a straight up project chick, but she wanted something more outta life for her and Bret, known to all as Bee, besides what the ghetto had to offer.

"What's up with you, Mieka?" Dee Dee asked, still making faces while waiting to hear what Mieka wanted.

"You seen your brother? I been paging his beeper and calling his cell phone all day and that nigga ain't even called me back yet," Mieka whined.

Dee Dee stood up and walked over to her dresser mirror. She stared at herself wrapped in the big beach bath towel and mumbled, "Nawh, I ain't seen him, you sack chasing ho." This was said in such a low tone that Dee Dee thought Mieka wasn't able to hear her words, but Mieka did hear what Dee Dee said, the words just weren't clear enough to make out fully.

"I couldn't hear what you just said, Dee Dee."

Dee Dee cracked a smile.

The doorbell rang just when Dee Dee was about to speak, which made her pause.

"Damn, who could that be?" Dee Dee asked no one in particular.

"What did you say, Dee Dee?" Mieka asked, understanding nothing.

"Listen, Mieka, somebody's at the door. I gotta go. Bye!" Dee Dee said, not giving Mieka a second thought.

"But Dee Dee . . ." And that was about all Mieka got to say before she heard the dial tone in her ear.

"That little bitch. Who the fuck do she think she is, hanging up in my face?" Mieka was pissed off. She quickly pushed redial, but before the phone began to ring she hung up and cussed out loud. "Funky bitch. Jay, where are you when I need some money?"

Dee Dee ran down the steps to the door and peered through the peephole. Prat was on the other side nervously looking all around. He had never picked Dee Dee up at her house before, but Dee Dee called him earlier so he could take her to the mall. Dee Dee wasn't dressed at all, so she was far from being ready, but when her eyes caught a glimpse of Prat in that gray, Phat Farm, velour sweat suit with all his jewels caressing his body, she instantly became horny—horny enough to fuck, which they hadn't done yet. She felt her nipples get hard just thinking about doing the nasty. Mainly Dee Dee preferred a good lick'em down low job from a nigga, which she would always get off the rip if she decided to let a nigga sample her goodies.

Dee Dee opened the door and stood right in front of Prat. She then dropped the towel, exposing her honey coated brown skin, slim waist, and hairy, bushy down low special that she chose to call "Tasty." Prat didn't know what to do as he stood there in shock, but Dee Dee was far too mature to play games when she wanted something. Knowing what she wanted was just a little something that she picked up from her big brothers.

"You gonna stay there and look like a fool, or come in and satisfy me?" she asked as she gave him a wink.

Even though she had his mouth watering and his dick rock-hard as she stood there butt ass naked in the doorway, the thought of her brothers pulling up made Prat second-guess the invitation.

"Yo, Dee Dee, what about your brothers? I ain't trying to trip with those cats," he said, still eye-balling her body.

"Prat, is you a man or a mouse? Cuz here I am basically throwing my pussy at you, and you acting scared as hell!"

Those words were strong and made him think. He threw the notion out of his head about her brothers and decided on trying to do the best impression of the porn star Mr. Marcus that he could with her fine ass. *Only one shot, cuz I may not get a second chance*, he thought.

He stepped in and closed the front door, thinking he was about to finally get the pussy. He moved in to give her a kiss, but she pushed him back, stalling him and his hormones. "Hold up for a sec. First of all, I gotta get mines off the top, Prat. Now you handle up down here," she hinted as she pointed to Tasty, "then you know what's poppin'."

Prat liked the way Dee Dee talked, all nasty and shit, but what he didn't like was the strong words she chose to use. To Prat, he felt only a nigga should talk like that, but he gave Dee Dee her props 'cause she was like no other female he had ever messed around with. He really liked Dee Dee just because of how she represented herself—no gimmicks, always keeping it real, and always saying what was on her mind.

Prat led Dee Dee's naked body over to the couch, and then motioned for her to sit down. She sat down and seductively scooted over to the left end of the couch positioning her back in between the armrest and the back of the couch. She wanted to get comfortable so she could receive pure pleasure. Dee Dee looked at Prat with a smile, then she patted her pussy which told him that Tasty was now ready to be tasted. Prat looked at Dee Dee and zoned out into his own thoughts. *Since we've been talking to each other for a while now*, he thought, *this should be the*

*start of us finally getting serious and starting a relation-
ship since she is now giving her body to me.*

"Prat, what is you waiting on?" she asked with a
tad bit of sass in her words.

Prat woke up outta his daze, not because he heard
what she said, but because she nudged him in his
head with her finger. He then grabbed hold of her
ankle and raised her right leg up in the air, resting it
on top of the backrest of the couch, which exposed
Tasty fully and openly. He noticed she had four
shades of color down low. Her body was brown, the
skin that surrounded Tasty and her inner thighs
were dark brown like the color underneath her
shaved underarms. The skin color on her pussy lips
was black, and the inside of Tasty was pink with a
tad bit of white cream.

He took his middle finger and stuck it inside her.

"Uh-uhhh, don't do that," she said as she flinched.

"Why not?" he asked, not getting the point.

"I just don't like nobody putting their fingers in
there cuz finger nails can scratch up my insides."

Prat thought about what she had just said 'cause
it was all new to him. He'd been with a lot of females and they loved the way he finger fucked their
pussies, but still, her words made him think about
how his long fingernails could scratch her insides up.
He respected her request and went straight to eating. His nose took in her scent, then his tongue took
in her taste as he licked and sucked. He was hard and
Dee Dee knew it, so that's why she raised her other leg
up and placed her foot at his crotch area. She pushed
his head back, then told him to take off his clothes.
He quickly did as she asked, except for his boxers. Dee
Dee stood up and eased her body close to his. Prat was

looking at her firm breasts and those two big black areolas that surrounded her hard nipples. Dee Dee turned and walked away from him, heading toward the stairs.

"Dee Dee, where you going?" he asked, not understanding her sudden move.

"I ain't no ho, Prat. I do have a bed."

Prat was relieved to know that their encounter was still a go. She turned back around and started up the stairs. As she walked up the steps he kept his eyes glued to her juicy booty switching away. Dee Dee made it to her room and laid on her bed. Prat walked in seconds later with his dick trying to bust outta his boxer shorts. Dee Dee turned her body around so she could scope out Prat's nude physique.

"Prat, don't move. Just stand there for a second," she commanded. Dee Dee was lying on her stomach with her head on her pillow, staring at Prat. Her feet were crossed at the ankles and her legs moved up and down.

"Stop? But why?" Prat asked, already having a clue as to why she made her request. He knew that he had a good looking body 'cause all the females he'd been with had told him so.

Dee Dee then motioned with a wave of her hand for Prat to turn around in a complete three sixty. That was her way of seeing the "goods." When he did as she asked, she began sucking on her finger seductively then shifted her eyes from the top of his body to the bottom.

"Damn boy, you got it going on!"

Prat smiled from the compliment, thinking she was talking about his body shape, but she was referring more to the size of his dick, which was looking bigger than what she had thought. Too bad she didn't give head. It just wasn't her style, but the thought did cross her mind.

Her ex-boyfriend, Mikey, had spoiled that type of pleasure for any other man in Dee Dee's life when he exploded in her mouth without warning. Dee Dee hated that so much that she was disgusted. She didn't eat for two whole weeks as she tried to get the taste outta her mind and mouth. It was just something about slimy shit that Dee Dee didn't like.

"Prat, would you do me a favor?" she asked with a sexy voice and a smile on her face.

"Yeah, you got it. What you want me to do?"

"Would you jack off for me? Cuz I've never seen a dude do that before," she asked with an innocent whine in her voice.

Prat was thinking Dee Dee was tripping for asking him to do that. Prat wasn't into masturbating, but for Dee Dee he would do it. He began, and she paid close attention to how he did it. *Long slow strokes! Long slow strokes!* she said to herself, making a mental note. Watching Prat jack off made Dee Dee kick her legs up in the air, holding her ankles with her hands.

"Come and get it," she said with lots of sexuality in her voice.

Prat stopped what he was doing and walked over to her body. He kneeled down to eat some more, but Dee Dee told him to get right on top of her. Prat looked on with excitement, thinking to himself that it was time to wax that ass. Dee Dee, on the other hand, was saying to herself, if Prat couldn't fuck with a dick that big, then he was surely gonna be let out the door with his clothes off. Prat slipped a condom outta his sock, then ripped it open with his teeth. Once it was on, Dee Dee felt the big head enter her.

She flinched a bit, but managed not to utter a sound. He positioned himself comfortably, then eased more of himself inside her nook and cranny. He felt her fingernails sink into his skin, and for once she was a lady to him, vulnerable as she succumbed to the size of his dick all up inside her pussy. Once he was on a roll, going in and out, she couldn't hold it in anymore. Word after word started flowing outta her mouth. Complete and incomplete words like, "Damn, nigga, you doing too much," or "Umm, shhittt, ouch!" Prat was giving it to Dee Dee's fine ass.

"Look Ronshay, I need you now and not later, so just set up another hair appointment and get over here, baby," Bee said as he looked around the airport lobby.

"All right, I'm on my way," she replied. Ronshay had just sat down in the salon chair when she got that call from Bee. She was trying to get all cute for her baby 'cause she knew he was coming home. She liked all the gifts he would give her and all the shopping sprees he would take her on, but she hated the game 'cause it would always bring up something unexpected, like her having to reschedule her hair appointment so she could go pick him up.

"Look Shuma, I gotta go girl. But can I get in tomorrow?"

"Girl, go on and pick up your man, cuz you know Bee is too fine to be waiting anywhere. Now get outta here. We'll do this later. Check this out though, Ronshay, if you see that fine ass brotha of his, tell him to get with a real woman and leave that skank Mieka alone."

Ronshay laughed as she stood up outta the chair. "I'll make sure I tell him, Shuma." Ronshay knew that Shuma was right. Just the other day she'd peeped Mieka out in the car with Rock.

Rock was rolling hard in the game, and while they were in his car, Mieka was just smiling like she was the owner of that BMW. Ronshay wasn't no shit starter, so whatever she saw she kept to herself, except when she talked to Dee Dee. Now that's only because she knew Dee Dee was tight-lipped on everything. Jay knew what Mieka was about before he got with her. Ronshay and Dee Dee felt it was Jay's problem, not theirs.

Mieka was known for getting the ballers and Jay fell for the shit. Rock was Mieka's ex who got married in Jamaica to his baby's mama, Danna. What was so bad about it was that he took Mieka to the Islands the week before he took his wife. Mieka still loved Rock, but she hated his wife, so to show she was still the shit she would ride around Memphis with Rock, just so it would get back to Danna and eat her up. Rock wanted Mieka, but because Danna had gotten pregnant first, he went ahead and married her, 'cause that was just how he was raised.

Roshay hopped in her Honda Civic and headed for the airport. She bumped the *The R* CD by R.Kelly. She was waiting for him to come to Memphis and shoot his video. His website said it was gonna be in three months.

* * *

Jay walked outta the bathroom at the airport in his business suit looking like he was a young black businessman. His Armani glasses made him look intelligent, so the whole camouflage shit was working. Jay and Bee both looked alike, except Jay sported a mustache 'cause his facial hair wouldn't form a goatee like Bee's did. Both of them looked the part of black businessmen in corporate America. Both had thick, three-sixty waves with an all around, super crisp edge up, and a smooth taper in the back. Jay caught up with Bee at the front lobby bar. Bee had already ordered two shots of Hennessy for them. Jay laid his black, shiny leather briefcase on the bar top and took his seat.

"I hope the Lakers beat San Antonio tonight," Jay said as he saw the commercial for the game on the TV that was mounted just above the bar mirror.

"The Lakers can't win everything, brah," Bee proclaimed as he took a sip of his cognac.

"I know that, Bee. I'm just saying, I want them to beat that ass." Jay took his shot and downed it. "Whooooh, that shit was strong," Jay said as he pounded his fist against his chest.

"Yeah, I know, but let's get outta here cuz Ronshay should be here by now." Bee left the rest of his Henny on the counter. As he got up and walked away, the bartender went to grab the tip and the glass that Bee left. Jay reached his hand out and put it on the white bartender's arm.

"Hold up, money," he said as he looked at the bartender.

"I'm so sorry, mister. I thought you were done," the bartender said.

"There's nothing to be sorry about. It's just that I'll finish it for him."

The bartender looked at Jay, wondering why the guy was dressed like he had money, but he was willing to drink after somebody else instead of buying his own. The bartender released his grip on the glass and began to wipe down the bar. Jay gripped the glass, then raised it up to his lips and downed the remainder of the liquid. "Damn, that shit is really strong!" He stood up and grabbed his briefcase. Bee was already outside when Jay reached the door.

Once he stepped outside, Ronshay was just pulling up to where they stood. As she pulled over, Bee walked happily over to her side of the car and opened the door. He extended his hand to help her out. Once she was out, she hugged him tight. She was truly in love with her man.

"Baby, I'm so glad you made it back safe," she said.

"Everything's always gonna be all good, baby," he said as he kissed her lips.

"That's enough of the smooches, ya'll," Jay interrupted.

"Hello, Jay," Ronshay said as she looked his way with her hug still tight on her man.

"It's good seeing you too, sis," Jay said with a smile.

Ronshay couldn't understand how two brothers who looked so much alike were so different, except for when it came to their sister, Dee Dee. Jay was more of a hothead type who was full of game with his mouth piece. Bee was more of the laid back type of cat, the undercover thug. He was fly as hell on the outside, but inside, a thug was waiting to escape and turn cold and lethal on somebody if the wrong button was pushed.

They all got in the car. Jay got in the back and Ronshay sat in the passenger seat while Bee took the wheel.

"Did ya'll have a good time in Texas?" Ronshey asked. She was really asking to see if they would slip up and tell on themselves about any bitches they may have met.

"It was cool," Bee said.

"Fuck that, Ronshay. It was hotter than a mutha-fucka down there," Jay jumped in and stated. As they hit the highway, Jay was starting to unbutton his shirt. Once he did, he pulled two birds from his chest that were taped to him.

"We gonna kill'em with this shit, Bee!" Jay exclaimed. Bee looked at his brother through the rear-view mirror and smiled. They were both glad that they made the new connect with the Costa Rican cat in Houston. To them the new connect meant cheaper prices than what they had been paying in Chicago, but of course most of the time it was delivered to them within the city limits. It also represented a come up, which they were seriously trying to do.

Tony was a good cat. Only 'cause Jay was fucking his cousin was he able to get introduced to him. Tony came down to Memphis one day outta the blue to see his cousin, Miya, and from there Tony met Jay. Miya had two kids, and because Jay took care of her kids, Tony respected that and took a liking to Jay. Tony had just gotten a new connect himself, and as Jay and Bee were being tested by him, he was also being tested by his people. Tony knew a lot of people, but he wasn't into front'n no one. He felt front'n little shit was bad business, but he had big plans for Jay and Bee 'cause he was feeling their style and he knew that business was a whole lot sweeter up there in Tennessee, especially if the product was rich in protein.

Right about this time, Dee Dee was feeling the pulsating from Prat's dick as it shit cum spurt after cum spurt inside his condom. She was relieved that the good pain was over, but she was a tad bit sad that the good sex was over. He had passed her test for not being a ten-minute brotha. Actually, she was surprised that he went for a nice thirty-something minutes. Through that time period, he put her body in every position one could use, including eating her pussy from the back.

Prat reached his head down to Dee Dee's chest and sucked one last time on her breast. She liked that feeling and wished he could go another round, but she knew once a nigga nutted, he didn't have another one in him right away. She raised up and headed for the bathroom. She grabbed a washcloth and soaped it up. But wiping herself clean was only temporary. As she walked back to the bedroom, Prat's eyes honed in on her nakedness. *Shit*, he thought. His eyes were glued to her whole sexy body. He wondered when they would do the nasty again.

Dee Dee got back in the bed, nestled right up against his body, and fell asleep. Prat fell asleep also, while holding her naked body tight to his.

* * *

Bee pulled up into the driveway, parked, and they all got out of the car. Bee waited for Ronshay to come around so he could kiss her. Ronshay was fine. Petite, but fine. No make-up was needed; her face was naturally cute. She was twenty-seven, but she looked like she was sixteen with that baby face of hers. Ronshay walked dead into Bee's arms and took in his big ol' hug. His choice of cologne filled her nose with a soothing scent that she loved a lot. Bee put Ronshay's hand inside the palm of his as they walked up to the house.

Jay was looking hard at the car parked on the street in front of their house. He didn't know whose it was, so he figured it must have been somebody for one of the neighbors. Jay stuck the key in the lock and opened the door. They walked in and saw clothes in the middle of the floor. Bee picked up the velour jacket in anger.

"What the fuck is this?" he shouted. Jay and Bee were now sporting fucked up mean mugs as they sensed some bullshit. Ronshay threw her hand over her mouth as she knew what was to come next with her bad tempered man and his brother who just wouldn't allow Dee Dee to enjoy her life. Ronshay knew that the car belonged to Prat, and she knew those clothes that were on the floor meant that he and Dee Dee were upstairs doing the nasty. Bee and Jay both stormed up the steps. Ronshay pounded her fist against her leg in frustration 'cause she knew what was about to go down if Dee Dee and Prat were upstairs.

The door to Dee Dee's room flew open, smacking the wall so hard the doorknob busted a hole in the wall. Prat and Dee Dee jumped up from the bed at the sound of the loud noise. Dee Dee's breasts were exposed to her brother's sight as she sat there in shock. She quickly pulled the cover up to her neck when she realized what was up. Prat was scared as hell. He didn't know what to do, but he knew those means mugs were a bad sign. Jay and Bee moved in, and Jay yanked Dee Dee's naked body right on up outta the bed, tossing her down to the floor.

"How the fuck is you gonna have a nigga in our crib? Have you lost your fucking mind, girl?" Bee shouted.

Prat was shaking 'cause this was serious. Their attention was focused on their sister. He looked at the door, thinking about making a dash for it, but they had it blocked off. He knew her brothers were crazy when it came to her. His eyes veered over toward the window, which was the only other exit. He didn't second guess the thought of escape. He decided to go for it. Prat hopped out the bed and dove out the window. He hit the ground hard, but unhurt. They all rushed to the window and looked out of it. They saw Prat lying on the ground, trying to get up.

"Run, Prat, run!!" Dee Dee shouted outta fear.

Jay and Bee shot their sister a heated stare, then broke into a run down the stairs and straight out the door. Prat staggered to his car to get in, but his keys were in his pants, which were in the house on the floor where he left them. Jay grabbed Prat by the shoulder, turning him around. Bee slung a blow at his head, striking Prat in his eye. He was already dizzy from the two story drop, so he couldn't really see the little bright stars floating around in front of his eye. Prat swung at the air trying to defend himself. His eye was swelling quick as fuck. Jay and Bee both delivered blow after blow on Prat, fuckin' him up something serious over some bullshit. Once he hit the ground, they stomped him with kick after kick.

The neighbors were outside looking at the brothers' show. One old lady looked at the naked boy being beaten down, then saw Dee Dee emerge outta the house dressed in a bathrobe, and she knew Dee Dee was the cause of her brothers doing what they were doing.

"Ronshay, help me before they kill Prat," Dee Dee begged.

Ronshay knew she was right, but she also knew that Dee Dee was partly to blame. They both ran over to Jay and Bee. They shouted at the brothers, but their words did no good, so they jumped on their backs. Prat had taken a beating, but he finally managed to rise up to his feet. His eye was swollen shut, and his face was bleeding from a gash that came from the concrete street.

"Get the fuck off of me, Ronshay," Bee shouted.

"For what? So y'all can hurt that boy some more? He didn't do anything wrong, baby, and ya'll fucked the boy up for nothing. Ya'll dead wrong."

Jay slung Dee Dee off of him and went over to lay some more punishment on Prat, but a loud BOOM stopped him in his tracks.

"Ya'll let that boy go on about his business. Ya'll did enough," the old lady shouted holding a shotgun. She knew something had to be done to save the poor boy who had taken too much punishment.

Dee Dee grabbed Prat's clothes and keys from inside. She rushed back outside and helped Prat inside his car. She drove Prat to the emergency room and waited there with him. The doctor came out to talk to her about Prat's condition.

"Doc, how's Prat?" she asked with concern.

"He's stable. There was no damage to his brain, but he does have two broken ribs, and that laceration on his forehead. The swollen eye will go down. It's just a good thing that his eyes didn't suffer any serious damage."

"Thank God," she said with a sigh of relief.

"Do you know who did that to him?" the doctor asked.

She felt bad about what happened to Prat, but there was no one who could come between her and her two brothers. She had always liked how her brothers protected her better than they did their own women, but she didn't appreciate what they did to Prat.

"No, I don't, Doc. It all happened too quickly. Can I see him?" she asked with tears in her eyes.

The doctor felt sad for her, so he allowed her access to visit Prat. Dee Dee walked in his room and saw that he had a patch over his eye. When Prat saw Dee Dee, he turned his head from her view. She walked to the other side of the bed, and he turned his head away again.

"Prat, I am so sorry. I didn't mean for that to happen. We just made love and I think I love you," she confessed. His good eye opened at the sound of those words, but he thought to himself that there could never be any *them* after what had happened.

"Look, Dee Dee, I ain't gonna tell the police what happened, but you need to leave, cuz that was just too much. Ain't nobody to blame but myself. I should have just followed my first instinct, but I didn't and now look at me."

She was hurt, but she knew he was right. She couldn't understand it, but she had come to feel strongly about Prat in just a little bit of time. She remembered the way he kissed her, the way he delivered his manhood inside of her, and the way he held her when she snuggled into his body before dozing off.

Chapter Two

Two weeks had gone by, and Dee Dee was still feeling badly about what her brothers had done to Prat. Prat was keeping his distance from Dee Dee, hoping to never see her again in life. She would blow his phone up all day, every day, just so she could hear his voice, but he never answered. He kept his word about not telling the law about who fucked him up, but not for the sake of Dee Dee. No, Prat was from the streets just like Jay and Bee, and he felt that the streets would be the place where his justice would get served and his revenge would taste sweet. He didn't know how he was gonna do it, but it was gonna get done.

Dee Dee was missing Prat in a way that was unbelievable. The day she gave herself to Prat had left her with a feeling that was eating her up, 'cause she never felt anything for a guy like how she was feeling for Prat. She sat on the couch plucking Dorito chip after Dorito chip outta the big bag. Dressed in nothing but her Looney Toons nightgown and a yellow bandana wrapped around her 'do, she sat watching her favorite soap opera, *The Young and The Restless*. Dee Dee was watching her show when her brother opened the front door and walked inside. Bee knew his sister only made that twisted face 'cause she was still tripping about him and Jay whooping Prat's ass. He didn't like seeing his sister act funny with him, even though he felt he deserved it. He and Dee Dee were very close—closer than her and Jay, so for them to be at war was killing him.

"Hey sis, what's up with you?" he asked, giving her a playful shove.

Dee Dee turned her head in his direction, looking crazy and mad as fuck as if her stare could kill him right then and there. *He got his nerve*, she thought to herself, rolling her eyes afterward.

"Look, Dee Dee, I know I'm not your favorite person on the earth right about now, but you already know we gonna look out for our lil' sis," he stated as he sat down next to her on the couch.

"Are you serious?" she asked sarcastically.

"For real though. Over my dead body will I ever let a nigga think that he can fuck you and split, then you'll be walking around here looking crazy cuz the nigga won't return your phone calls. Actually, you should be thanking us," he finished.

"Bee, I'm twenty-three years old, so that makes me legal, as well as a woman who can think. You and Jay ain't my momma, and y'all sure ain't my fuck'n daddy, so it would be nice if y'all just let me live my life so I don't have to worry about if every nigga I meet is gonna get their ass whooped by my two crazy, overprotective brothers," she proclaimed as she stood up and walked into the kitchen.

"Dee Dee, I'm sorry about homeboy, but none of this shit wouldn't have never happened if you would have took that shit to a hotel or something where we wouldn't have found out. You know what, Dee Dee? You can kiss my ass. I ain't about to explain shit to you when you already know the business."

Bee was through wasting his breath. Anything they did to a nigga was over two things. Either over their money or over their sister, and neither one of those things was brand new to Dee Dee. Since they'd made it back from Houston with those bricks, shit had been moving quickly. The word on the streets was that Jay and Bee had that good shit. Niggas dubbed it "Texas Tea." They didn't cut the dope, nor did they sell any weight outta the bricks. It was simply ounces for a gee. By selling it like that, they would be able to get more from Tony when they went to re-up, which was gonna have to be soon cause they were almost out. By sticking to their plan, they now had seventy-eight grand stashed away with nine ounces left to get rid of.

Jay was sitting in his all black Lexus Coupe, bumping some Tupac while rolling a phat blunt. He was just finishing the rolling part when his celly started ringing. Jay grabbed it off the dashboard, checked the name, and flipped it open with hesitation.

"Yo, what the deal playboy?" Jay asked as he flamed up the blunt.

"Jay, what it be like?" Nasty asked. Nasty was one of the cats Jay and Bee did business with on a regular. Nasty wasn't a dealer, but he always found somebody who wanted to get the work or the hookup.

"You tell me homie, cuz time is money."

"You think Precious will want to see me in those size nine jeans she love wearin' so much?" Nasty asked, stating the amount of dope he needed to make the sell.

Jay's eyes got big as fuck when he heard the number. He took a big toke of the blunt, then blew the smoke out so he could speak. "You ain't confused about the size she really wear, are you?" Jay asked in code to make sure he knew the price on nine ounces.

"It's all cool, playa, as long as she still looking the same way how I seen her the other day. Feel me?"

"Yo, let me get at you in a few cuz I gotta track her ass down first," Jay said, telling him in code that it was gonna be a minute until he got the dope ready.

"Yo man, I need to see her, brah, like now, so don't have me on line for more than a sec, cuz I just may be out."

Jay knew that Nasty meant that he probably wouldn't be able to keep the nigga who wanted the dope there long. Jay closed his flip phone and stepped outta his ride. Just when he was about to walk toward the house to get shit ready, he heard a horn blowing down the street behind him. When he turned around, he saw Mieka rolling up.

"Damn, why now? Outta all the times in the world, why fuck'n now?" he asked himself out loud as she pulled into the driveway. He walked over to her red Honda Accord to see what she wanted. The window rolled down and Jay felt the cool air of the A/C escape as it cooled him off some on that hot day.

"Jay, where you been? I been calling you all day and you haven't called me back not one time. You got somebody else?"she asked in a shiesty, innocent way like she was pouting.

Jay could see right through Mieka's fine ass. He knew she was full of bullshit, but that was just one of the reasons he made her fine ass his girl. He knew when she pouted like that it meant that she wanted money. He didn't mind 'cause money was how he hooked up with her in the first place. When he met her at the club, he told her that he wanted to buy up the store on her ass if she would let him take her out. Since then he'd been spending money like clockwork, but not without getting something in return. Mieka understood the mechanics involved or needed to be involved when a bitch had to keep her man satisfied. There was nothing that she wouldn't do.

Shit, girl, you make a brotha wanna hit that ass looking that damn good, but you lucky I gotta handle some business right now," he stated, slapping her on her phat ass after she climbed out of the car.

"So you ain't got time to spend with me, Jay?" she asked, not really caring as long as she got what she came over for.

"I got business to take care of right now, but it's on and poppin' in more than one way when I'm done."

She made the "tsk, tsk" sound as she turned around. Jay didn't like that move of hers one bit.

"Mieka, I'mma tell you this one time and one time only."

She looked at him, not expecting what he was about to say 'cause she had made that move just so he would give her a lot of spending cash.

"Don't ever turn your fuck'n back on me like

that, cuz that's disrespectful. Do you understand?" He held a firm, but soft grip on her arm.

"But you supposed to chill with me, not run the streets all day," she volleyed, trying to soothe his heated attitude.

"Shit, if I didn't run the streets, then how the fuck could I give you cash like I do?"

She wasn't gonna dispute that, 'cause his money was like water to her. Once it hit her hand, it was gone. She put her arms around him and went in for a kiss. Jay put his lips on hers and locked their embrace. He put his hands on her phat ass and felt on it like she was butt naked.

Bee came outside and stood on the porch as he looked at Mieka's black ass getting felt up by Jay. She was cute, jet black, and thick in all the right spots, but Bee knew she wasn't shit.

"Yo, brah! Y'all gonna stay in that position all day or what?" Bee asked as he held up a blue Wal-Mart bag in his hand.

Mieka broke her kiss off and spoke.

"What's up, Bee? Where's Ronshay?"

Bee didn't know why she was asking about his girl 'cause they didn't even talk to each other except for saying "hi" and "bye."

Mieka is so fucking fake, he thought to himself. "She at work, but Dee Dee is in the house." He knew Dee Dee didn't care for Mieka either, and Mieka would get exactly what she was looking for fucking with his little sis.

"Look, we need to talk, Bee," Jay said as he and Mieka walked up the steps. They all went inside the house. Jay and Bee headed into the kitchen to talk about what Nasty wanted.

Mieka went and sat in the chair by the couch where Dee Dee was lying.

"What's popping, Dee Dee?" she asked as she slipped her feet outta her shoes.

Dee Dee looked at her feet, thinking, *this bitch act like she's at her crib or something.*

"Dee Dee, you ain't speaking or what?"

I ain't trying to speak to your funky ass, she thought, wanting to say it out loud.

"I just don't feel like talking right now, Mieka."

"That answers my question about why you're dressed like a bum at four in the afternoon."

Dee Dee threw Mieka the evil eye 'cause she felt she was too fucking nosey. Mieka turned her head to see what Jay and Bee were doing in the kitchen, 'cause Dee Dee was watching the soaps, which was something Mieka wasn't into.

"I gotta piss," Mieka said.

Dee Dee felt she could do without knowing what Mieka had to do. For all Dee Dee cared, Mieka could have just pissed on herself. Mieka grabbed her purse and bounced upstairs to use the restroom.

Once she was done, she stood by the steps trying to hear if anyone was coming. Once she felt that the coast was clear, she crept into Jay's room and headed straight for his closet. Jay had about a hundred shoe boxes in his closet, but there was one in particular where he kept his money. She didn't see the one that he kept the money in, so she cursed out loud. Mieka heard someone coming up the stairs so she rushed back into the bathroom. She played it off by flushing the toilet and cutting on the sink water.

"Meika, where you at?" Jay asked in a loud tone.

Mieka had just opened the bathroom door to see that Jay had his hand reached out to open it himself.

"Hey boo, I was just washing my hands," she said, lying through her teeth.

"Look, five bills should be enough to cover your shopping, all right?"

Mieka gave a fake smile, but inside she wasn't too excited about five hundred dollars when she had shit already picked out that was gonna cost damn near close to what he was offering. She knew Jay had more money to give her than what he did, but she couldn't figure out why he would play her out like that right then. He reached inside his pocket and pulled out a knot of cash. Her eyes got big cause she wished she could somehow have what was in Jay's hand. Jay peeled five crisp, one-hundred dollar bills from the knot, then held them out for her to take, but when she reached out, Jay pulled his hand back in a playful way while smiling.

"Why you playing?" she asked, propping her hand on her hip.

"Who playing? You know what daddy want," he stated as he looked downward.

"This is yours, so anytime you want this, don't ask. Just take it, cuz you know I'm game for whatever when it comes to you," Meika said as she moved in close to him.

She now had his back pinned up against the wall. Her lips were on his as they kissed while her hand massaged his crotch through his baggy jeans. Jay leaned his head back and let her kiss and suck all over his neck. While Jay was enjoying himself, Mieka slipped the money outta his hand and held it tight in her fist, still doing her job to please him. She went down to her knees. After unzipping his zipper, she took his dick outta his pants and put it right into her warm mouth. As she worked her head skills on his dick, Jay felt like he needed a shot of her pussy. The head was off the hook, but when she gave head she broke him down to where he had to hit the ass even if he was in a rush.

He finally couldn't take it anymore when she made his dick head tickle. He pulled her up from off her knees and put her face forward against the wall. He reached his hand around her waist and unfastened her pants and started pulling her panties and pants down. It was a task, 'cause Mieka was thick as heck, and her pants seemed as if they were two sizes too small. He had to shift them from side to side to get them to move an inch, but he soon had them down to her ankles. Her phat, jet black ass sat right in front of his face as he was bent down. He spread those big ass cheeks apart and saw the chocolate factory. Jay looked at his all gold and diamond Movado watch on his wrist. He knew he didn't have much time to waste, so he went right to work. With dick on hard, he raised up, stuck it inside her warm, wet pussy, and pumped like he was in a race. Mieka instantly started making moaning noises. She knew what Jay liked to hear. Hell, she knew what all men liked to hear from a female while they were fucking them. The moans just intensified Jay's fucking ability, but Mieka knew that it would help Jay bust his nut quick like a virgin getting pussy for the first time. She turned the heat up a notch when she started speaking to Jay all nasty like. Then she started slamming her phat ass back against his dick like she was fucking him. Before Jay knew it, the pressure in his nut sack was building up and he knew his climax was near.

Dee Dee got off the couch. Mieka's words about her having to pee had rubbed off on Dee Dee, along with the help of the soda. She made her way up the stairs. Because she had on her house slippers, her approach went undetected by Jay and Mieka.

"I'm about to nut, baby," Jay said out loud.

Dee Dee wondered what the fuck was going on as she heard those words come outta her brother's mouth. She slowed her approach 'cause she knew from the closeness of those words that he was in the hallway. She had to check it out, so she crept up the last two steps with ease, then poked her head around the corner. She instantly started silently laughing at what she was now seeing. To Dee Dee, Mieka was getting fucked like a prostitute in an alley somewhere. Dee Dee saw the money in her hand and knew her brother had fallen for the ol' okey doke, one of Mieka's scheming ass scams. Dee Dee couldn't believe they were fucking right in the hallway. She couldn't wait to tell Ronshay about what she was looking at. She knew Ronshay would get a good laugh outta that story.

Jay pulled out and let it all ride as he squirted on Mieka's back. "Oh yeah, baby. Now that was good as fuck," Jay uttered.

"Momma take care of her baby, don't she?" Mieka reached her hand around to her back and smoothed the cum out all over it.

"That nasty bitch. Ooh, I can't wait to tell Ronshay," Dee Dee said in a low tone as she made her way back downstairs.

Dee Dee was still laughing as she got back down-stairs, and Bee saw her. He didn't know what was so damn funny to her when just a second ago she was madder than a son-of-a-bitch, but he was about to find out.

"What's so damn funny, Dee Dee?" She didn't say one word. All she did was point upstairs in the direction of Jay and Mieka. When they both started coming down the steps, Bee saw Mieka tucking her shirt back into her jeans. He looked at Dee Dee, then at his brother. Jay gave Bee a wink of his eye. Bee then knew that Dee Dee must have seen some-thing, the something being Jay and Mieka getting down. Mieka headed straight for the front door, but stopped when she saw Bee grab his brother's arm.

"You ready?" Bee asked.

"Yeah, let's ride cuz I'm already starting to get sleepy," Jay shot back.

Mieka gave Jay the cold stare 'cause he knew that she didn't like for her business to be put on front street, even to his own brother.

"See you later, Dee Dee," Mieka said as she opened the door. Dee Dee just waved her hand, not even looking her way. Mieka hissed, and then said to herself, *that bitch thinks she's something special. I shouldn't have even wasted any of my breath speaking to her.*

Jay slapped Mieka on her juicy, phat ass, which brought her up outta the daze she was in. He kissed her on the cheek as he escorted her out the door and to her car. Once she was in her car and had it started up, Jay leaned in and got a nice kiss.

"I'll see you later on, OK?" Jay said.

"You better, cuz you said tonight is all for me, remember?" she reminded him as she made puppy dog eyes.

Jay gave her another kiss, then assured her that it was definitely on and poppin' after business was concluded. Jay and Bee headed for Jay's ride. Mieka blew her horn as she pulled off.

While Bee drove, Jay rolled a blunt knowing he needed something in his system to keep him up. Bee already knew that Terry Tee needed some work 'cause he had called him earlier, so that's where their first stop had to be.

Once they reached Sunset Apartments, where Terry and his girl lived, Jay put the blunt out. After entering the black, steel security gate, Bee drove to Terry's unit. Sunset had some nice ass apartments, but Bee felt that the cost was just too high. When they reached the unit, they spotted Tawanna walking toward the trash dumpster.

When they got out the car, Tawanna walked their way. That's when they saw her sporting a nice, big, black eye. Tawanna usually looked cute and all, but today that black eye had her looking fucked up.

"Tawanna, I know you ain't been fighting with these hoes out here," Jay said.

"Yes, I have, and he gonna stay in the county jail until we go to court," she said as she got inside her red Cherokee truck.

"What you mean by saying he?" Bee asked.

She looked at both of them with a sorta mean look and exclaimed, "Y'all muthafuckin' boy Terry did this, and he ain't gonna get away with it."

Hearing that coming from her, they both looked at each other then got back in their car. Tawanna pulled alongside them and told Jay to call her later on so he could come and get his stereo outta her apartment that he lent Terry a while ago. He agreed, and she peeled out the parking lot madder than a muthafucka.

"Damn! Terry fucked her up, didn't he?" Jay exclaimed.

"Shit, that nigga hit her like she was a dude. Did you peep that big ass bruise on her leg?"

"Yeah, it looked like a shoe print, didn't it?"

"Man, we brung this dope all the way out here and now look," Bee said, holding up the bag. They didn't like carrying dope back and forth like that for fear of the police stopping them, so Jay called Nasty to see if he was still on and poppin' with his people who wanted the dope.

"Yo Nasty! Sexy said she'll see you," Jay said.

"Cool, playa. Tell her fine ass to meet me at my pop's house." Nasty wasn't doing this shit to be nice. He was more so trying to get a nice percentage outta the deal. He told dude who wanted the dope either a hundred off each ounce or a sixteenth off of each one. Either way, Nasty was walking away with eighteen hundred or more.

They pulled onto Chester Street, which is where Nasty's old man lived. Once they reached the beige, two-story house, Nasty was waiting outside. He waved them to come into the garage. Bee checked his .38 Snub Nosed, and Jay did the same with his 9mm Glock, just in case. Bee grabbed the bag and they walked coolly into the garage, but they were on alert for any bullshit to jump off.

"What's cracking, fellas?" Nasty asked as he looked at the blue Wal-Mart bag in Bee's hand. Bee sat the bag on top of the beat-up, wooden work-bench as Nasty closed the door.

"Hey, fellas. This is Manny, that cat I told you about. These are the brothers who been serving the killa shit, Manny!" They all gave dap to each other. Manny was a short, stocky, old school playa, so Bee and Jay weren't too alarmed about a jack move, but they were still on alert.

"Nasty, I ain't never seen this nigga before. How you know his ass ain't the people?" Jay asked outta Manny and Bee's hearing range.

"He's cool, man! The nigga been around longer than us," Nasty shot back, trying to ease Jay's doubts.

Jay became at ease after looking Manny over. He knew Nasty had never fucked them over before by bringing somebody over who was hotter than a fire-cracker from working for or with the police.

Bee looked over at his brother, knowing that he was drilling Nasty about the cat who wanted to get on. Bee got the look he was looking for from his brother when Jay blinked his left eye twice.

"Hey fellas, look. I know what y'all thinking, but I don't get down with the fuzz. All I'm trying to do is get on so I can get this money. Hell, if my cousin wasn't outta town right now, I wouldn't even be fucking around, especially by dishing out nine grand for nine zones. Now I heard how good this Texas Tea is supposed to be, so I gotta have it to hold me off until my family gets back."

Jay and Bee both wondered who the fuck was dude's people, but since asking questions can get you hurt in the dope business they let it ride and got down to business. Bee opened the bag and took out one zone and the digital black scale they brought with them. Jay walked over to the window to see if he could spot anything unusual. He had an irking feeling in his bones since they arrived, but still he couldn't place it since everything outside looked cool.

Manny picked up the ounce that was wrapped in a plastic sandwich bag. "God damn, this shit is strong," he said loudly as he sniffed at the bag, smelling its power. Manny quickly pulled the brown bag outta his pocket and set it on the table. From that good, strong smell he knew he could make a killing. He didn't even care to check the other shit out 'cause time was money, and with the dope he now had, he was ready to go.

"Look, the cash is all there. Fellas, I can wait till y'all done, but I got other business to handle if y'all know what I mean!"

Jay and Bee looked at each other. Bee held the stacks of bills up in the air to show Jay that it all looked good, even though he wasn't done counting yet. Jay gave the OK to his brother, so Bee pushed the bag over to Manny. That was it as he gave all of them daps and left.

Nasty already knew that he was supposed to meet Manny later on at Dan's bar so he could pick up his payment for setting up the deal up between him and the brothers. Bee raised his head as he finished counting the nine gees. Jay asked if it was all there and Bee told him that it was all good.

Nasty was looking like a hungry dog, waiting for someone to toss him a bone to eat. Jay spotted Nasty as he watched Bee sticking the money in his pockets, so he walked over to him and wrapped his arm around his shoulder.

"Look, playa, that was nice looking out on the sell. Now, do you have a problem with getting hooked up tomorrow?" Nasty knew that Jay and Bee were two of the few niggas that were in the game who were straight up and about their business, so he had no problem with getting his later on. What he would be getting from Manny tonight would hold him anyway. Nasty said OK and gave Bee and Jay some pounds as he walked them outside. Once they drove off, Nasty went right inside the house and called his girl so she could come and pick him up.

Jay and Bee went back to smoking as they rolled down Main Street. The night air was cool and the moon was full, lighting up the whole sky with the help of all the stars.

"Man, we gonna need to re-up soon, Bee," Jay suggested as he blew out the weed smoke. When he heard his brother say those words to him, it made Bee realize that something was missing. Then it hit him.

"Jay, hurry up and go back to Nasty's crib," he demanded abruptly.

"What we need to go back there for? Nasty know we gonna take care of him tomorrow," Jay replied, looking at his brother with one hand on the steering wheel, coasting.

"Brah, I done fucked up big time!!!"

"How?" Jay asked, now paying full attention as he stopped smoking.

"Remember when I was counting the cash? Well

when you gave me the OK to let the nigga gone about his business, I didn't take the other nine out the bag when I passed it over to him," Bee explained, clutching his fist.

Jay whipped his ride right in the middle of the street as he busted a U-turn, then floored the gas. Once back at Nasty's crib, they hopped outta the ride, eager to holla at Nasty. They walked straight to the garage door hoping that Nasty could lead them to ol' boy. But they saw that the lights were off in the garage, which meant that Nasty wasn't there. So Jay figured it wasn't nothing else to do but go knock on the front door, even if it was twelve thirty in the morning.

While Jay walked up to the front door, Bee stood there tripping, wondering how he could slip up like he did. The trashcan sitting on the side of the house was overflowing with trash. The smell was unbelievable. Bee was so heated with himself that he kicked one of the bags that was on the ground. The cat that was hiding in the trashcan jumped out, knocking the can over. A light upstairs flicked on, no doubt from the noise. Jay ran back to the side of the house with his Glock drawn, expecting his brother to need help. Just when Jay was about to ask Bee what was up, they heard the sound of the window right up above them screeching as it was being raised. Jay and Bee looked up, waiting for Nasty to stick his head out, but when the head finally appeared out, they found out that it wasn't the head of whom they expected.

"Hey down there. What y'all doing on my property," the old man shouted.

Jay reacted quickly, seeing that it was Nasty's father. "Sir, we came by to see Nasty."

"I wish that boy would quit having people call him by that name. His given name is Latrell. Anyway, he's not here. He left with that girl of his a little bit ago," the old man stated.

Jay and Bee both apologized for bothering him then walked back to the car. Upset and now getting irritated, they drove around hoping to spot one of them. Nasty didn't have a celly, nor a beeper, so there was no way of getting in contact with him. The girl Nasty kicked it with was a new chick that he had just started seeing, so Jay and Bee didn't know where she stayed.

Bee asked his brother if he thought the nigga Manny would bring the dope back. Jay turned and looked at his brother giving him a face that said, *Are you serious?* Both of them knew the real truth, which was anybody who got caught slippin' in the game had to just chalk it up as a loss, but not these brothers. They was out there trying to come up, and taking shorts wasn't the way to come up. Jay and Bee were on the paper chase, which meant anyone who got in their way would pay the price, even if the brothers were the ones at fault.

A few days later, Dee Dee was awakened by a loud noise. She got up out of her bed and walked over to Jay's room. She paused for a second when she saw Mieka's sheisty ass in Jay's room going through all his shoeboxes. *This bitch got her nerve,* Dee Dee thought. Dee Dee turned around unnoticed and went downstairs to see if her brothers were in the house. She looked in the kitchen, then in the other rooms downstairs, and found no one. She looked out the window to see if Jay or Bee's car was outside. She saw nothing except for Mieka's car in the driveway.

"Where the fuck is the money?" Mieka shouted out loud. Dee Dee looked back upstairs. She knew Mieka was up to no good, going through Jay's shit, but that all was about to change. Dee Dee walked back upstairs and headed straight to Jay's room. When she looked through the cracked door she saw Mieka with two shoeboxes on the bed. She was sticking money in her purse. *This bitch is stealing, just robbing my brother blind*, Dee Dee thought. Dee Dee pushed the door open quietly, and then cleared her throat loudly. Mieka turned around quick as fuck in a startled way, dropping a stack of money on the floor right in front of her. Dee Dee had her back against the wall with her arms crossed over her chest and a smirk on her face.

"Hey, Dee Dee," Mieka said, not knowing what else to say because she knew she was busted. The thought of Dee Dee telling Jay about what she was doing haunted her 'cause she didn't want to get her ass kicked and dismissed.

"I thought you was asleep girl," Mieka said as she picked up the scattered money.

"I was, until a thief in my house woke me up."

Mieka looked up and stared at Dee Dee with an expression on her face like she wasn't trying to steal.

Dee Dee switched her pose to where her hands were planted on her hips, giving off a little ghetto body language.

"Dee Dee, I wasn't stealing. Jay asked me to come and get this money," Mieka tried to explain.

Dee Dee knew Mieka was lying through her fucking teeth. She knew Jay didn't like anyone touching his money. She also knew Mieka had been stealing from Jay for a while, but she didn't care 'cause she knew that a thief always got busted sooner or later.

"Mieka, do you think I was born yesterday or something?" Dee asked as she walked over to the bed.

"OK, Dee Dee, maybe he didn't send me to come and get this money, but your brother is balling, making all this cash, and now he wanna give me chump change. When we first hooked up, he wasn't tight on his money like that."

Dee Dee didn't care for what Mieka was talking about 'cause it was all bullshit. The bottom line was that Mieka was in her house, uninvited, and stealing from her flesh and blood. Dee Dee reached for the phone that rested on the nightstand. She felt that she had heard all she could stand from a lying, stank bitch like Mieka.

"Hold up, Dee Dee, I just told you why I did it," she whined.

"Now that isn't supposed to make me forget about this, now, is it Mieka?" Dee Dee asked, smiling devilishly.

Mieka wanted to just jump on the bed and start whooping Dee Dee's ass, but she knew that would just add to her problems.

"Look Dee Dee, how about me and you go shopping? I know how much you like that," Mieka suggested, trying to ease shit over.

"Shopping! Now come on, Mieka. What do you

take me for? A sucker? I probably got more clothes in my closet then you got in yours. Now, what I do need is a ride. Can you buy that?" Dee Dee asked, putting it out there, testing the waters. Dee Dee saw that Mieka wasn't letting anything ride outta her mouth, so she reiterated her last words. "Well, can you?"

"Damn, Dee Dee, you really are like your brothers, but I respect that."

Dee Dee waited for the answer that she was looking for 'cause to Dee Dee the matter was non-negotiable. It was either the ride or have Jay put that ass to sleep. After coming to her senses, Mieka finally agreed. Dee Dee was now satisfied, so she went in her room to get ready 'cause their deal was for today only, which is how Dee Dee saw it anyway.

Mieka knew that she would now need some extra money, but to take more from Jay would be insane as he would be sure to notice, seeing as she had taken three thousand out already. Mieka figured that she would just have to go into her own stash. She cringed just at the thought of making her rainy day stash deplete.

Mieka restacked the boxes, hoping that she was putting them back in order. She made sure, though, that the money boxes got placed back in their original spots, trying her best not to leave any signs that they had been fucked with. When she finished, she thought about burning off on Dee Dee, but soon changed her mind when Dee Dee came outta her room as she was walking down the steps. Dee Dee was happy that she was about to get her very own ride. The thought about how she was about to get it made her a little uneasy, but then again, she thought about how Mieka had been killing her brother all this time without him saying anything. This was her moment to get her a ride, even if it was at the expense of Jay's pocket.

They both got in Mieka's ride. When Dee Dee closed the passenger door Mieka looked at Dee Dee as if she was crazy as fuck. Dee Dee hadn't just closed the door. She had slammed it, but not intentionally. Still, Mieka was looking at Dee Dee like she done lost her fucking mind. But Mieka had to chalk it up as a lesson learned, 'cause Dee Dee was holding a trump card against her which would stand up in any ghetto court hearing, if there was ever such a thang.

After leaving the second of the two car, Dee Dee became irritated with the spots that Mieka had chosen to take her. She finally spoke up.

"Mieka, we been to two car lots already and both of those muthafuckas was a piece of shit. And they didn't have anything that I liked, so what's next?"

Mieka acted like she didn't even hear Dee Dee. She was only trying to find Dee Dee a ride, not a gotdamn Lexus or something. As they rode around she finally spotted a nicer car lot that looked like it had some affordable potential. She pulled into the car lot and parked. They both got out. Mieka spotted one car and called Dee Dee over to come take a look, but on her way, Dee Dee spotted something that she knew she just had to have. Mieka saw Dee Dee posted up on a beige 1999 Acura Integra. The pricetag on the windshield read $6,599 with the letters A/C underneath the price, like for that price it wasn't supposed to come with it.

"Mieka, this is it. I gotta have it. Isn't it just the

cutest thing?" Dee Dee said with excitement, but also adding sass to it just to piss Mieka off.

Mieka's blood was boiling and her pocket was burning from how much the car would cost, but, nevertheless, she had to buy it or deal with losing her money-making man. She saw a white salesman coming her way so she dropped the attitude that Dee Dee had caused her to get.

"Hey there, girls. Is there anything that ol' John here can do for you? Now before you answer that question, I just want to let y'all know that at this here car lot we do business the right way. No credit. No job. Bad credit. Welfare checks. Social Security checks. We can help you get a car at John's. As long as you got money, John will fix you up with a ride. Now, what can I do for you two divine ladies?" he asked with a wink of his eye.

Mieka said to herself, *I know this crooked ass ain't referring to me as a welfare recipient.* Mieka went straight for the jugular. She knew that car dealer was full of shit, so she knew what she had to do.

"Look, here, John, I got five thousand for this car—cash," she stated, knowing that he had paid less than that for it.

John went into deep thought. He knew if she had five grand, then she had to have even more on her. Hell, all the rings on her fingers and all those gold necklaces that were wrapped around her neck said that she wasn't working for McDonald's. He was about to deny her offer and raise it, but Mieka was one step ahead of him, giving him a look back that said, *Don't blow this sell and be stuck with trying to sell this car for another five months.* Yes, Mieka was beyond hip to the games that car salesmen played, thanks to her ex, Rock.

"You got five thousand cash with you right now?" he asked, looking hard.

Mieka reached her hand inside her purse and pulled out a knot. All that green made the white man lick his lips as if the money was a juicy Porterhouse steak. "It looks like we can do business, little lady," John stated, extending his arm out to show her the way to his office.

While Dee Dee was getting the feel of her new ride, Mieka yelled to her so she could come inside and sign her name on the dotted line. Now in the office the white man told her to ink her signature on three pieces of paper that he had resting on his desk in front of him. Once done with the signing, he gladly handed Dee Dee the keys, the title, and her thirty-day tags. Dee Dee was out of that office quick as fuck with a smile on her face that was the size of the sun itself, and brighter.

When Mieka came outside Dee Dee had already placed the tag in the window and was pulling outta the parking lot. Mieka yelled Dee Dee's name, but she was already pulling onto the street about to merge with the traffic.

"I can't believe that heffa," Mieka said as Dee Dee disappeared in the traffic. Mieka was heated. She had paid for the car, and really didn't even know what it looked like or how it drove. Mieka wished bad shit on Dee Dee right then and there. She even prayed to God, asking for Dee Dee to get smacked by a Mack truck.

Dee Dee was riding down the street chilling away

when she saw a car wash. She knew she had to be the one to give her baby its first bath, but after that she promised herself that the same crackheads who washed her brothers' shit would wash her shit too. She pulled into the car wash, and when she stepped outta the car she caught all the fellas' attention with that fine body of hers. Dressed in a halter top with some hip hugger shorts and some wooden clogs on her feet, she went to work.

After Dee Dee was done washing her baby she stepped back and admired the luster and shine the bath helped bring out. Dee Dee was happy she had a car, a car that wasn't a piece of shit, and looked almost new. No more would she have to beg her brothers to let her borrow their rides. No more would she have to bum a ride from others. Dee Dee was now riding good in her clean Acura.

When she got inside the car she felt that something was missing. She couldn't put her finger on what it was right then, but she knew there was something. The stale smell of a car being parked on a car lot was still inside the interior, so she went to get some air fresheners to bring life back to the inside. When she reached the air freshener machine, Dee Dee smiled 'cause what she felt the car was missing was now looking her dead in the face. Every car should have something hanging down from the rearview mirror, and now she had something to hang from hers to give her car life.

Dee Dee hopped in and closed the door. With the air freshener now dangling down from the mirror, she just had to give it a twirl. Dee Dee turned the radio on, thinking to herself that she couldn't wait to bump some of her favorite CDs in her ride.

But for now, since she didn't have any with her, she'd settle for the radio station which was playing one of her jams by Busta Rhymes and The Flip Mode Squad.

As she rode down the street, Dee Dee decided to cruise through her old hood. Once she hit the corner she was there. Everything and everybody was out and making shit happen. Her mother had long since moved them from this part of town to keep them safe. Jay loved the streets and Bee followed his older brother wherever. This neighborhood was where Jay and Bee got their hustle on.

The fellas who were hustling on the block spotted Dee Dee's driving the unfamiliar ride. With her brothers not being around, some of them saw this as a chance to seize the moment by trying to get her to look, or better yet to get her to stop. Dee Dee paid them no mind. As she turned the corner, she damn near had a heart attack at who she saw shooting dice. There were her brothers, chillin' on the corner, winning some money. She knew she wasn't allowed over in this part of town. Jay and Bee weren't having that shit. Dee Dee got herself together and busted a left at the next street, flooring the gas pedal to get the hell up outta there, for fear of catching drama.

Dee Dee calmed down after getting outta the area. Caught up in a song, she didn't even realize that the red light she was stopped at had turned green. Just when she was about to take off, she noticed the light switched to yellow. The people that were behind her were pissed off. They were waving their fists, sticking their middle fingers up in the air, and shouting obscenities.

Dee Dee floored the gas, leaving the angry people still stuck at yet another red light. She felt bad for what she had caused, but when she saw the green, two-door Riviera with chrome Enkei rims pass by her, she almost broke her neck as she turned around and tried to get a glimpse of Prat. He was moving so fast she didn't think she could catch him if she tried. She waited till there was an opening in the other lane, and once she felt it was clear, she busted a U-turn, catching road rage honks from other drivers. She hit the gas, running through three red lights just to be able to talk with Prat.

When she finally caught up with him, she spotted him parked in front of a red brick house. She was about to stop, but she changed her mind when she saw a female coming outta the house, headed for his car. The female gave Prat a long kiss with her hands on his cheeks. Dee Dee was crushed. She eased by the car, taking in a close up. She hurt so much that her eyes flooded with tears. She sat on the side of the road for an hour before heading back to the house with more shit on her mind than the law allowed.

Both Jay and Bee were at home with their women. Bee was drinking a MGD, while Jay and Mieka were smoking a blunt. Dee Dee stormed in the house, slamming the door behind her. Everybody looked her way and wondered what that was all about. Mieka's first thought was that Dee Dee had wrecked the car already. Ronshay got up and went to see what was bothering Dee Dee. She saw Dee Dee crying and Ronshay knew that the one thing a girl needed when tears were dropping was a friend. Ronshay knocked on the door softly before entering.

"Go away. I don't wanna be bothered," Dee Dee yelled.

"Hey girl, it's just me," Ronshay said as she peeped her head through the door.

"Ronshay, I ain't trying to be rude, but I really don't feel like being bothered right now," Dee Dee stated as she laid her face down on her bed.

"Dee Dee, come on, girl. This is me—Ronshay. Now you can't tell me that something isn't eating you. What it is, I can't imagine, but those tears are telling me that you're hurting bad."

Dee Dee raised her head up off her pillow. "Ronshay, I don't know what it is, but I can't stop thinking about Prat or what my brothers did to him. I'm crying cuz I just seen him kissing another girl, although I can't blame him after what they did to him. I just don't get why I'm feeling like my whole world has crumbled, you know?" Dee Dee confessed as she wiped away her tears.

Ronshay felt Dee Dee's pain. The tears in Dee Dee's eyes and the words were starting to make sense to Ronshay. Dee Dee was hooked on a nigga, which was unlike her.

"Say girl, I never knew the one and only Dee Dee to be sweating some nigga. Shoot, if I didn't know any better I would think that you was in love, or was the dick just that good?"

They both started laughing hard. Ronshay was glad what she said was funny enough to lift Dee Dee's spirits. Dee Dee knew what Ronshay had said was true. Dee Dee was sexy, cute, fine, and deep down she was just like her brothers—crazy. When it came to hooking up with a nigga Dee Dee did the choosing, not the other way around.

Meanwhile, downstairs Mieka rushed outside the house, leaving Jay and Bee inside. She was hoping that the car wasn't fucked up. Mieka couldn't wait any longer. She had to see what was up with the car.

Jay and Bee were thrown for a loop at all the shit that had just happened around them. Dee Dee came in the house tripping. Ronshay took off upstairs like she was Dee Dee's momma, and Mieka ran outside like she was about to be sick or something. Jay and Bee went to check on Mieka first, and as soon as they stepped onto the porch they spotted the beige Acura Integra in their driveway. Mieka was happy to see the ride was still intact, but Jay and Bee were heated that somebody had parked their shit in their driveway. They spotted the thirty day tag taped to the back window of the ride.

"Who the fuck parked their shit at our house?" Jay asked out loud, not to anybody in particular.

Mieka jumped at Jay's loud tone of voice. Now she was sweating bullets, knowing that the inevitable was about to go down. She kept her mouth quiet and slowly crept back up on the porch. Jay was checking out the thirty day tags while Bee scoped out the inside. What he saw made him call his brother.

"Jay, check this out." He pointed at the purse in the front seat. They both knew the purse belonged to, Dee Dee. Mieka was really sweating bullets now. Her heart was pounding fast as hell. This was one day she wished she wasn't over there. She cursed herself for buying Dee Dee that car. Now it had all come back to haunt her. Dee Dee didn't follow the plan they had discussed, which was to keep the car outta sight for a while until they could come up with a good lie on how she got the ride. No, Dee Dee had the muthafucka right smack dab in front of two crazy niggas' faces.

"Bee, you know who ride this is?" Jay asked, looking at his brother.

"Nawh, it's probably some little nigga car that she fucking with," he replied, smiling, feeling cool that they didn't have to whoop anybody over a car.

The thought that the car belonged to some young nigga made Jay upset. All he could imagine was that the car belonged to some young punk who was hotter than a firecracker, hustling on some block in front of the police.

As they talked, Mieka slipped back inside the house hoping to holla at Dee Dee before her brothers got to her. She shot up the stairs, heading for Dee Dee's room. When she got there she slowly pushed the door open just to see Ronshay and Dee Dee sitting on the bed talking.

"Dee Dee, we need to talk, girl," Mieka said with a straight face.

Ronshay couldn't believe that Mieka had barged in on them like that, and the look on Ronshay's face was telling it all as it screamed out the words, *Damn bitch, can't you see we were talking?* Ronshay didn't trip, though. She rubbed on Dee Dee's right leg gently then told her that she would holla back after they got through. As Ronshay headed for the door, Jay and Bee busted in. Ronshay jumped back quick as fuck to avoid being hit by the opening door. Mieka's mouth cold dropped 'cause she knew shit was about to hit the fan.

"Dee Dee, whose car do you got?" Jay asked shouting.

Dee Dee wasn't up for none of her brothers' bull-shit so she blew up. "It's my damn car." Mieka's heart sank dead into her stomach 'cause she knew more questions where about to be asked which would most likely lead to her having to answer some. She wanted to just slip out the door and dis-appear. If she did, she felt that once Jay hooked back up with her she would be able to smooth things over with a little world class head job, and some of her bomb ass pussy skills.

"What the fuck you mean by saying it's yours?" Jay asked, looking at Dee Dee curiously.

"Did I fucking stu . . . stutter?" she shot back as she got out of the bed and walked to the window.

Everybody in the house was shocked to hear her say that, including Ronshay. But Mieka wasn't shocked. She was beyond shocked. She was scared shitless.

"Hold up for a sec, Dee Dee. Where the hell did you get money to buy a fuck'n car at because if I'm not mistaken the last time I checked you asked me for some money?" Jay inquired with a mean streak lacing his voice.

Everybody was looking on, waiting to hear her response. Dee Dee looked at Mieka. Mieka was silently begging Dee Dee not to tell on her, but then Dee Dee figured why not kill two birds with one stone, 'cause she felt Mieka's time was up anyway with all the sheisty shit she had been carrying on with.

"Ask your girl, cuz she the one who bought it for me."

All eyes went straight to Mieka, who was trem-bling with fear. She didn't know what to say, and Jay wanted answers.

"Where the fuck did you get money to buy somebody a car, cuz the last time I checked I can't remember letting you borrow any money," he said, displaying a killer look on his face. Jay had an idea about where she had gotten the money from, but he couldn't figure out why she would spend Rock's cash on somebody else. He had heard stories about her creeping around with Rock from other females, but he dismissed those rumors 'cause he knew the females that told him those thangs were just jealous hoeshating 'cause they wasn't in Mieka's shoes. But now he had some kind of proof 'cause he knew he didn't give Mieka enough money to buy a ride like what was outside.

"You think I'm playing games, girl? You better start saying something," Jay shouted, sending chills through everybody that was in the room.

Those words brought Mieka outta her shocked mode. She just told herself to stay tough. She stared right back at Jay with a girly expression that said, *don't be yelling at me*. Jay changed his persona real quick as his arm raised and his hand locked onto her throat with force. He shoved her back against the wall, signaling to her that he was serious and when he wanted to know something that meant he wanted an answer right fuck'n then. Mieka was gasping for air as she tried to break Jay's hold from her neck, but he wasn't budging. Jay's grip was tighter than a pair of vice grip pliers. She tried to say the words "please stop," but they came out muffled because she was being choked to death.

"You gonna tell me what I wanna know?" he asked, tightening his grip. Mieka blinked her eyes twice as if Jay knew that meant yes. He must have known 'cause Jay released his grip and Mieka slumped down to the floor on her butt, holding her throat.

"Start talking," he stated, standing in front of her.

Mieka knew she had to say something if she didn't want to wind up with her body jacked back up against the wall.

"Jay, baby," she sobbed with tears streaming down her cheeks. "I only took the money from you cuz you didn't give me enough."

Jay's mouth dropped open when he heard the words "from you" come outta her mouth. And the words "you thieving bitch" popped right into his head. He couldn't believe that she had stolen from him. He was so heated that he reached out to yank her up. Her eyes got big as hell at seeing his hand, but Jay released her shirt and told her to get her funky, stealing ass outta his house. Mieka got up off the floor looking silly. She looked at Jay, who only held the bedroom door open so she could keep stepping. She then looked at everybody else. The last person she stared at was Dee Dee, and she felt she had to say something to her.

"Thanks a whole fucking lot, Dee Dee. I hope you're happy now," she stated as she walked outta the room looking stupid.

As Mieka left the house, Bee patted his brother on the back. Once Jay turned around, Bee spoke.

"Brah, I'm 'bout to check the stash, all right?"

"Yeah, do that, playa, cuz me and your sister here is about to rap on some shit," Jay responded.

Ronshay followed Bee to Jay's room to count the money 'cause she knew Jay was about to go off on Dee Dee, and she didn't want to be in the line of fire of blood relatives unless it involved Bee.

"Dee Dee, you stole from me, your own fucking brother?" he asked, staring at her back.

Dee Dee turned around and sat on her bed. "Nawh Jay, your bitch stole from you, and if you wasn't so pussywhipped you would have been able to see that she been stealing from your ass all along."

Those words stung Jay so badly that he raised his hand and slapped Dee Dee across her face. Dee Dee's hand quickly went to the stinging area on her face, but she didn't utter one word. She just stared at Jay, and rose up off the bed. Jay wanted to tell his sister that he was sorry, but he wasn't about to admit he was partially to blame for what happened.

Dee Dee reached into the top drawer of her black dresser. What she pulled out had Jay all fucked up, 'cause she was pointing the same 380 chrome gun at him that he gave to her to protect herself.

"Bitch ass nigga, I should pop your funky ass for hitting me," Dee Dee yelled.

Ronshay and Bee immediately stopped counting money and rushed back to the room. Both of them knew those two acted a fool during arguments, but what they were now looking at had them fucked up. Dee Dee had a blank expression on her face as she held the gun straight out, pointing it at Jay with two hands locked on the steel.

"What the fuck is ya'll doing?" Bee asked, looking shocked as hell.

"Dawg, your sister tripping," Jay whined, standing scared at gunpoint. Dee Dee had her target locked and the look on her face was the same stare that Jay and Bee got when they had it in for a buster ass nigga or bitch.

"Dee Dee, please put that gun down before somebody gets hurt," Ronshay pleaded.

"This nigga slapped me. I ain't putting shit down until he apologizes."

"You slapped Dee Dee, man?" Bee asked, now realizing what had happened.

"He won't get a chance to do it again and that's for real. Now if he don't get on his knees in ten seconds and apologize, he's going straight to the hospital. Trust," Dee Dee said boldly.

Dee Dee started counting and Jay still wasn't budging, not until Bee laughed and told him that their sister didn't look like she was playing. Now she was on eight, and when she got to nine she pulled back the chamber like she was an expert in handling a gat. With the sound of the chamber cocking back, Jay's eyes bugged out, but when she released one of her hands off the gun and angled the gun down in a tilted position, showing she was serious, Jay quickly dropped down.

"Now apologize, punk," she shouted.

"I'm sorry, Dee Dee," he said.

"I'm sorry, too," Dee Dee said, then released a back hand bitch smack on Jay's face, making his smirk disappear. Jay rose up quick as fuck with a crazy, heated look. Bee grabbed him to prevent him from reaching Dee Dee.

"Chill out, playa. She just got you back, plus you didn't have any business hitting her in the first place," Bee said honestly as he held his brother from the back.

"Fuck both of ya'll," Jay shouted in anger as he struggled, breaking his brother's hold then walking out of the room.

"Dee Dee, you're a cold piece of work, but you were dead wrong for pointing a gun at your own brother," Bee stated.

"Nawh, he was wrong, Bee, for putting his fuck'n hands on me," she exclaimed, still heated.

After seeing Dee Dee act like she did, Bee knew his sister would never take any shorts from a nigga, let alone from a female.

Chapter Three

Jay was sitting in his car mad as hell about what had happened in the house. He pulled a blunt outta the Philly box, needing something to help calm his nerves. The flame from his lighter was so high when he fired up that it caught the peach fuzz on his face. He shook that off, but he was still pissed off.

Jay and Bee were now outta dope, especially after leaving those nine ounces in the Wal-Mart bag with the rest of the dope they gave Manny. Nasty was supposed to give Jay a call at nine letting him know Manny's whereabouts, but still no word had come from him. They couldn't find where Manny was earlier because he had gone outta town. Nasty had been hard to find also because the little dope that people gave him went straight in his and his girl's noses for three days straight.

Manny knew he had come up when he saw nine extra ounces in the bag. Honesty wasn't on his priority list, so he wasn't going to give shit back. He had paid his dues as a youngster, getting swindled here and there. Now, by being a playa in the game, he felt that Jay and Bee had slipped up, and if they were ever to come at him asking where their dope was at, he would just play stupid and ask what dope.

As Jay took drag after drag on his blunt he started easing into a calmer state of mind. He didn't like the fact that he had hit his baby sister, nor did he like how his sister pulled a heater on him. Looking on the bright side of things, Jay felt that Dee Dee had shown him something that was really impressive. The way she held that gun, the way she caught him by surprise, and the way she exposed Mieka and her stealing ways told him that his baby sister had the words, "The Baddest Bitch," written all over her. Thinking of the qualities that she possessed brought a smile to his face. The thought of him, Bee, and Dee Dee working together to build an empire was something he wanted badly, and now that she had shown him she could handle herself, he wanted her to learn the ways of moving and handling dope.

His phone suddenly started to ring, which made him fumble the blunt onto his lap. The fire from the blunt singed his pants, making him move franticly in his seat as he patted out the fire. When he finally found the blunt, it had scarred his leather interior seat with a burn hole.

"Ain't this about a bitch," he shouted in anger, looking at his now fucked up interior.

The phone was still ringing when he grabbed it. He flipped his celly open and placed it to his ear.

"Yo, what's up people?" he said into the phone.

"Peoples, it me," Nasty responded.

Jay was happy that Nasty had called 'cause it

could only mean one thing—that he had located Manny.

"Tell me something good, Nasty."

"Well, he's back."

Jay clenched his teeth at the thought of Manny being back in town. He figured now they could get paid back what homeboy owed them, one way or the other.

"Give me that nigga's address, Nasty." After hearing all that he needed, Jay decided to roll over to the address himself. When he got there he contemplated going up to the door and kicking it in, hopefully finding Manny inside so he could pistol whip the shit outta him until payment or the dope was in his hands. He had opted on that move when the door suddenly opened and he saw Manny come outside dressed up all slick and shit. Manny hopped in his Mercedes S-Class and pulled off.

Jay decided to give Bee a call at the house and tell him about Nasty finally calling. Bee was relieved to hear the news. Now he felt that they could get paid for the shit Manny owed them. Bee asked Jay where he was at, and Jay explained to him how he had just trailed Manny to a bar over on Loan Avenue called Johnnie's. Bee told him that he was on his way, but Jay slowed his brother's roll by telling him that he wanted him to bring Dee Dee along. Bee didn't understand why Jay would need or want their little sister to come along when they were trying to handle business in their usually ruthless way. Jay told his brother that he would explain everything when they arrived.

Jay sat in his car slouched down, smoking on a blunt and listening to rain hit his ride. To be a Monday, he noticed that the bar had a crowd, at least that's what he suspected from the look of all the cars parked in the parking lot. As he sat eyeing the door of the bar, he contemplated what he wanted his sister to do, but first he had to get Dee Dee to agree to help them out. He knew it wouldn't be an easy job persuading her, 'cause she was a hothead, not to mention how he knew she would probably still be mad at him for slapping her. The one thing he knew he could offer Dee Dee was the right to keep the car if she did what he wanted. The weed flowed outta the blunt and into his mouth. A little smoke escaped outta his nose as he held the smoke in, getting high.

Bee finally got his sister to agree to come along for the ride, but she made it known to Bee that it was only 'cause of him and not because of Jay. She loved her brothers and all that they did for her, but she couldn't forget how they had wronged Prat by beating him down, and she sure the fuck couldn't forgive Jay for putting his hands on her.

She sat in the car with her arms folded across her chest, looking forward. Her eyes pierced through the windshield. Bee kept looking over at his sister, knowing from the expression on her face that she was still upset. He bumped the song "Notorious Thugs" on his CD player by Biggie featuring Bone Thugs. He loved Biggie's flow and the music that the Bad Boy Camp put out 'cause their sound got him hyped. At times like this, when shit was gonna go down, he played that one particular jam by Biggie—"What's Beef"—for a boost.

When they finally made it to the bar, Jay pumped on his brakes until Bee got the hint that it was him. Once the flashing lights caught Bee's attention, he took a closer look to see if it was his brother like he thought. It started to rain heavily, making it hard to see anything. Bee pulled up alongside his brother's ride and parked. Jay got out of his car and covered up from the pouring rain. He shook the rain off, opened the backdoor of Bee's gray Pathfinder, and got in. He gave Bee some dap and rubbed his sister's shoulder.

"What's up, brah? And you too, lil sis?" Jay greeted.

Dee Dee sighed in disgust. She was still pissed off.

"Why you wanted me to come over here?" she asked, staring him down with eyes that could kill. She had asked the question that he knew he had to answer.

Bee looked on with open ears, wanting to know the answer also. Jay sat back in his seat. He pulled a blunt outta his Phat Farm shirt pocket and lit it up. With a strong toke of the weed he gathered his words. Dee Dee turned her head around and stared at him, waiting.

"Listen, Dee Dee, I asked Bee to bring you along cuz I need your help," he stated.

"Now you want my help, huh! After you done slapped me? Nigga please!"

Jay expected that, but he had an ace up his sleeve, so he played his hand out. Bee still had open ears, ready to hear what his brother proposed.

"Dee Dee, if you do this for me, we'll let you keep the ride that Mieka bought with our money, plus we'll give you five grand to spend on yourself for whatever your heart desires," Jay proposed as if he was making a big corporate deal.

"Nigga, is you gonna tell me why you got me out here in the damn rain or what?" Dee Dee asked, wanting to know the deal. She had already made up her mind to do whatever he wanted, but she had to play it cool with a mean mug and all. She needed the car, and the five grand was a bonus that she could definitely use.

"Look, Dee Dee, it's a nigga in that bar right there that owes us a lot of cash, and I want you to get his ass to take you to a motel so we can check that nigga." Bee silently agreed with his brother's smooth plan.

What Bee and Dee Dee didn't know was that Jay didn't plan on letting Manny leave that hotel breathing. Jay knew that Manny wasn't gonna give the money back, and if they had to set the nigga up to get payment back, then he felt that he might as well off the nigga. Dee Dee felt that the proposal was easy enough to do just to keep the car and earn five gees.

"So what he look like?" she asked.

Bee rubbed his hands together as Dee Dee agreed to do the deed.

Jay explained to his sister what Manny looked like, and that was all she needed to know. Dee Dee was already wearing a Gap, tight fitting, baby blue shirt and some boot cut jeans that showed off her ass good as fuck. Her hair was slicked back into a pony-tail, so she didn't have to do anything with it.

They watched Dee Dee as she entered the bar. She looked around and saw the bar had a mixed crowd of older folks. Blues music and the smoke from cigars and cigarettes filled the faintly lit room. All the men's eyes were on Dee Dee as she made her way toward the bar. She rested her Coach purse and her cell phone on the bar's counter top. Dee Dee grabbed one of the pieces of paper outta the little black container that was mostly used for writing down somebody's name and number. She wrote a little short note to Prat, which she planned on placing on his windshield under the windshield wiper. When the older white lady walked over to her and cleaned off the spot, Dee Dee hurried and placed the note inside the flip lid of her phone.

"Hey sweetie, what can I get you?"

Dee Dee was a homebody, so ordering drinks was foreign to her, but she remembered her brothers' discussions on their favorite drinks.

"Let me get a glass of Belvedere," she requested.

The bartender looked at Dee Dee with surprise, then she looked at the selection of liquors behind her. The choice of drink Dee Dee requested was so far off that bar's selection that the bartender second guessed herself and looked at the drinks as if they really might have what Dee Dee requested.

"Baby, you know this ain't a club, right?" Sandra, the bartender, stated to cover up her amazement at Dee Dee's choice of drink.

"Yeah, I know! But I changed my mind anyway."

While Dee Dee was in the middle of ordering, she was interrupted by the words of a man.

"Sandra, let me get two seven and sevens," Manny requested as he took the stool next to Dee Dee. "One for little momma here, and the other one for me."

"And who might you be?" Dee Dee asked.

"Me? I ain't nobody but a guy who wanted to buy a pretty young thing like you a drink," he responded.

"Well, I don't except nothing from nobody I don't know on a first name basis."

"If that's what it will take to keep our conversation going, then I should tell you that my name is Manuel, but my friends call me Manny," he stated with a smile.

Jackpot, Dee Dee thought. She knew from looking at him that he wouldn't be hard to convince to take her to a hotel. *Damn, this nigga's cologne smells cheap as fuck*, she thought, secretly holding her breath. Manny looked her up and down, lusting for her young, fine body.

"Here you two go," Sandra said as she placed the two drinks on napkins in front of them.

"Thanks, San, and keep the change," Manny insisted as he gave her a crisp twenty.

"Thank you," Dee Dee said to Sandra for being so nice.

"Now, where were we? Oh, I remember now. I was just about to ask what name people call a sweet thang like you," he flirted as he took a sip of his drink.

Dee Dee was nervous there for a sec, but she blew it off real cool-like. She then picked up her drink, stuck one of her manicured fingers inside it, and started stirring around the ice cubes. Once she saw that she had his complete attention, she pulled her finger out and gave it one of those feminine, seductive sucks. Manny quickly picked up on the vibe she was giving off. He didn't waste any time in asking her if they could leave together. Dee Dee smiled, not answering his question yet. She was thinking about what her brothers wanted her to do.

"Look, Manny or Manuel, I'm gonna cut the

games, OK? If you got the cash to spend to get a piece of this ass, then it's on and poppin'," she stated.

His eyes got big. He knew it had to be something about her when he first saw her walk through the front door.

"You sell pussy, huh? Well it ain't nothing wrong with getting your hustle on, now is it?"

She looked at him and smiled. He downed the rest of his drink, then told her that his money was burning a hole in his pocket. Dee Dee picked up her cell phone and stuck it in her purse. She thought about just leaving the piece of paper she wrote on to give to Prat, but she decided to take it with her. She raised up outta her seat to see that Manny was ready and waiting, grinning away. As they headed for the door, Dee Dee knew to get him to take her to the closest place possible so as not to lose her brothers on the way.

Jay and Bee passed the blunt back and forth talking about the trip they would soon have to make back to Texas to see Tony. As Jay toked on the blunt, Bee nudged him in his arm, signaling him to check out who was coming outta the bar. Jay vibed at the sight. He didn't know how his sister had done it, but she had. Jay wanted Manny's ass so badly that he just wanted to get out the car and rush the nigga, putting one in his head for dodging them. He took two deep breaths just to calm down. He knew there wasn't any use in him fucking shit up when his little sister had everything going just as planned. Jay liked Dee Dee's style. She had handled her business with ol' boy. He could only wonder what she had told the fool to get him to leave with her. Both Jay and Bee watched on as Dee Dee looked their way. She got inside the passenger seat of Manny's ride, and Bee and Jay watched them drive off in the Benz.

The rain had let up some, making it easier for them to follow their sister and Manny. Bee was telling himself that if that nigga Manny laid his hands on his sister to hurt her in any way, then it was on and poppin' with a whole clip of nine bullets to Manny's dome. They spotted the Benz up ahead as it pulled into the Howard Johnson Inn that was to the right of them. Jay and Bee both watched as Manny exited the car, heading for the office.

Dee Dee quickly got on her celly to call her brothers. While she waited for them to pick up, she kept darting her eyes from the office to all the cars that looked like they were gonna turn into the parking lot. Finally Jay picked up. He listened carefully to his sister, which was the first time he had done that since they had been living. She asked where they were and he told her to look for the car that had its left blinker on. Jay spotted Manny coming back out the door of the office, heading straight for his sister. With no time to waste, Jay told his sister that it was show time 'cause Manny was on his way toward her. Dee Dee quickly turned her head and saw Manny getting closer. She whipped her head around quickly, trying to spot her brothers, and she did. She saw the two shadows of men in the SUV over in the corner with its yellow light blinking. She knew to call her brothers back once Manny was in the shower and vulnerable.

Manny opened the passenger side door, letting Dee Dee out. He was all smiles as she looked at him. She nonchalantly looked over toward her brothers, then felt Manny's arm wrap around her waist, gesturing her to come along. She wanted to throw up at the thought of him touching her like he was. They stopped at room 136. Manny slipped the key in the lock and opened the door. The room was nothing but an average hotel room. The queen size bed rested between two wooden nightstands that had two brass lamps bolted down to them. A twenty-six inch color TV with a cable box connected to it rested on the dresser next to the A/C unit. Dee Dee eyed the bathroom door, which was closed, then made her way to it.

Manny closed the room door and tossed his coat onto the desk chair. He slapped his hands together and said, "It's on and poppin' as soon as she brings her ass up outta there." He dove on the bed, rubbing the sheets. He then made himself real comfy as he kicked off his shoes. He practiced fucking positions, thinking about all the ones he wanted to use on Dee Dee.

Jay and Bee chilled, smoking a blunt and talking about different shit. In the back of Bee's mind he wondered how his sister was holding up in that room with Manny. He really feared for his sister's safety, thinking that Jay didn't fully understand how dangerous shit could get for their sister if something was to go wrong. In Jay's mind he was thinking about the plan that he had for his sister, which would take anybody to the highest level of the game.

Dee Dee opened the bathroom door and stepped out, looking like a cold stallion that hasn't yet been broken in. Manny looked at her as she stood barefoot with nothing on but her bra and thong. His mouth was wide open, letting flies in. Her breasts

looked like perfectly rounded chocolate-covered or-
anges as they bulged in her bra. He wanted to lick
every inch on her brown-skinned body. Those wide
hips, those lusciously thick thighs, and those nice
smooth legs had him unable to wait any longer.

"Hey, little momma. What you say you come on
over here and have a seat?" he suggested as he patted a spot on the bed next to him. Dee Dee thought
he must have lost his mind if he thought that she
was gonna do that.

"Slow your roll there, Tonto. Don't you wanna
take a bath before we get started? And if you ain't
got them dollas, then ain't shit really poppin', and
my clothes getting put back on me," she stated
coldly.

Manny didn't have a clue as to what her asking
price was gonna be, but he didn't care. All he
wanted was that young pussy of hers. He pulled out
a stash of big faces, showcasing nothing but fifty and
one hundred dollar bills.

"This is twenty gees right here, baby. Now if that
little sweet cunt of yours can hang all night, then
you just may take a lot of this home with you," he
said as he waved the money around. "Now be ready
when daddy come outta the bathroom from getting
all clean like you said, all right?"

Once the door closed, Dee Dee rushed over to
her purse and grabbed her celly to let her brothers
know it was on and poppin'. When she grabbed her
celly she also pulled out the note she wrote to Prat.
She went back to the window and flipped the celly
open, unaware that the note had fallen out. She dialed Jay's cell phone as she peeped outta the window, looking at them. Jay answered his phone and

was hit by a slew of words telling them to move their asses 'cause Manny was in the bathroom taking a bath.

Dee Dee could see them clear as day making their way from the ride to the room. Once they made it, she opened the door to let them in. Bee noticed that she had a towel wrapped around her upper body. He quietly asked her if she fucked the nigga, but he really wanted to yell it 'cause he was overprotective of his little sister, but he kept calm. Jay, on the other hand, didn't care if she fucked the nigga or not, as long as she got the nigga to where they could carry out their plan.

"Little sis, you did good. Now, we'll take it from here," Jay stated while pulling his heater out.

"He's in the bathroom thinking that he's about to get some ass," she stated, answering Bee's question.

They all took their positions, waiting for Manny to come outta the bathroom. Bee hid on the side of the bed that wasn't visible to anyone who came outta the bathroom. Dee Dee got underneath the covers in the bed while Jay stood to the side of the bathroom door, waiting. They all heard the water cut off. Jay raised his hand, placing his finger over his mouth to tell everyone to be quiet. The door opened and Manny stood in the doorway with nothing on.

"Girl, I hope you're ready for this cuz I'm about to bring the pain to your sweet young pus . . ." was all he was able to get outta his mouth before Jay whacked him in the back of his head with his gun, sending Manny straight to the floor.

"Nigga, don't ever talk to my sister like that," Jay stated, towering over him.

Bee raised up from the floor while Dee Dee started putting her clothes back on. Manny wasn't really able to hear shit that Jay had said 'cause the blow to his head had his ears ringing something serious. He struggled and managed to rise up on his hands and knees. He placed his hand on the back of his head and felt the gash back there. Blood was dripping like it was water coming outta a broken pipe.

"What's going on?" Manny asked groggily.

"Fool, you know what's going on," Bee stated. "Now the question is where the fuck is our dope?"

"Yeah, nigga, where the fuck is the dope that you owe us?" Jay interjected, thrusting his Timberland-clad foot onto Manny's bare ass, sending him back down to the floor.

Manny raised his head up, looking straight at the two brothers. He instantly recognized them. He knew the position he was in was a fucked up one.

"Look, fellas, I'm sure we can work this whole misunderstanding out," Manny pleaded.

"I can't tell that you want to work anything out with all the ducking and dodging you've been doing," Bee stated, aiming his piece at him.

"Yeah, fool. Now look what you got your fake ass pimp self into," Jay said.

"Look, I know you want your dope back, and I can give it to you, but it ain't like I stole it from y'all."

"Bitch, who the fuck you think you talking to? You think that we went through all this trouble just to hear you try and weasel your way out of this?" Jay countered.

"Look, how 'bout I give the dope back and pay y'all for what you could have sold it for? Now that sounds like a plan, don't it? That way it ain't no hard feelings, even with the lump on my head."

"How 'bout you keep that and I take something else from your punk ass?" Jay suggested.

Bee looked at his brother, wondering what the fuck he was talking about. The plan was to get the cash or the dope, and here the nigga Manny was willing to give them back even more than what he owed, but Jay was confusing him. Manny knew what the fuck Jay was hinting toward when he said what he did. He knew that he had to entice them in a different way 'cause everything else had failed, and he wasn't trying to take a ride in that stretch black.

"Man, look. I just got ten bricks of some good shit from my cousin. Y'all can have that shit. I ain't tripping, just let me make it," Manny enticed and pleaded at the same time.

"Ten bricks. Where the shit at?" Jay asked, feeling the ten.

Manny didn't hesitate to give the 4ll on where he had the dope stashed. All he wanted to do was make it out alive so he could get straight, then come back and show all three of them just who the fuck OG Playa Manny really was. Once they were sure that they understood where the dope was truly hidden, Jay went back to his original plan.

"Where your clothes at?" Jay asked. Manny pointed to the bathroom area, then Jay forced him up. While Manny was walking into the bathroom Jay grabbed a pillow off the bed.

"Here, cover yourself up, nigga. My sister don't need to being seeing you butt-ass naked." Manny took the pillow and did as he was told. He looked at

Dee Dee and wondered how the fuck could he have let his little head get him in something that his big head couldn't get him out of, all because of some pussy. Manny reached down to get his pants, but when he did, Jay placed his foot on top of them, stopping him.

"What's the deal, man?" Manny asked, not understanding.

"This is the deal, muthafucka," Jay said in a heated way as he slammed the gun across the front of Manny's face, sending him motionless to the ground.

Bee and Dee Dee just looked on at Jay who sat on the edge of the tub. Manny knew he wasn't gonna make it outta there alive, so he tried to yell for help, hoping that somebody would hear him. But the only part of the word "help" that escaped his mouth before Jay rammed his right Timb into Manny's rib cage was the letter "h."

Jay walked out of the bathroom and took his sister by the arm. He asked her to kill Manny. The way he said it he was dead serious. Manny looked on, hearing their discussion word for word. Jay took her hand and placed the gat in it. Dee Dee quickly felt something she had never felt before in her life—the power of holding a 9mm. It seemed as if she became cold like the steel in her hand. Jay stared at his sister as she looked hard at the gun. Dee Dee wasn't down to shoot anybody, especially not somebody for Jay.

Dee Dee, Jay, and Bee walked back in the restroom and Jay told her to do it, but Dee Dee couldn't. He told her all she had to do was put the pillow over his head and squeeze the trigger, and then the job

would be done and she would be partnas with Jay
and Bee. Manny knew if she didn't do it then one of
her fool ass crazy brothers would, so he decided to
make a dash for it. Manny leaped up from the floor
and rammed Dee Dee into Bee while she was still
looking at the gun. They both fell into the dirty tub
water Manny hadn't bothered to let drain. Jay was
caught off guard 'cause he didn't have his gun.
Manny crashed Jay into the wall, knocking over the
nightstand and shattering the lamp's light bulb. Jay
had been in many fights, but none where he had to
tussle with a 230 pound short, stocky nigga. Jay
found himself being choked from behind as Manny
tried to squeeze the life outta his body while talking
shit.

"You tried to kill the wrong nigga muthafucka.
Don't you know who the fuck I am, bitch?" Manny
spoke into Jay's ear as Jay started to feel himself
drifting. A muffled bang was all that Jay heard.

Bee went and grabbed his brother off the ground,
telling him that they had to move fast. Dee Dee was
still standing where she had pulled the trigger, killing
Manny by putting one in his head. Jay snatched the
gun outta her right hand and tucked it in his pants.
He yanked the pillow that she had placed up against
Manny's head outta her other hand. As the brothers
yanked all the sheets up off the bed, wiping everything down, Dee Dee went in the bathroom and did
the same. Once she was done, she remembered the
money was in Manny's pocket, so she grabbed that
shit without her brothers even knowing.

They opened the door and saw that it was pouring down rain again. They covered up with the sheet

from the bed, then bolted out the door, headed for the car. Once inside, Bee drove off while Jay looked at his sister, smiling. He knew she was tripping, so he passed her a blunt and told her to smoke 'cause it would make her feel a whole lot better. Two puffs and Dee Dee was all mellow.

Chapter Four

Bee was inside a rental car blowing the horn so his brother would hurry up and come out. He didn't want to miss their flight. Miya walked Jay to the front door wearing a red, silk nightgown on her well-shaped body. Her long, black, straight hair was pulled back in a ponytail, but it was still long enough to reach her lower back. Jay liked being with Miya. She could always bring a smile to his face. The way she talked in her deep Costa Rican accent made him know he had a real jewel, especially when she said the word "Poppi." Now that Mieka was out of the picture, Miya had Jay's attention. Miya grabbed Jay's arm, which made him turn around just to see those little, bitty soft browns staring him in the face. He couldn't help himself from not taking a few minutes longer, even through the horn was still calling him. Miya's presence was overwhelming. Her beauty was captivating even as she stood in front of him from just waking up. Jay wrapped his arms around her body and pulled her in close and tight.

"Baby, when I get back we gonna go do something fun, just you, me, and the kids." Miya's eyes got big at the sound of those words, so she gave him a nice, long, wet kiss to show him that she was game.

"Poppi, tell Tony I miss him and for him not to let business interfere with him going to church." Miya was a firm believer in the Bible. She knew what Jay, Bee, and her cousin, Tony, did, but she overlooked that. She always prayed for their safety because that's about all she could do, seeing as they was grown men and no one could tell them what to do. Jay gripped a handful of her ass and gave her a quick kiss.

"I'll make sure I do just that. OK, little momma," Jay stated. Bee started blowing the horn again, but stopped when he saw the door to Miya's crib open.

"Miya, let that boy come on before we miss our flight," Bee shouted.

"And hello to you too, Bee," Miya replied with a wave of her hand.

"I'll see you later, OK," Jay said, giving her one last quick kiss. Bee waved, motioning for his brother to hurry up.

Their flight was scheduled to take off in an hour and they still had to battle the Memphis traffic to get there. When Jay got inside the rental he gave his brother some pounds, then got comfortable in his seat.

"Man, Miya gonna have to start letting you go without any of that Spanish fly, cuz she got your ass not wanting to handle business."

"Shiiitttt. Nigga, you know I ain't nothing but a paper chaser so that will never interfere with business. Besides, if it wasn't for her we wouldn't have ever hooked up with Tony."

Jay reached in his pocket and pulled out a blunt. Bee reached in his pocket and pulled out what he never left home without, which was Biggie Small's CD. He slapped it in the CD player and pushed the track button until it reached the song he loved hearing. He liked how versatile Biggie was with his rapping skills, and that's why he couldn't get enough of the track where Biggie teamed up with the cats from Cleveland, Bone Thugs-N-Harmony, to make a classic joint. They puffed on the blunt as they cruised down the highway. The music had them in a mellow mood, which was cool 'cause they had business to take care of. Bee started to rap along with the song, but he always found out that he couldn't keep up with the cats from Bone's flow, so he just sang the hook. The next song "Juicy" came on and that was more to Bee's speed.

Bee looked at his watch and noticed that they had made up some time in getting to the Avis car rental parking lot. As Bee parked the car in front of the return and exit booth they quickly started to clean out the car. They both got out of the car dressed in collegiate apparel. They had everything to go with their Rice University sweatshirts and turtlenecks. The duffel bag, the backpack, and other stuff that would make anybody that was looking on think they were attending college there. Bee walked toward the booth to return the keys while Jay grabbed their belongings outta the trunk. Once that was done, they hopped on the shuttle bus that had just pulled up.

The driver reached the airport lobby doors and let everyone off. Bee and Jay carried their bags inside the lobby, heading straight for the Southwest service counter. They got plenty of stares from people, but none of the stares were bad. The stares that they liked the most were from these two black females who looked good. Even though they were both in happy and suitable relationships, they were also men. Jay couldn't help but to stop and make a quick conversation with the sexy females, which turned into an exchange of phone numbers. Bee and Jay could hear the sistahs speak about how they looked so much like twins. They didn't mind that people thought they were twins. As a matter of fact, it was just one of the many tricks that they had up their sleeves to use when necessary.

They finally reached the service desk and got checked in. The sistah that was assisting them was looking good, and from the bright ass pink colored fingernail polish she had on, they knew ole girl was a project chick. With all that business taken care of, they were off to board their flight.

Dee Dee stepped outta the house and onto the porch with the rotating fan in her hand. Ronshay was sitting in the chair sipping on a glass of tropical flavored Arbor Mist wine. Dee Dee's portable radio was providing them with good tunes to listen to as the sun delivered some punishing temperatures. Dee Dee plugged the fan up and angled it right smack dead on them. Now they were really chilling.

"Oooh, girl, that's my song."

"I tell you, R. Kelly could get this pussy anytime

he wanted to," Dee Dee mentioned with excitement.

"I don't think he would care for your coochie too much, Dee Dee."

"And why not?" Dee Dee asked, feeling a tad bit ticked off.

"Girl, you know that nigga only like to fuck around with youngsters."

They both laughed 'cause they knew it was true. The thought of R. Kelly fucking around with minors made Dee Dee sick, especially when the nigga had women who wanted to fuck the nigga's brains out every second if he would let them.

"But you know what?" Dee Dee asked.

"What, Dee Dee?"

"The nigga may like that jail bait shit, but he can sho' sing his fine ass off."

"You can say that again." Dee Dee held her glass out toward Ronshay so they could make a toast. A red Escalade turned onto Dee Dee's street and when it got close to their house it slowed its roll, almost coming to a complete stop. The ride was phat, and Dee Dee and Ronshay wouldn't have minded having it as their own personal ride. The horn blew three times, but no one got out the ride.

"Do you know whose car that is?" Ronshay asked.

"Naw, girl, but I have seen it around a couple of times," Dee Dee replied. "Let's wave at whoever it is and see if the nigga get geeked up enough to get out," Dee Dee suggested.

They both waved, and just like they thought, a red-skinned nigga, dressed in a Karl Kani outfit, stepped out of the car.

"Ooohh, look, Ronshay. The nigga got it going on, don't he?" Dee Dee stated, looking for confirmation.

"I guess, if that's your cup of tea," Ronshay responded.

Dee Dee liked how ole boy was carrying himself with his dress code. He walked around the other side of his truck and leaned on the side. He posted his red and white Nike Air Max sneakers on the Armor All-ed twenty-two inch chrome wheel. The sight of two sistahs chilling on a hot day gave him all the reason to think that both Dee Dee and Ronshay were available. He leaned his Fendi shades slightly down on his nose so he could see them better.

"How y'all sistahs doing today?" he asked. Ronshay knew her place as Bee's girl, so she let Dee Dee do all the conversing.

"We could be doing a whole lot better if this damn heat wasn't this damn bad," Dee Dee responded.

He thought he was really getting somewhere with the convo, but he didn't know that Dee Dee was one tough female to slick talk. Since Dee Dee was the one doing the talking, he decided not to play his hand wrong by try'n to get both of them involved in conversation.

"Excuse me, but do you think a brotha can get a couple minutes of your precious time over here?" Dee Dee liked how homeboy said the word precious because that's just what she felt her time was.

"Should I go talk to him, Ronshay?" Dee Dee asked, wanting the go ahead sign.

"Dee Dee, you ain't no baby, so I'll leave that decision up to you to make," Ronshay stated, patting her hand on Dee Dee's left leg.

Dee Dee gave Ronshay a slight smile, and then let it disappear as she decided to stand up and go see what homeboy was working with. His eyes got big as fuck when he saw her stand up. He gawked at Dee Dee's thickness in her tight, home-cut, blue jean shorts. He liked everything about her, including that sassy walk she was displaying. He quickly changed his pose from cocky to thankful. Dee Dee stopped right in front of him with hips dipped, arms crossed, and bubble gum popping. He knew the pose she was giving off meant that he better have something to say that would really make her want to stay, and not have her regret that she even gave him the time of day.

"Look, let me start off by introducing myself. I'm Alastair, but my peeps call me Al," he stated.

When he let the name Alastair come outta his mouth, Dee Dee's first thought was that the name sounded like a white boy's name. But as she thought about it, she realized that his name was truly unique and different, much better than plain ole Ty, Mike, Tre or any of the other names that niggas in the ghetto had.

Ronshay watched on, and when Dee Dee didn't turn around and walk away in the first five minutes of being over there, she knew that Dee Dee was feeling what the guy had to say. Ronshay got up and walked in the house. She felt that it was no use in her watching a love connection go down when she could be in the confines of the A/C. The only reason she was on the porch in the first place was because Dee Dee wanted to be nosey and talk about people. Ronshay didn't mind the girl gossip 'cause she too was ready to talk about people. The both of them were really cool with one another, and Ronshay was happy to have a man like Bee and a friend like Dee Dee, who just so happened to be her man's sister.

The conversation had gotten so good that Dee Dee accepted Alastair's invitation to take a seat inside his ride.

"I still can't believe your momma named you Alastair," Dee Dee commented.

"Actually, it wasn't my momma that gave me the name."

"Then who did?" She asked.

"Well it was all my old man's idea. His momma's name was Alice so that's where it started. Now as far as the second part of the name goes, I have no idea."

"Aw, that is so cute. Most men always wanna name their sons after themselves so their name can go on, but your dad did it so your grandmama's name could live on."

Alastair liked the way she laid that down because the name never appealed to him. He felt a brother in the 'hood wasn't supposed to be addressed by Alastair out loud, so he just cut the name down to Al. Whenever he did tell someone his name, or wrote his name down, they could never get it right. When they tried to pronounce his name it always came out wrong. Like Allstar, A-stair, or Alasta. He couldn't understand how so many people that he encountered in his life could not pronounce his fucking name right, so that's why he just stopped going by his full name. Two things were for certain, though, which were that the name was an icebreaker, and deep down he really did love his name. The thing about it was he always wondered if a female could ever like the name enough to call him by that every day, which he so desperately wanted.

Dee Dee leaned back and started inspecting Alastair's ride to see if he had anything to hide. She didn't give a fuck if he didn't like it, because he had asked for it when he asked her to get in.

Dee Dee liked what she saw in Alastair, but for her, enough time had been spent talking to a guy that she didn't even know. She knew it was unlike her to even fall into a game like that, but something inside her told her to go for it. She drew a blank for a second and thought about what her brothers would do if they caught her in the car with dude. She knew it had to be something about homeboy that was good for her. She also knew that in order not to have any rain on their parade, she should let them part on a good note.

"Al, I gotta say that my first impression of you was that you was a cocky muthafucka who thinks you're the shit, but after talking to you for a sec, I gotta say that you're a cool dude." After Dee Dee spoke those words, Al began to feel victorious until she finished the rest of what she had to say.

"And even though I enjoyed our little talk, I gotta be going. You saw that I got company and shit." Alastair didn't bother to try and entice her any further because what she just said was right. She did have company. He got out of his truck and walked around to her side of the ride. Dee Dee watched as he became a straight gentleman by opening the door.

I bet he be doing this slick shit with every female that he ain't got the pussy from, Dee Dee thought to herself.

Dee Dee stepped out the car and walked away, heading for the front door. Alastair was thrown for a loop with her leaving and not saying anything, not even goodbye. Alastair knew that she was feeling him, but the walking away and not speaking threw him off. He figured if that was the case, then she would have never even came and saw what he wanted. He couldn't allow the fine, sassy mouthed sistah to get away just like that, so he ran up behind her and grabbed her arm.

"Boy, what is your problem," Dee Dee said as she jerked her arm back outta his clutches.

"Look, I'm sorry for grabbing you like I did, but my problem is you, and how you could just walk away from me like that."

"And! Oh, don't tell me it's a new law that went into affect that says a female that don't even know a nigga can't walk away without telling the nigga bye," Dee Dee said, flipping the script.

Alastair just shook his head 'cause he knew that a female like her, that had a mouth like what she had, could be nothing but trouble. But he had no idea how much trouble awaited him. Dee Dee's attitude reminded him of his own mother, who had long since been deceased. Even though his mother never whooped his ass when he acted up, he still was mad at her for leaving him.

"Look, Ma!"

"Ma! My name is Deondra, but people like you call me Dee Dee," she shot back fiercely.

"OK, Dee Dee. Let me try this again." Dee Dee looked on, waiting to hear what brother man had to say.

Ronshay was headed back out the door, but she quickly put the brakes on when she got there. She was gonna turn around, but she figured she would just be nosey and eavesdrop on their conversation.

"Now, you can't get mad at me for this, cuz this is exactly what we was doing earlier," Ronshay whispered to herself with a grin.

"Dee Dee, I would be a fool if I left here and I didn't get your phone number, so could you please be kind enough to a brotha and let me get the digits from a sistah I really think is smart, funny, feisty, and beautiful?" Dee Dee was touched by his words, but not enough to give him the digits.

"Al, I don't think that would be such a good idea."

"Should I even ask why not?"

"Well, it looks like you already did, but let's just say I got two big problems that would give you a headache."

Alastair had no idea that Dee Dee was referring to her two crazy ass, overprotective brothers. She knew if she gave Alastair her phone number that sooner or later he would bump heads with her brothers, and the shit that happened to Prat and the other niggas she was feeling would happen to him.

Alastair's first thought was that Dee Dee was referring to some kids. He scoped her body up and down and couldn't see any traces that a baby had came from her body, but the word "problem," and the thought of her having two kids, was enough for him to just chill and fall back. He raised his hand up in the air in an "I give up" gesture and walked away.

Dee Dee didn't like it that he didn't ask her what her two problems were, and the thought didn't cross her mind that he walked off because he figured that she had kids. Her train of thought wasn't even close to her thinking that could have been it. Dee Dee stood on the porch and watched Alastair drive off. Ronshay opened the screen door and posted up on the other side with her feet keeping the screen door from closing.

"Nice going, Miss Smooth! I can only guess what he's thinking your two big problems are."

"What you mean?" Dee Dee asked as she walked back over to take a seat in her chair.

"Well, the way you made it sound was like you had two babies somewhere around here, and you know a nigga can't see himself playing daddy to nobody else's kids but his own."

"You think that's what he thought for real?" Dee Dee asked.

Dee Dee pondered on what Ronshay had said for a sec. Ronshay just replied by pointing her index finger at her own head. Dee Dee picked up her glass of Arbor Mist and began sipping on it.

"Well, that's his loss, not mines."

But actually Dee Dee felt that it really was her loss 'cause it had been a long time since she'd been in the company of a brotha she was feeling. Alastair had it going on from head to toe, and Dee Dee liked the way his conversation had kept her attention.

Chapter Five

Jay and Bee stepped outside the lobby doors of the Houston Hobby Airport's lobby. When they looked around they saw a hand sticking outta a black Lincoln limo, waving them to come over.

"That's our ride, little brah," Jay said to Bee. As they got closer, Tony let the window down and told them to put their bags in the trunk. Once that was done they got inside the car.

"To the house, Miguel," Tony ordered. The driver wheeled the big limo outta the airport and into the merging traffic.

"So fellas, did y'all have a nice flight?" Tony asked as he handed them both glasses of bourbon on the rocks.

"It was cool, you know," Jay replied, speaking for the both of them.

"That's good cuz we got a lot of shit we need to do."

Jay wondered just what Tony meant by that. The driver entered the beltway. As they rolled though the city, Jay and Bee looked out the window and noticed all the buildings being built just off the highway.

"Man, Tony! It's a lot of shit being built around here," Jay commented.

"I know. That's why I'm investing my money in a construction company, so I can grow like they are."

Jay felt what Tony had said, but for Jay, growing was stacking that paper until he couldn't stack no more.

"You're quiet today, Bee. Something wrong?" Tony asked.

Jay looked over at his brother and saw that he was in dreamland. That was one thing that separated Bee from Jay. Bee wanted a legit business for him and Ronshay to run. Bee was funding Ronshay's college education so she could get her degree in Business Management. Bee looked at all the buildings that were going up as the way of the future, and the way for his own future. A while back he had gotten the idea that he wanted a construction company.

"I'm cool, Tony, just sightseeing. You know," Bee stated as he reached in his pocket to get a Black & Mild cigar.

"What you got there, my friend?" Tony asked.

"It's just a cheap cigar that everybody in the hood smokes."

Tony raised the window that was in the middle of him and Jay.

"Since that's a cheap cigar I can't let you smoke that while I'm smoking one of these," Tony stated as he pulled out three Cuban cigars. He passed one each to Jay and Bee, then clipped his and lit it. Bee raised the cigar to his nose and smelled it. He then examined it because this was the first time he had seen a Cuban cigar, let alone smelled one.

"Tony, ain't these banned in the states?" Jay asked.

"That's right, but so is cocaine and that don't stop us from getting it in the states, now do it," Tony pointed out.

The driver pulled onto a dirt road. Jay and Bee noticed about ten horses walking around, grazing on the grass.

"Awh, Jay, they got horses out here," Bee said excitedly.

"Do you ride, Bee?" Tony asked.

Bee told Tony no, but said that he had always wanted to. As they got closer they saw three Spanish men walking around a track with three beautiful, black, muscular horses.

"Damn, Tony, what y'all giving those horses? Steroids or something?" Jay asked, noticing the magnificent definition in the horses' chiseled bodies.

"Those, my friend, are what you call thoroughbreds, which just so happen to belong to the man y'all gonna meet tonight—Señor Valdez. This is all his."

The limo finally came to a stop and the driver came around to open the door. Tony stepped out first just to be greeted by a Spanish lady who took his hat. One of the Spanish men who was walking the horses came running over to the car.

"Pedro, grab the bags and take them to the guest room," Tony ordered.

"Si, señor," Pedro replied.

Jay and Bee stood outside the limo checking out

their new surroundings. The place was spectacular. The idea of being on a ranch made Jay think he was in Mexico or something. Tony summoned Jay and Bee to come with him into the house. They followed, but not without getting a last look at their surroundings. *Ronshay would love this place*, Bee thought to himself. Ronshay had never been outta Memphis, and Bee didn't like her not seeing the sights, but she didn't want to see nothing at this point in time except a degree, so they could leave Memphis for good.

Jay and Bee followed Tony into a room that was as big as their own living room and dining room combined. The table was long enough to seat ten people.

"Are y'all hungry?" Tony asked. They both told him yes, so Tony told Sarah, the maid, that they were ready to eat now. Tony told them to go ahead and have a seat at the table, which they did.

Sarah rolled a silver cart filled with food into the room. She placed a tray on the table that had a whole cooked chicken on it, with vegetables surrounding it. She then placed three bowls on the table which contained mashed potatoes, gravy, and a garden salad. Tony was the first one to get served, and the first one to dig in and eat. Bee and Jay followed soon after they received their own plates. While eating Tony let out a loud belch that sent Bee and Jay into laughter.

Now with all of them having full bellies Tony asked them to accompany him on a stroll around the ranch, which would really be a tour for them. They reached the stables, and once again Bee thought about Ronshay and how much she would enjoy herself on this ranch. Bee walked up to the three log gated fences and tried to summon one of the horses the way that you would a dog. Tony saw that Bee was really taking a liking to the horse, so he grabbed a handful of straw outta the trough and handed it to Bee.

"Hold it out and watch what the horse does," Tony suggested. As Bee held the straw out, one of the horses came up and started eating right outta his hand. Bee was all in the horse's grill, which showed him the horse had some big ass yellow teeth.

While Bee enjoyed himself, Tony took Jay on a walk to the other end of the stables.

"Hey, Tony, before I even forget, Miya told me to tell you not to let the business stop you from staying humble and praying." Tony slapped his arm around Jay's shoulder and laughed as he gave Jay a little shake.

"That's my favorite cousin for you. Always about God." As they came to a stop, Tony rested his snakeskin boots against the bottom of the wooden fence.

"Jay, a lot of things have changed since y'all's last departure." Jay didn't know if that meant bad news or what 'cause he couldn't understand how stuff could change in only two months time.

"Like what, Tony?" Jay asked.

Tony took two more Cuban cigars outta his pocket and handed one to Jay. "Look, right now I'm in a position to make a lot of money, but I can't do it by myself. If you and your brother want in, then I'll gladly welcome y'all in as part of my crew." Jay was all ears, and from what Tony had just mentioned, he was already game.

"What part will me and my brother play in this, Tony?" Jay asked. Tony lit up his cigar and passed the lighter to Jay so he could use it. Tony took a toke and blew out a cloud of smoke.

"My friend, the part that you and your brother will play is the part of our Tennessee connect. And if y'all can handle that, then we'll all be rich in no time." Jay's mind instantly started registering dollar signs.

"How much will we get at a time?" Jay asked.

"Is a bill at ten a piece all right?" Tony asked.

"Nawh, that's cooler than a fan, Tony," Jay shot back.

"OK, then. One hundred kilos of cocaine will be distributed to you every week and payment is to be made every month on the first."

Jay was stunned because he didn't think the deal would be this big. A hundred kilos was way too much for him and Bee to handle, at least by them-selves. *One hundred bricks! Damn!* He thought.

One of the field hands ran toward them, calling out Tony's name. Tony turned around to see who it was.

"Señor Tony! Señor Tony! We got a problem!" The field hand yelled.

"Like what, Marco?" Tony asked with a serious look on his face."

"Come, Señor! Come this way," Marco said as he escorted Tony toward the barn.

"Wait here, Jay," Tony told him.

When Tony reached the barn, Marco swept away the hay that covered the big wooden door on the floor.

"Señor, I counted the top two layers three times and I keep getting the same number of kilos missing."

Tony threw his cigar down to the ground in rage. He was fully pissed off that someone would steal from Don Valdez. Telling Valdez some of his shit was missing without showing him the culprit would make Tony look irresponsible.

"I take it that you don't know who did it. Si?" Tony asked Marco.

"Señor, I didn't take it," he stated, trying to clear himself.

Tony was so mad at that answer that he grabbed the horsewhip off of the wooden beam and swung it, hitting Marco right across his face. Marco fell to the ground holding his face. Tony knew in his head that Marco didn't take the shit, but he felt that Marco shouldn't have given the answer that he had.

"I want everybody in here in five minutes. Comprende?" Tony demanded.

"Si, Señor Tony! Si!" Marco replied before running off to summon the rest of the workers.

Bee walked over to Jay and asked him where Tony went. Jay told him that something was going on over in the barn. Jay brought his brother up to date by telling Bee about what Tony had proposed.

"No shit, brah," Bee said with excitement.

"No shit. But how the fuck is we gonna push one hundred bricks a week?" Jay asked, still unsure of a method.

"Don't sweat it cuz it's on and poppin'. All we gotta do is put a crew together and handle up."

"Yeah, that's all cool and shit, but what about if one of those niggas come up short with Tony and 'em shit. You know this is the big time and that means they will hold us responsible," Jay stated, holding his head.

"Man, don't sweat it. Everything will work itself out. It gotta work out cuz this is what we been wanting, a straight come up."

In the meantime Tony had all the workers lined up. Tony knew one of them had the coke stashed somewhere on the premises. He had to find it, and the one that was fool enough to take it, before Don Valdez arrived. He asked all of them one by one where they had been and who could vouch for their story.

Jay decided to go check on Tony, since there were no other people around, which made him suspicious that something was wrong. Bee followed his brother over to the barn. When they reached the door, Jay could see that everybody was in the barn, including Tony.

"Hey, my friend," Tony said as he spotted Jay standing at the barn entrance.

"Man, Tony, I'm sorry for interrupting y'all, but I thought something had happened to you," Jay said.

"Something happened all right, but as you can see, I'm OK."

"That's good, but like I said I apologize for interrupting," Jay reiterated, then started to walk away.

"Hold up, Jay. Maybe you can help me out."

Tony waved Jay and Bee over to where he was standing. They walked over to him, eyeballing the Spanish people that were standing in a line like they were in the army.

"So what's poppin', Tony?" Jay asked. Tony walked over to the door in the floor. He then summoned Marco to come lift up the big, heavy door. Jay saw that Marco's face was fucked up with a long, red ass mark going damn near from one side of his face to the other. *Damn, homeboy shit is fucked up,* Jay said to himself. Tony motioned with his hand for Marco to open the door and Marco was quick to do so. Jay's eyes got big as fuck when he saw all those kilos down there. There was enough shit there to supply every big city and town in Tennessee.

"Got damn. That's a lot of shit," Jay commented. Bee couldn't see from where he stood, but Jay's comment told him that there had to be dope in that floor.

Bee took his eyes off the door and looked back at the people who were standing at attention. He noticed one of the cats sweating real bad, wiping his sweat away real nervously. But he didn't know why they were in the barn in the first place, and he didn't know why the guy was sweating like he done stole something.

"Jay, what would you do to someone who stole something from you?" Tony asked as he put his arm around Jay's shoulder.

"Man, ain't no doubt I would level that muthafucka," Jay answered.

"The word level means to kill, right?" Tony asked, not really understanding.

"Yeah, that's right."

"Good, cuz one of Don Valdez's people done stole from him."

Now Jay and Bee knew why everybody was in the barn. Bee also figured out why homeboy was acting nervous. Tony walked down the line asking every last one of the workers if they took the stuff, and all of them said the same thing, which was, "No, Señor." Bee called Jay. Jay walked over to see what Bee wanted.

"What's poppin', little brah?" Jay asked.

"You see dude right there with the brown boots on."

Jay played it off and took a look like he would do when he would peep something out on the cool in the hood. "Yeah, but what about it?" Jay asked.

"Well, dude caught my eye like he did something wrong, and I peeped this out before I knew anything about somebody done stole something from Tony."

Jay walked outside the barn and called Tony over. Tony walked over to see what Jay wanted, and when Jay told him what Bee peeped out, Tony became enraged and happy at the same time.

Tony looked at the worker whose name was Chewy. Chewy started working for Don Valdez not too long ago, so that made Tony realize he had his man, but he wanted concrete evidence. Tony called Marco and Pedro over, then told them to go search Chewy's room. When they came back they had two duffel bags with them.

"Open them," Tony demanded."

"Si, señor," they both answered.

When Chewy saw the bags, he decided to make a dash for it. Tony turned around to see Chewy had taken off running. Tony ordered Pedro and Marco to chase after him. Neither of them were in any shape to catch the young, speedy Chewy, so Bee decided to handle up. Like a pure sprinter in the hundred yard dash, Bee was off. Tony saw Bee moving with the speed of lightning and wished that he could run like that. Bee had made up enough distance to where he could touch the thief, so he did. Bee threw his whole body forward as he dove onto Chewy's back. Chewy struggled with Bee but after Bee got his grip on him, he laid two thunder rights to his forehead, stopping any more resistance.

Pedro and Marco finally caught up, breathing hard as hell. They dragged Chewy's ass back to the barn like a sack of shit. Tony had dismissed everybody else so he could tend to the thief.

Once in the barn, Tony chained Chewy's hands to both sides of the wooden beam poles. Now Chewy was pleading for his life with his arms outstretched and locked up tight. Bee had seen a lot of drug cartel movies where they had to deal with people, and the way Chewy was chained to those poles told him that dude was gonna get fucked up. Chewy kept pleading as Tony, Bee and Jay walked away, headed back to their tour of the compound. Pedro and Marco were ordered to stay behind and secure the dope back in its space.

It was already past six o'clock and Tony still hadn't heard from Don Valdez. Tony was starting to get worried because Don Valdez had gone back home to Costa Rica to handle family matters with the heads of the Costa Rican Cartel.

Tony knew that Don Valdez and Don Angelo Ruiz, head of the Ruiz family, had bad blood between them, and Angelo wanted Don Valdez dead. While Tony was pouring Bee, Jay, and himself a drink, the phone started ringing. Tony picked it up and heard Don Valdez's voice on the other end. After being told he was on his way to the ranch, Tony hung up the phone and downed his bourbon.

Four black Suburbans with deep black tint on the

windows trailed each other down the road that led to the house. When they reached the house Tony was outside waiting. The first two trucks pulled up, then stopped. Six men got out of each SUV and stood alert. They were all heavily armed with automatic weapons. The other two trucks continued up to the house. The first truck stopped, and six more heavily armed men got out and examined their surroundings. This was a regular routine because having someone like Angelo as an enemy made Don Valdez a marked target.

Don Valdez emerged from his truck and looked around his property. He was dressed in a black suit with an eagle head cane in his hand to steady himself as he walked. Tony couldn't see Don Valdez's eyes because they were being protected from the sun by his black, diamond encrusted Versace shades. Tony made his way to Don Valdez and greeted him. He then told him that their guests had arrived safely. When they entered the house, Tony summoned one of the maids to get Bee and Jay and have them brought into Don Valdez's library. Tony introduced them to Don Valdez, and right away he took a liking to the two.

"So you two are ready to take charge of our shipments in Tennessee, huh?" Don Valdez asked, then coughed. Tony motioned Jay to go ahead and answer.

"Me and my brother was born ready, Señor Valdez."

"I like your answer. That was good. Now you two understand how we do business, don't you?" Don Valdez asked.

"Not exactly, Señor Valdez."

"OK, now listen up! Once you're in, you're in. There's no out and if you agree to those terms, then we can do business," Don Valdez stated.

Jay was cool with what Valdez said 'cause the streets were all he knew, and the streets fit him like a glove. Bee, on the other hand, had no intentions of staying in the game once he reached a mil.

Bee wanted to say something, but he decided to stay quiet because he really felt that no one could make him do anything that he didn't want to do, unless they had a gat to his head.

"What you say, little brah?" Jay asked.

"I'm game," Bee answered.

"We accept, Señor Valdez," Jay answered.

"That's good. Now that we have that taken care of, let me show y'all how I take care of people who steal from me."

They all walked to the barn, except for the women who got out of the truck with Don Valdez. Don Valdez ordered some of the heavily armed men to stand point outside while they went inside. Don Valdez walked up to Chewy, grabbed him by his cheeks, and squeezed on them hard.

"You steal from me, you little piece of shit!" Don Valdez shouted, then jabbed Chewy in his stomach with the point of his cane. Chewy started coughing from the pain.

Don Valdez wanted to see Chewy's punishment delivered. The two henchmen took off their suit coats and revealed double strapped shoulder holsters with gats in them. They took turns working Chewy over with blow after blow. Jay and Bee looked on at the shit they was doing, which to them looked like something outta a movie.

After a massive beat down, Chewy slumped over, dangling from his arms in the chains.

"Wake him up," Don Valdez ordered. One of the henchmen grabbed a bucket of water and tossed it on Chewy's face. He woke up, coughing.

"Pull his pants down," Don Valdez ordered as he stood up. "My friends, in third world countries the punishment for stealing is to have yours hands cut off, but in my family the punishment is this." Don Valdez grabbed Chewy's penis and slid the eagle head end of his cane to reveal a long knife. With one swing, Don Valdez now held Chewy penis in the air above his head.

"Now leave the maricon there to bleed to death," Don Valdez ordered.

Chewy dangled there crying, screaming, and bleeding to death. Now Bee could see that getting out of a deal with Valdez might not be as easy as he thought.

Chapter Six

Dee Dee was sitting on the couch eating a bowl of Fruity Pebbles cereal as she watched her favorite soap, *The Young and The Restless*.

"Can't you see Stephanie ain't nothing but a tramp, Derrick?" She said to the TV, referring to the characters on the show. Just when the show was getting good the door bell rang. "Dammit," Dee Dee shouted, upset at being interrupted.

Dee Dee placed her bowl of cereal on the coffee table and went to answer the door. She didn't bother to look through the peephole as she opened the door.

"Take that, bitch. Now what!" Mieka shouted as she threw a can full of yellow paint all over Dee Dee.

Dee Dee couldn't believe what had just happened to her. The paint was all over her body and face. She was bent over trying to rub the paint outta her eyes. Mieka had got her good, and as Dee Dee stood there defenseless, Mieka thought about rushing her and putting a world class ass whopping on her, but she was having herself a good ole time just laughing at how Dee Dee looked.

Dee Dee kept wiping, and soon she was able to see Mieka standing in front of her laughing and pointing at her. Dee Dee was now mad as fuck, and she had her hand balled up in a fist, ready to set it off. Dee Dee came up from her bent over position with a crushing right hand that hit her target, which was Mieka's face. There wasn't any doubt that Mieka felt Dee Dee's power 'cause the punch sent her floating backward, hitting the wall of the house. Dee Dee was furious at Mieka, and therefore she had no love for her as she rushed in to give Mieka more of what she come for.

"Bitch, you done fucked up throwing some paint on me, but it's on and poppin' now," Dee Dee shouted as she grabbed Mieka by her hair.

Dee Dee jerked and yanked Mieka everywhere while she held Mieka by her hair. Mieka grabbed Dee Dee's hands and tried to break her grip, but all Dee Dee did was yank harder. Dee Dee yanked so hard that Mieka was free, but minus a handful of her own hair that was now in Dee Dee's hand.

As Mieka felt the plug spot that was missing from her weave, she decided that it was time for her to do her thang. Mieka just went crazy and started swinging all crazy and shit like a wild woman. Dee Dee wasn't able to block all the wild swings coming at her, so some landed, including one that put a nice, big scratch on her face. Dee Dee could feel the scratch burning her face from her nose to her ear.

The fight between the two had attracted a hood crowd, mainly from all the yelling they were doing.

People couldn't believe that Jay's girl was fighting with his sister, but they didn't know that Jay had long ago given Mieka her walking papers. The crowd was so nosey that people actually sat down in Dee Dee's front yard. The crowd didn't interfere by trying to break the two up and the two didn't notice that the crowd was there.

Dee Dee was now on the rail of the porch, about to be pushed over it by Mieka, who was showing all of the onlookers that she was the strongest outta the two. Dee Dee couldn't stop herself from going over the rail once her feet came outta her shoes. Dee Dee went over the rail, but not without pulling Mieka down with her. They both hit the ground, landing in the flowerbed, which was muddy. Mieka got herself together first so she grabbed a handful of the mud and slammed it in Dee Dee's face.

"Take that, bitch," Mieka shouted. Dee Dee was now spitting mud outta her mouth. Mieka didn't stop her attack. She grabbed Dee Dee's hair and made her get up.

"GET YOUR STANK'N ASS UP, BITCH!" Mieka shouted while slapping Dee Dee in the face like she was a rag doll.

The shouts from the people in the crowd were being thrown out like it was a Mike Tyson fight.

"Damnnnn! She slapping the shit outta Dee Dee," one of the dudes in the crowd yelled.

"Whoop her ass, Dee Dee," another shouted.

"Yeah, don't let her do you like that, especially not in your own yard," a short, chubby chick with some big ass mismatched curlers in her head shouted.

Those words struck home with Dee Dee. Somehow she mustered up the strength to stop the tears from coming, and to finish fighting. Dee Dee grabbed Mieka's left breast and squeezed. She knew Mieka had gotten her nipples pierced while she was with Jay, so she used that to her advantage.

"Let go, Dee Dee," Mieka whined.

"That's it, girl. Work that bitch!" the chubby chick shouted.

Dee Dee let go of her grip and caught Mieka with another fierce right hand to the mouth. Mieka fell to the ground, so Dee Dee decided to help her up. Dee Dee gripped Mieka's shirt and yanked. She yanked so hard that Mieka's shirt ripped open, revealing her breasts.

"Damnnn, baby! Let me suck those big ole titties," a crack head shouted. The shit was so funny that the whole crowd started laughing.

Mieka sat on the ground with titties exposed. When she finally saw the crowd there she quickly covered herself with both hands. Feeling straight embarrassed she got up off the ground and made a dash for it, but not without Dee Dee catching her and slapping mud right back into her face. Now it was Mieka's turn to spit mud out. Dee Dee shouted every cuss word in the book at Mieka as she hightailed it to her car. Mieka got inside her car and started it up, but before she could take off she had to witness the remainder of the paint that was in the can being poured on her ride, including the windshield. Mieka hit the windshield wipers and created one big ass mess. As Mieka pulled off, Dee Dee chucked the paint can at the ride, hitting the back window and breaking it.

"It ain't over, bitch," Mieka shouted as she looked back and spotted Dee Dee standing in the middle of the street waving her to come back and finish what she had started.

"Damn, girl! You whooped her ass," one of the dudes commented.

"Yeah, Dee Dee! I didn't know you could go like that," another cat said.

"Girl, don't you know I started to jump in and help you whoop that bitch ass, but you looked like you was handling up and all, you know!" the chick with the rollers in her head stated.

"Janelle, you need to quit telling that fat ass lie cuz you know you wasn't gonna do shit but go back inside and feed your face," the first guy said.

"Fuck you, Rodney! And while you talking shit, nigga, it ain't nothing for me to take these rollers out my head and punish your little skinny ass," Janelle shot back as she began to take one of the rollers outta her hair.

"Chill out, Janelle! You know I was just kidding, so what you say we go in your crib and eat some of that food I smelled you cooking?" Rodney said.

"Fuck you, Rodney. I ain't got enough food but for me and my six babies. So, sorry Charlie. Better luck next time," Janelle responded.

"I didn't want none of that welfare food you got in that house anyway," Rodney shouted as he walked off. Janelle turned around and faced Dee Dee.

"Girl, come on in the house and let's get you taken care of. Your brother gonna kill the both of y'all when he finds out his girl and sister done got into a fight," Janelle exclaimed.

"Jay don't fuck with that bitch no more."

"Whattttt! Jay done kicked Mieka to the curb? And here I was just thinking she was creeping on Jay riding around town with Rock. Unnn Unnn Unnn! Well, her loss cuz Jay sho is fine. I tell you, your brother could get some of this at any time, Dee Dee," Janelle stated as she shook her head, thinking nasty thoughts.

Dee Dee just looked at Janelle, thinking that her brother would have to be totally drunk to even think about touching Janelle with a ten-foot pole.

They reached Janelle's front door and walked inside the house. Janelle's crib was laid out, but the roaches just fucked everything up. Janelle had Dee Dee take a seat at her shiny kitchen table. When she came back, she had some medicine for the scratch on Dee Dee's face.

"Come on, girl, so you can get cleaned up." Dee Dee followed Janelle up to the bathroom, where she had already started running the water in the tub. "When you get out of the tub, we gonna take care of your face," Janelle stated while holding up a bottle of alcohol.

"Janelle, I can't take a bath over here."

"And why not, girl?" Janelle asked.

"And what am I gonna put on?" Dee Dee asked, as she looked at her own fucked up clothes.

"Seeing as how you're too small to fit in any of my clothes, I guess I can go to your crib and get something for you to put on."

Dee Dee just nodded her head in agreement, 'cause at that moment in time, her body started to feel the effects of fighting, which was the soreness and pain from where the blows had landed.

Janelle took off, telling Dee Dee that she would be back in a sec. Dee Dee stood up and looked in the mirror. She put her hands on her hair, feeling disgusted at her fucked-up hairdo. She began to take off her clothes so she could get into the tub. Once undressed, she stared at her still sexy body. Janelle had all sorts of Bath & Body Works stuff on her shelves, so Dee Dee took some of the bath bubble balls and plopped them into the water. She then added some of the vanilla bubble soap. Once that was done, she stepped one of her feet into the water, then the other. It was a little hotter than she would make her own bath water, but at this point, it was just what her aching body needed. As she eased down into the water, she let out a sigh, then sank all the way in.

With her head leaning back on the rubber headrest, Dee Dee was now at ease. She closed her eyes and reflected on her fight with Mieka. She still couldn't believe Mieka had brought that bullshit to her house, and just like Mieka said, it wasn't over. Dee Dee knew she would have to punish Mieka, only this time she would have to give Mieka a dose of her own medicine by catching her unprepared.

Janelle knocked on the door and peeked inside.

"Girl, you have too many outfits over there in that closet of yours, so I just got you this sweat suit, OK?"

Dee Dee was thankful that Janelle was showing her so much love, even though she knew that Janelle was lying about jumping in and helping her out.

"Since you got that face cleaned up already, I guess my ass will doctor it up right now. Cool?" Janelle asked.

Dee Dee just threw her hands up in the air, signaling that Janelle could do whatever. When Janelle put the alcohol swab on the scratch, Dee Dee flinched from the burning feeling.

"Damn, Janelle! That shit stings!" Dee Dee shouted.

"Cut the games, Dee Dee. What you thought, the shit was gonna feel good, or what? I bet you don't get into another fight again, huh?"

Dee Dee looked up at Janelle with devil eyes and said, "That bitch gonna get dealt with, Janelle. I ain't playing. The bitch came to my crib and fronted like that. Hell! Fuck naw! Her ass is mines," Dee Dee stated as she started washing up.

"Listen, girl. The bitch got served, and you did the serving, so just calm down and finish washing up. I'll be downstairs waiting," Janelle told her, then walked out.

Dee Dee started getting all the paint off her body, then she washed her hair. Once dressed, she walked downstairs. The scent of home cooking was in the air, and it had her taste buds standing at attention.

"'Bout time," Janelle said as she placed two plates of soul food on the table. "Come on and get some of my good cooking I done fixed."

"It do smell good, Janelle," Dee Dee complimented.

"What you mean it do smell good? Just wait till you put some of these candied yams in your mouth, or my smothered pork chops, then you'll see."

Janelle went back into the kitchen to get them something to drink, while Dee Dee sat down and quickly sampled everything on the plate. Everything tasted perfect, like it was Thanksgiving or Christmas. Janelle entered back into the room with two glasses of Orange Crush soda.

"Girl, this food is the bomb," Dee Dee stated with a mouthful of mustard greens.

"I told you," Janelle shot back with a jazzy-head snap. They sat there and talked as they ate. They shared laughter at stuff they knew about people's dirty laundry.

Once they were done eating, they headed over to Dee Dee's crib to clean up the mess from Mieka throwing the paint, but when they got there, Dee Dee saw that there was no paint, just a wet spot like someone had already cleaned up.

"Dee Dee, I cleaned that mess up for you, and it's on the house," the crack head shouted as he rode past on a little kid's bike.

"I can't believe Mikey did something for free. He must got a big ass rock hid somewhere to do something that generous," Janelle stated.

"Mikey's OK, Janelle. It's just too bad that dope got his ass hooked," Dee Dee said as she waved to say thank you to Mikey.

Chapter Seven

Jay found a two-story apartment complex that they could use to handle business. Tony told him to keep the money he brought down to cop with, and to use it to set up a safe house which they were gonna need. Jay liked the brown brick building. It had eight apartments in it which could serve different purposes. He was waiting on the construction man that Tony had set up to install a security system and a hidden compartment where the dope could be stored. The building cost more than what Jay and Bee had, but Tony covered the other hundred thousand, courtesy of Don Valdez.

Bee just turned onto the block where the niggas from his hood hung out. When he parked his ride, Nasty walked up to greet him. Jay stepped out of his car and quickly gave Nasty some love as Nasty's hand was already extended.

"What's the dilly yo, playa?" Nasty asked.

Bee put his arm around Nasty's shoulder and motioned for him to take a walk. As they got clear of all the rest of the niggas who was hustling, Bee broke it down to him.

"Listen, Nasty, I want you on my team."

"And what exactly do I have to do to be on this team, Bee?" Nasty asked with some curiosity.

"Look, it's some big thangs about to happen, and if you want in, you'll get paid," Bee explained.

"I'm down with that, but Bee, I ain't killing nobody unless they try and kill me first."

Bee knew that Nasty was referring to the death of Manny, but Bee let those words slide, cause no one knew that they were involved. All they knew was that it seemed kind of odd that the nigga they was looking for wound up dead.

"Nigga, you couldn't kill a fly, so why would you think I would involve you in something like that? Besides, from what I hear, you're a lady's man." Nasty laughed because everybody knew he had gotten his name from doing all kinds of freaky shit with the hos. Nasty gave Bee some dap and told him to just let him know when it would be on and poppin'. As Bee walked back to his ride, a little shorty ran up to him.

"Bee! Can a nigga get a job?" Bee looked at the youngster called Lil Man. Bee would always turn Lil Man down whenever he asked for work. He just didn't like the idea that Lil Man was hustling at the age of sixteen, but now plans had changed, and Lil Man had popped the question at the right time and moment.

"Yo, Lil Man! Today is your lucky day," Bee stated.

"What? You gonna put me on, Bee?" Lil Man spoke with a look of excitement on his face.

"Lil Man, call this number tomorrow at this time and we'll talk," Bee explained as he handed him a piece of paper with a phone number and time written on it.

"Man, Bee, thanks. I promise I won't let you down."

Bee liked the way that sounded. He even thought to himself that he could probably mold Lil Man into a real smart hustler.

"Lil Man," Bee called out. Lil Man came back to see what Bee wanted, and Bee told him to keep what they had discussed on the down low.

"It's on and poppin', big homie," Lil Man said, reaching his hand out to give some dap.

Bee pulled off, feeling good with lining up his first two recruits. Now it was time to talk with Terry Tee and his brother, Junior. Jay had left all the recruiting up to Bee, so that's just what Bee was doing—recruiting real niggas from their own 'hood.

As Bee cruised down the street heading for Terry Tee's crib, he spotted a nigga he couldn't believe was back in Memphis. He quickly pulled his ride over to the curb and slammed on the brakes. The screeching noise from the car tires was so loud that homeboy reacted quickly, reaching into his jacket for his heater. But when he laid eyes on Bee, who was getting out of the ride, a big ass smile leaped onto his face.

"D-Dawg! Man, when you get back into town, and why the fuck haven't you got with a nigga yet?" Bee asked as he wrapped his arms around D-Dawg. D-Dawg had been Bee's real, true homie since they were young. They had lost contact with each other when D-Dawg left Memphis after shooting one of the Robinson boys and moved to Cali. Ever since then it'd been nothing but Crips banging for him. Every summer D-Dawg would come back to Memphis, but that seemed too short of a time to kick it for two homies who had so much in common.

"Look at my nigga," D-Dawg shouted as he looked Bee over.

"Nigga, you gonna answer my question or what?" Bee asked with a serious face.

"Chill out with that ugly look. Shit, it's bad enough that you was born ugly!" D-Dawg was laughing, but Bee was dead serious about being given an answer. "Look, Bee, I just got in town."

"You mean to tell me that you're just getting here?" Bee asked.

"Man, I'm just getting here. Here's my Greyhound bus ticket if you don't believe me," D-Dawg stated as he reached into his pocket to get the ticket.

Bee stopped his boy in his tracks from retrieving the evidence, 'cause the story was good enough. Bee hadn't talked to his moms in about a month, so he asked D-Dawg how she was doing. D-Dawg was kind of shocked that Bee would ask him something like that, but then again, he knew the story about how their moms hated what they were doing.

"You know the Robinson boys got hit up a while ago, huh," Bee told D-Dawg as they walked over to Bee's ride.

"Why you think I'm back? But you know those suckas don't wanna tangle with the West Coast rider." D-Dawg was a full-fledged gang banger, and when he shot one of the Robinson boys, niggas really respected him. Even though he was born and raised in

Memphis, the nigga represented L.A. like he was born there. Bee didn't mind 'cause he liked hearing the stories of the California lifestyle. That banging shit fitted D-Dawg to a tee, 'cause he was already crazy in the head. Try talking slick to D-Dawg, and one would probably find himself getting his dome split open. Bee was happy to have his nigga back in town, and with D-Dawg on his team, he could really plan to pump the block.

"So what you been up to?" D-Dawg asked.

"Man, shit has changed a lot in the past two months."

"What you mean, like muthafuckas getting shot or what?" D-Dawg asked, waiting to hear the answer.

"Naw, ain't no shit like that. What I'm talking about is that me and Jay is about to be getting some major weight in a minute."

"What is major in your vocab, and what is a minute in your world, cuz you know you think your ass is a college boy, all philosophical and shit."

"Look, man, we got this connect with these hard hitters, and D-Dawg, when I say hard hitters, I mean like the fucking cartel."

"Get the fuck outta here!"

"D-Dawg, we just got back in town from meeting with the niggas in Houston. The head nigga, Don Valdez, chopped this nigga's dick off right in front of us because the nigga stole a hundred bricks from him."

"Now that is the big time. What the fuck y'all done got y'all self into?" D-Dawg asked.

"I know it's some deep shit, but right now it's

time to get this paper. So, are you in or out?" Bee asked, looking hard for an answer as they stopped at a red light.

D-Dawg turned and looked at Bee, then he reached his hand in his jacket and pulled out his all black .45 semi-automatic heater.

"We're down for the come up, so let's get this cash, my nigga." Bee gave a smile back, then floated through the traffic, heading to Terry Tee's crib.

Jay was in his car smoking on a blunt when he spotted a white man pulling up in a van. It was a working van, but the color of the dude's skin threw Jay off because Jay was under the impression that everybody Tony knew was Hispanic. Jay stepped out of his ride and approached the dude.

"You must be Jay," the man said.

"How did you know that?"

"You look just like your brother."

"You met my brother already?" Jay asked.

"Not really, but these photos of y'all helped me to know who I'm looking for." Jay was shocked to see the guy had some pictures of him and Bee.

"Hold up, man! Where you get pictures of us at?" Jay asked, not recognizing the background in the photos.

"I can tell that y'all really don't know what y'all got yourselves into, huh? These people play for keeps, and when I say for keeps, I mean not only do they got pictures of you and your brother, but if y'all ever fuck up, then everything that y'all are connected to will disappear. For good." The white man's words struck home with Jay, and the man knew that his words were heard because the expression on Jay's face told it all. The man went on to tell Jay that he was in the same situation, which shocked Jay.

They walked inside the apartment building and Jay showed him around. After going through the whole place, the man went straight to work. Jay sat around and watched how the stuff was being done so he could have a little insight on the know-how side of things. Once the white man was done, he showed Jay how to operate the sliding dummy wall. Jay was amazed at what he was looking at. He couldn't believe that the wall could move like it did, and he wasn't able to tell it was fake. Jay looked at the wall over and over again and still couldn't detect anything that would make him think that something could possibly be hidden behind there.

Next Jay learned how to work the camera and the rest of the security system, and just like that, Jay was a pro. He couldn't wait to show Bee. The man told Jay that the wall could hold a hundred million in big bills only, and about five thousand kilos of cocaine. He told Jay to fill the place up with coffee grounds so that a dog couldn't detect the drugs, and to use only Colombian coffee because it was the best in the business at the fifty-two fake out.

With his job concluded, the white man shook hands with Jay and walked off, leaving Jay to digest all the information he had imparted.

Chapter Eight

Detectives Gary and Perkins were on their way to interview a young boy whose brother had been gunned down on the lower east side of town. When they pulled onto the street, there was a block full of black people standing around, which made the detectives feel insecure. Even though they were packing legal heat, and had a license to kill, they still knew to be cautious.

"Perkins, these people don't like us coming in their neighborhood, so why do we even bother?" Gary asked, wanting to get the hell up out of there.

"Yeah, they may not want us here, but the truth of the matter is that they need us here. Look around, Gary. Would you want your daughter or son talking to people who did God awful things to them? I can't blame them, and neither can you once you open your eyes. But remember this: we got a job to do and that's just what we're going to do."

"All right then, but if I get shot out here by one

of these black people, you just remember to take care of my family," Gary said seriously. "Now which one of these buildings does the boy stay in?" Gary asked as he looked around.

Perkins pulled the notepad out of his suit coat and flipped it open. "Here we go. Jamal Jenkins, son of Mary Jenkins, Apartment 44C." The two white cops stepped out of their unmarked police car and faced all the black stares that were darting at them.

"I tell you, the things I do for MPD," Gary stated. There's Building C right there. Now come on." Gary pulled up his pants to straighten them out, then he took off his suit coat so he could show the onlookers that he had one nice looking 9 mm Beretta in his shoulder holster, just itching to start popping. Perkins looked back and saw Gary broadcasting.

"Come over here, Barney Fife," Perkins shouted. Gary stepped with pep as he noticed Perkins had moved ahead.

They both walked up to Building C, and stood there for a second looking for Apartment 44. Once they were standing in front of Apartment 144C, Gary beat Perkins to the punch and quickly extended his hand to deliver three knocks to the wooden door. They waited. The door finally opened, and a little boy stood there looking up at the two white men.

"Kenny, get your butt back in here before momma whoop you," an older boy shouted.

"Excuse me, young man, but would you happen to be Jamal Jenkins by any chance?" Gary asked with a smile.

"And who wanna know?" The teenage boy asked.

"I'm Detective Perkins, and this is Detective Gary. We just wanted to ask you some questions about your brother."

The teenage boy looked at the white cop like he done lost his damn mind. "My brother is dead, so what you should be doing is looking for the person that killed him," the teenage boy stated before slamming the door in their faces.

"I told you, Perkins, these people don't want our help," Gary stated as he turned to walk away. He looked back and saw Perkins still standing in front of the door the boy had slammed in his face. "Perkins, are you coming or what?" Gary shouted, glad to be able to get away from the rough enviroment.

Perkins walked away from the door, still dumbfounded as to why the kid didn't listen to what he had to say. Perkins didn't think like Gary did. Gary was an ex-military man, and Perkins was a churchgoer.

They hopped back in their car and drove off. While Gary did the driving, Perkins sat in his seat going over his notes in his notepad. He spotted some notes on yet another murder that was unsolved.

"Gary, remember the guy they found dead in that motel room?" He asked.

"You mean the guy over at the Howard Johnson?" Gary asked.

"That's him. What do you say we head back on over there."

"For what?" Gary asked.

"Maybe we couldn't get any assistance from that kid, but maybe we can solve this one." Gary just looked at his partner and started to wonder what the hell was going through his head.

Gary turned left on Central Avenue and coasted down the road till they finally reached the Howard Johnson Inn. They walked into the office and asked the young rock "n" roller looking white kid to give them the key to room 101. The white kid hesitated, but when Gary pulled the left side of his coat back, revealing one of his guns and his shiny shield that was clipped to his belt, the kid quickly grabbed the key and handed it to him.

"Thank you son," Gary said sarcastically.

Once they reached the room, Perkins ripped the yellow tape off the door, Gary opened the door, and they walked in. The room was left the same as when they had found it because the investigation was still ongoing. Gary just stood in the doorway as his partner snooped around like a hound dog looking for clues. He searched the room and didn't find anything. Gary was laughing on the inside, but he didn't let on to his partner. Instead he turned and faced the big window that had its curtains closed.

"Maybe if you had some sunlight in this place you might find something," Gary stated as he yanked the string down that would open the curtains.

A piece of paper fell to the floor as the curtains opened. Gary didn't notice it so it just stayed there. "I guess it ain't nothing here after all, Gary," Perkins said, disappointed.

"I told you. Maybe next time you will listen to your partner." As Gary walked out of the spot he was standing in, Perkins spotted the paper on the floor.

"Gary, you dropped something." Gary looked down to where Perkins was pointing his finger. The paper didn't look familiar to him so he picked it up. When he looked at it, he was surprised to see that it had something on it. The note said: *Prat, I miss you. Will you please call me. Dee Dee 243-7922.*

"If this ain't a clue to breaking this case, then I don't know what is!" Gary shouted.

Perkins reached his hand out to inspect the paper. Sure enough, the paper said what Gary had read out loud.

"Now who should be listening to who, Gary? Now all we gotta do is see how this Dee Dee character is connected to this homicide," Perkins stated with a smirk. They went back to the police department and called the number.

"God damn it!" Perkins shouted.

"What's going on here?" The Sergeant asked.

"Nothing, Sarge," Gary said, covering for his partner's outburst.

"Don't tell me nothing, cuz I know what I heard," the Sergeant stated.

"Sarge, I just thought we had a lead on that Howard Johnson Inn homicide, but this cell phone number is out of service," Perkins jumped in.

"Well, find out who the cell phone carrier is and follow up. We could use the publicity if we crack this case, so you two get to work cuz this is now y'all's sole case."

Gary threw his hands over his face in anger 'cause the last thing he wanted was to be stuck on a homicide that didn't have any leads.

"Why don't you send this paper to the lab and see if they can get a print off of it? And while you're at

it, have them go back over to the room and fingerprint the window, seeing as how the paper was in
the curtain. Just maybe if we're lucky, we'll find
something that we can use," Gary said, figuring he
might as well do something since he was now ordered to be on the case.

"Look at my partner. And here I was thinking
that you were all muscle and no brains," Perkins
teased with a smile. Perkins stopped one of the
rookie officers and had him take care of the tasks for
him after sealing the piece of paper in a manila evidence envelope. He then handed it to the rookie to
deliver.

Chapter Nine

Dee Dee decided to take a nap, and while she did, she dreamed about when she pulled the trigger and murdered Manny. She had seen the whole episode in her dream as if it was happening all over again. Only in this dream, she was by herself, and when she ran outside the hotel room, the whole got damn police force was waiting, pointing all kinds of heaters at her. Then they blasted her to the other side of the world.

Dee Dee woke in a cold sweat with her shirt soaked. She was scared to death 'cause never in her life did she have a dream haunt her like that one. She felt her whole body to make sure she had no blood or bullet holes in her. The only thing she felt was her shirt drenched in her own sweat. The dream was as real as they came.

Dee Dee went upstairs and got undressed so she could take a shower. Her brown skin was smoother than a baby's butt. She knew that she had the total package, but she didn't have the nigga she wanted to quench her burning desire for love and to be loved.

She stepped out of the shower and walked to her closet to see what she could wear on this cool day. She hated the way the weather would switch climates right in the middle of the summer. She put on her tight, pink JLO shorts and a white JLO matching sleeveless T-shirt with JLO printed on the front in big pink letters. She walked to her dresser mirror and opened her wooden jewelry box with a see-through glass top. There she plucked out her big, round hoop earrings and her rings that she hardly wore. Dee Dee reached down and opened one of the drawers that contained her socks. She was happy to see that she had a pair of clean pink footies with the white ball at the heel. Now that her outfit was complete, she slapped on her DKNY watch and some of the Dreamy for Women perfume. She loved the way the Dreamy perfume smelled on her. It smelled sweeter than candy and lovelier than the smell of a flower. She walked back to her closet and grabbed her brand new, all white Nike Air Cross Trainers with the matching pink Nike swoosh. Matching and flexing was her thang when she wasn't playing couch potato.

Dee Dee stepped out the door with her white Louis Vuitton purse, and got into her ride. She flipped down her sun visor to check herself out one last time. What she saw was that she needed some lip gloss, so she reached in her purse and grabbed it. With her lips now glistening, she was out, headed for the mall.

Twenty minutes later Dee Dee pulled inside the

mall parking lot and found a place to park. With the sun shining brightly, she slid on her Baby Phat pin-tinted shades. When she walked through the doors to enter the mall, she found herself wanting to shop. She hit store after store, buying handbags, shoes, and a few outfits. Now Dee Dee had two big bags of clothes to lug around the mall. She smelled something good, so she headed toward the food court. What she smelled was meat being cooked, but at that moment she didn't feel like messing with something that could get stuck in between her teeth and fuck up her cute appearance, so she decided on a hot pretzel instead.

Three dudes got in line behind her and started making little remarks that they thought were cute. Dee Dee was laughing on the inside, 'cause what they were saying was lame as hell to her, and she felt that if that was all they were working with, then they needed to go to the University of Game so they could get schooled real good. Now it was Dee Dee's turn to step up to the counter, but before she did, one of the dudes got brave enough to reach his hand out and touch her butt. Without hesitation, Dee Dee turned around and swung her purse, catching the bug-a-boo who was brave enough, right in the face. Dude's nose started bleeding instantly. She didn't mean to, but she had managed to break his nose.

"Bitch, you broke my fucking nose! I should kill you, bitch!" Dude shouted. Before the incident, neither Dee Dee, nor the guys could see each other's faces as they stood in line, but when she stood there after popping dude in the nose, his homeboy recognized just who Dee Dee was.

"Yo, Man! That's those nigga's Bee and Jay's little sister," he stated as he backed up.

"Nigga, I don't care if the bitch was Jesus' sister, the bitch broke my fucking nose." Dude that recognized her didn't want any drama with Dee Dee's brothers, so he just walked away. The other cat was heated 'cause she swung on him and caused damage, and now he wanted her to pay. The crowd that had formed was looking on wondering what would happen next. Dee Dee was scared, but then again, she wasn't. That's why she reached her hand inside her purse to get her knife. Dude knew what time it was when a broad reached inside her purse, so he swung, knocking her purse out of her hand and onto the ground.

It was Dee Dee's lucky day 'cause Alastair was in the mall and walking her way. He didn't know she was over there, nor did he know that she was in the midst of becoming a punching bag. What he did know was that the loud noise meant that someone was about to start some shit, so he moved quickly to be nosey. Everybody in the mall was used to seeing shit like this episode go down, 'cause this was a mall was on the rough side of town.

Dude went in and grabbed Dee Dee by her throat. Dee Dee's eyes got big. She couldn't think of shit to do and all she could think of was that she wished her brothers were there.

Alastair spotted Dee Dee being manhandled by dude, so he shoved his way through the crowd already gathered around the commotion. Alastair didn't bother grabbing dude's hand to get him to release his hold on her throat. No, he just gave dude a straight chin checker from the blind side. Dude stumbled sideways until he lost his balance and fell to the ground. Dude stayed on the ground bleeding badly from his nose. It didn't take a brain surgeon for all the on-lookers to figure out that homeboy was dazed, 'cause he was looking disoriented from that straight right that Alastair had delivered.

Dee Dee got herself together and gave dude two fierce kicks, one to his face and the other to his rib cage. She wanted to do more, but Alastair spotted six mall police officers rushing over. Alastair grabbed Dee Dee and carried her in the other direction. She shouted that her bags were back at the scene, so Alastair put her down and took a chance on going back for her stuff. He grabbed her bags, and that gave the onlookers a chance to point him out to the security guards as one of the fighters. The police of-ficers turned and started after him. Alastair moved through the crowd and met Dee Dee. Without stop-ping, he grabbed her hand and told her to move her feet 'cause the law was behind them. Dee Dee had been a high school track star, so she was able to keep up with Alastair while he kept his grip on her hand, leading the way to the nearest exit.

Once outside, he headed for his truck. The police officers were still hot on their tails. Alastair had Dee Dee duck down and ease on into his truck on the passenger side. He then eased into the truck from her side and quickly got up out of there.

When Jay made it back to the house, Janelle had told him all about what had went down with Mieka and his sister. Once he saw that scratch on his sis-ter's face, he instantly backpedaled out of the door and went in search of Mieka. Janelle watched Jay peel off, hoping that she had gained some type of brownie points with her tattling.

Dee Dee knew from the way Jay had grabbed her face to examine it, that someone had beat her to the punch in telling him. Even though Mieka was the bitch he once trusted, he felt that she had really fucked up by putting her hands on his sister.

Jay whipped his ride through the streets searching every 'hood, all the way until he reached Mieka's crib. He pulled into her apartment complex and saw that her ride wasn't in her regular parking spot. He knew that she figured it would be wiser not to park her ride where Dee Dee's two crazy brothers would find it, so Jay drove all over the whole complex searching every parking space.

Just when Jay was about to leave, he spotted someone running across the courtyard. He thought it looked like Mieka, but he couldn't tell. He decided to say fuck it and move on. Jay reached above his sun visor and pulled one of the rolled up blunts out of the strap that was connected to the visor. He put the flame to the tip of the blunt and puffed to get it going real good. He inhaled the greenery deeply. The drag was so strong that Jay damn near coughed his insides up.

"Damn, this new shit is good," he said to himself. He took another toke of the greenery then rolled off.

On his way out of the parking lot he spotted a white Diamante with rims, parked sideways in the parking lot. Jay crept in slow motion up to the ride to see who it was. Now he was side by side with the car. His eyes locked onto the nigga who was driving the ride. They both looked at each other with a stare down match. Jay tried to think of where he knew the nigga from, but nothing was registering. The dude nodded his head.

Jay slowly moved his right hand onto his heater, ready to let it ride. Jay then returned the same nod. As Jay's car kept moving in slow motion, passing dude by, they both looked back to see if one or the other wanted some drama. Jay saw that nothing was popping, so he put the blunt back in his mouth and peeled off out of there.

Mieka came outside to the Diamante and asked Rock what Jay wanted. All she could do was watch the exchange between them from a distance. Mieka thought that they were talking, but they were really just ready to get it on. Rock knew Jay was the nigga that Mieka was kicking it with, but he brushed it off because he was still hitting the pussy at will any time he wanted. Mieka hopped back in the car and asked Rock again about what Jay had wanted. Rock just brushed her question off and slid his hand in between her legs. Mieka didn't care about too much, as long as she could be in the company of Rock, the nigga she both loved and hated.

Rock was a big, yellow nigga. He only wore expensive gear and sported nothing but the most expensive designer shades and shoes. From being an ex-linebacker for the Miami Hurricanes, he had built up a persona about himself that he was the shit. He had established a bail bonds company in town after he blew his knee out after only two years in the pros.

Rock knew that the nigga Jay didn't know who he was from the stare he was giving him, but he didn't like the stare, so he figured he would set the nigga straight at a later time and place.

By the time Jay made it back to the house, Bee was already there and drilling Dee Dee about the big scratch on her face.

"You see what that funky bitch that you had did to my baby sister," Bee shouted in anger.

Jay looked at Bee with the same heated eyes they were both born with.

"What the fuck is you talking about, nigga?" Jay shot back, slamming the door closed.

Bee was dead serious about what he had just said. Dee Dee was his heart, even though she had the same mentality that the two of them had. Bee couldn't stand to see her with that scratch on her face, knowing that someone had put it there.

"I'm talking about this scratch on her face," Bee stated as he grabbed Dee Dee by her chin and turned her head so he could see what he was talking about.

"The next muthafucker that grabs me by my damn face is gonna get fucked up just like that bitch Mieka got fucked up," Dee Dee said loudly.

They both looked at their sister in surprise.

"What you mean like she got fucked up?" Bee asked. Dee Dee went on to tell them the story about what happened from start to finish. When she finished, Jay and Bee both gave each other high fives.

Dee Dee looked at her brothers and thought those two niggas was just as crazy as the niggas on the street talked about. She threw her hands up in the air and walked into the kitchen.

"Aw, sis, don't be like that," Jay shouted.

"I ain't got time for you two and all that foolishness y'all got with you," Dee Dee shouted from the kitchen.

Bee was about to go after his sister to see if she was cool, but got stopped in his tracks when Jay grabbed his arm. "Look, man. We got to talk," Jay stated.

"About what?" Bee asked.

"Man, you know this shit is about to get real deep, right?"

"Yeah, but ain't this what you always wanted?" Bee asked as he looked into his brother's eyes.

"Yeah, it is, but I know this ain't what you really wanna do, at least not for the rest of your life," Jay said with sympathy toward his brother's future.

"Look, bro, I ain't gonna be in this shit for long cuz once I reach a mil or two I'm out."

Jay looked at his brother with concern and dread about the future. There was no way he would let some muthafuckas touch his brother, let alone kill him, so right then and there he started planning for a way to get his whole family out of Tennessee when the time came, including their momma.

Jay sat on the couch and listened to Bee tell him about how he had everybody ready to move the shit when it arrived in a couple of days.

While they were watching TV, Jay's cell phone started ringing. He flipped it open and spoke to the female on the other end. Shala had called him for her cousin Darrel, who had just gotten out of jail. Darrel didn't know Jay and Bee personally, but he was in direct need of the hookup, and since he knew Shala used to fuck around with Jay back in the day, he asked her to put it in motion. Jay told Shala it was on and poppin', and for her to give him about thirty minutes. Jay told Bee that they had a lick for the last of the shit they hit Manny up for, so Bee went and grabbed it out of the stash spot in the garage. Jay met Bee out in the car and they took off.

Dee Dee walked to the door and looked at her no-good, hustling brothers as they pulled out of the driveway.

Chapter Ten

Since the day Alastair had saved Dee Dee at the mall from what was sure to be an ass whooping from ole boy, things started to fall into place.

Alastair once thought that when Dee Dee said she had two big problems she was referring to the fact that she had kids, but that was one of the things she made clear to him that wasn't true. Dee Dee found herself wanting to pick up the phone and give him a call. She still had Prat on her mind, but Alastair was exactly what the doctor ordered to take her mind off Prat. She decided that since it was Friday, she would go ahead and make the call.

Alastair was at the pool hall kicking it with the fellas when his cell phone started ringing. "Talk to me," he answered.

Dee Dee stayed quiet for a sec, then she uttered, "Al, this is Dee Dee."

"Hey, Dee Dee! What's up?" he said with happiness clearly in his voice.

"Nothing much. I was just thinking that if you wasn't busy, then maybe we could meet somewhere."

Alastair liked the way that sounded, so he quickly gave her an answer, asking her where a good spot was for her to meet.

"How about the bowling alley on Riverdale?"

Alastair wondered why she would want to meet way out in Honkyville. Dee Dee figured that since this was the first time they would be alone, it wasn't any use in hanging out somewhere in the 'hood and chance her brothers spotting them and causing havoc. No, Dee Dee wanted to enjoy this sunny day with Al without interference from her two overprotective big brothers.

They hung up with each other and Alastair called his pool game quits with the fellas. His homeboys weren't too happy with him departing 'cause Alastair was the one with the stick on point who was winning all the cash.

"Sorry fellas, but my future wife is waiting on a nigga," he stated while counting his earnings. He then parted ways as he broke outside.

He hopped in his Escalade and headed for the other side of town, over in Honkyville. He liked how the homes over there looked, but Alastair's crib wasn't no shim shack. He had a one-story ranch style crib just outside of town in Rossburgh Township. The game he was in was treating him nicely to where he was living like the white folks in Riverdale.

Alastair pulled into the bowling alley parking lot and parked. Before he even had a chance to cut the engine off, Dee Dee opened the door to the passenger side of his ride and hopped in.

"Well, hey there, Miss Sneaky," Alastair greeted her, stunned.

"Sorry about the intro, but I spotted you when you pulled in," Dee Dee stated, taking off her slippers.

Alastair was all eyes as he scoped out her pedicured feet. Dee Dee plopped her feet up on the seat and tucked them underneath her butt. Alastair got his focus back to reality after scoping her out fully.

"I thought you wanted to go bowling," he said.

Dee Dee looked at the bowling alley, staring at all the white people inside, then told him, "Not with all those white people in there. Actually, I wanted to go to the carnival over there." Alastair thought about what she had just said, and thought that her idea could turn out to be really fun.

They pulled into the dusty road. The first thing he thought was that he was gonna have to have his ride detailed all over again in the morning from all the dust it was now collecting. They pulled up to the ticket booth and got a ticket to park. Alastair traveled as slow as he could as he looked for a parking spot.

Once they parked, they both stepped out of the ride and marveled at the colorful bright lights that lit up the whole carnival. Alastair looked over at Dee Dee and took it upon himself to wrap her up from behind with his arms. Dee Dee didn't bother to shake his embrace off, but instead she welcomed it as she put her hands on his. Alastair was shocked that she did that, but then again, he knew that he stood a chance seeing as how she was the one who asked him out. When he first met her, he knew that she had a feisty side to her, but here he was, seeing that Miss Feisty also had a genuine female side.

He took hold of her hand and led her to the entrance of the carnival. They talked about all they were seeing. They laughed at the funny faced clowns and the little people and inhaled in the smells of popcorn, cotton candy, funnel cakes, and hot dogs.

As they walked, Dee Dee damn near fell backward as she realized what had touched her when she bumped into the lady with the genie outfit. She tried to hide behind Alastair, but he kept moving out of the way as the lady kept saying, "He won't bite. Go ahead and pet him." The python the lady was holding was yellow and big, and that's the part that Dee Dee didn't want to have no part of.

Once away from the lady and her snake, Dee Dee copped an attitude with Alastair, giving him a straight hard punch in the arm. He took the pain and gave her an apology for not helping her. Still, Dee Dee was upset. She kept rubbing her arm as if the snake had left something on her. Alastair took it upon himself to make up for his behavior. He told her not to move as he went over to one of the game booths to get her a prize that he thought would put a smile on her face.

He talked to the man working at the booth and told him that he wanted him to rig it so his girl could win whatever she wanted. The man told Alastair that it would cost him a hundred dollars for him to pull it off. Alastair agreed and pulled out a knot that had nothing but big faces wrapped up in it. The worker's eyes got big as fuck when he saw all the money that the black brother had. He only wished that he would have asked him for a higher price.

Alastair walked back over to Dee Dee, who was still pouting, and had her go play some of the games with him. The first one they played was the one where you sit in the seat and try to aim the water gun at the bull's eye so your horse can win the race, which neither did. They lost to a little white kid. Dee Dee didn't mind losing to other people, so long as she beat Alastair, which she did, and she made sure she bragged about it all the way to the next game. Alastair was glad that she was feeling better, even though he had to intentionally lose the game.

The second game was the one where you threw darts at the balloons on the wall. Alastair cracked up at how bad Dee Dee's aim was, 'cause she didn't hit shit, but neither did he, intentionally.

Dee Dee was wired now. Alastair saw Dee Dee run for the place where he had worked the deal out with the guy. His eyes were stuck on Dee Dee's phat ass poking out of the Baby Phat blue jeans she was sporting. He just stood there and admired her from the back and wondered what it would be like to make love to her. The tight, red Baby Phat T-shirt had her titties looking more beautiful than any model's he had ever seen in a magazine.

"I see you must be scared to compete against me, Al," Dee Dee shouted as she saw Alastair standing in the back. To him, her smile was breathtaking, and he wanted so badly to put his lips on hers and sample them.

Before they started the game the worker looked at Alastair and gave him a wink, signaling to him that everything was a go. The worker had given Dee Dee some rings that were bigger than the ones that everybody else would normally use so she wouldn't have a problem with getting the red ring on the tip of the glass bottles. The first one she tossed she hit, and got overexcited. Alastair just smiled and looked on. The next five that she tossed, she also hit, and she became hysterical with joy. Alastair had the regular red rings, and when he tossed, he missed. He was really trying to make them onto the bottle tops, but nothing was up as he missed each time.

"We have a winner!" The worker shouted as he rang the school bell. Dee Dee ran and jumped onto Alastair, letting her happiness turn into affection as she gave him a quick kiss. Alastair was shocked, but Dee Dee was even more shocked when she felt herself like the way the kiss felt. She raised her head and just looked into Alastair's black eyes. What she was feeling was kind of the same way that she felt when her and Prat made love, but she knew that Alastair was no Prat. That kiss brought Prat into her mind, though. She still needed to talk to Prat, and for that reason, she didn't think that she could move in the direction that she knew she was supposed to go with Al.

The worker cleared his throat loudly so he could get their attention. He felt that his side of the deal was fulfilled, so it was time for them to choose the prize and get on about their business so he could tend to his other customers. Alastair gently let Dee Dee down. For a minute they were about to walk off and leave their prize, but the worker called them back. Dee Dee became happy again when she saw all the different stuffed animals that she could pick from. She pointed to the biggest one and asked if she could have that one. Dude wasn't trying to give her that one, but he soon changed his mind when he looked at Alastair and saw the black brother giving off a look. He handed Dee Dee the big white and brown dog, and when she took it, she could barely hold the big ass thing. Alastair quickly stepped in and took control of carrying the stuffed animal. He threw the animal over his shoulder and carried it as they walked to other parts of the carnival.

Dee Dee was happy at the way her day was spent, and with whom she spent it. Alastair tucked her stuffed animal in the backseat of his SUV and opened the passenger side door so Dee Dee could get inside.

As they headed back to the bowling alley, Dee Dee found herself wanting to spend more time with Alastair. When he pulled into the parking lot, Dee Dee looked at him from the side and thought how good his lips had felt on hers. She wanted to just reach over and lay a big wet one on him, but she felt that she had already did enough of that at the carnival when she won her prize.

Alastair got out of his ride and walked over to open her door. Dee Dee watched as he crossed in front of the truck, heading to her side. When she got out, Alastair took her into his arms and held her tightly around her waist. They both felt the heat. Alastair leaned his head in to make lip contact. His lips touched hers and Dee Dee damn near melted. The passion was stronger than she could have ever imagined.

While her lips were still connected to his, she opened her eyes and was shocked when she saw Prat's green Diamante roll by, bumping. She broke her embrace and headed for her car without saying anything to Alastair. Alastair was stunned to see her break camp on him like that. He had no idea what he did to make her leave like that, nor did he know that Dee Dee was still caught up on a dude named Prat.

Dee Dee sped down the street, hot on Prat's tail, but soon got yet another shock when she heard sirens and saw red and blue lights flashing behind her. She looked in her rearview mirror and saw the police right behind her. She banged her fist on the steering wheel and cussed out loud. She couldn't believe her luck. Her day had started off good, but now she had the police behind her about to give her a speeding ticket for sure.

Dee Dee signed the pink piece of paper stating that she would pay the fine or have a warrant issued for her. At this point, all she wanted to do was get to her bed and call it a day.

Chapter Eleven

The dope had finally arrived, only Jay and Bee had no idea that the shipment would be larger than what it was. Two hundred bricks of that white stuff sat in front of them. Dee Dee looked at the dope that her brothers were pulling out of the duffel bags.

"Dee Dee, turn that thermostat to the right," Jay told her. Both Jay and Bee looked on, waiting to see the expression on their sister's face when the wall started to move.

Dee Dee looked at the thermostat and wondered why the fuck Jay would want her to turn the temperature up on a hot day like it was. When she turned the thermostat, she freaked out as the wall started to move.

"What the fuck!" Dee Dee shouted as she jumped back. She looked over at Jay and Bee, who were cracking the fuck up. "Y'all make me sick with your punk asses," Dee Dee stated with her middle finger stuck up in the air.

"Naw, sis, it's just that you should have seen your face when the wall started to move," Bee teased.

Dee Dee didn't pay them any more attention. Instead, she checked out the wall and what was behind it.

"This is some slick shit rigged here, but what the fuck is it for?" She asked, not being hip to the game.

Jay carried ten bricks to the wall and stacked them on the shelves, answering her question. Once she saw what they were doing, she began to lend a hand. Jay looked at his sister and paid close attention to her as she scoped out the dope.

"You know, sis, they say that it's one law to this game, and that is ''n'ever get high on your own supply.''' Jay made sure to put that in her head.

Dee Dee looked at Jay, then at the dope she had in her hand. She figured that if niggas were crazy enough to spend all their money on this just so they could get high, then she would never go out like that.

"So, y'all gotta sell all of this shit?" Dee Dee asked, then tossed Jay the brick she was holding.

"Sis, this is gonna have us living phat like Puff Daddy. You just wait and see," Jay stated. Dee Dee didn't doubt what her brother just said, she just wondered at what price, 'cause that was a lot of dope.

Jay distributed dope to all the people that were on their roster. Terry Tee got the most, which was twenty kilos, because that was Jay's main man. The rest of the fellas got ten, except Lil Man, who only got a big eight at a time 'cause of his lack of experience in the game.

Everything was going good, but with all that

stuff, Jay and Bee knew that they had to expand. They had cousins up in Cashville, aka Nashville, and they had set it up so they could go up there and pay them a surprise visit before they got the next shipment.

Jay was still on his mission to get his sister as hip to the game as he could, and the first thing he did was get her acquainted to getting dope from the apartment complex on a regular. Jay would call Dee Dee to drive over there and grab some of those keys, but he instructed her to always look her best and walk to the grocery store to drop it off to whoever needed it.

Right now Dee Dee was at the apartment complex. Jay and Bee waited in one of the other apartments that he had laid out. The purpose for that crib was to have niggas that were on their team come and drop the cash off. If they got big ideas about robbing them at that apartment, then they would be in for a shock when they came and found out that no one and nothing was there. Jay was really good at deception, so that was the main reason that he only used that apartment for collection and nothing more, not even for pleasure. Bee didn't have a key to the apartment. The only cats that knew that they collected in the apartment were Terry Tee and D-Dawg, but they didn't know that Jay or Bee never did anything else there, so the two brothers and sister watched their people closely and kept the secret just between the three of them.

One by one, everybody was showing up with a shit-load of money to turn in, and when all was collected, Jay, Bee, and Dee Dee slid the money down the trash shoot, which was rigged so that it would go directly to the safe house apartment for counting.

They all walked out of the apartment and headed to the safe house. When they were inside, Jay went straight to the security cameras and looked to see if there was anybody outside of the building lurking for a come up. Jay marveled at the security layout 'cause it was something that every big hitter needed, but wasn't smart enough to have.

When they counted the dough, Jay and Bee were surprised to see that Tony's money was all accounted for.

"Man, Bee. Tony gonna like this shit," Jay exclaimed as he was stacking money on the shelves.

Bee took the last of the money out of the counting machine, and then handed it to his brother.

"How much money is all of that?" Dee Dee asked as she looked on.

"Just put it like this, sis. We got our connect money when he come through, and a little extra to do what we want to do, feel me?" Jay stated as he tossed his sister a stack of money.

"This is ten grand y'all," Dee Dee said after she counted the cash.

"We know, sis. Do as you please with it cuz you worked hard for it," Bee stated.

Dee Dee didn't have the slightest clue as to what he was referring to, 'cause to her, she hadn't done a damn thang. Dee Dee was about to open her mouth to say something that would probably cost her the ten grand, but something that her mother always told her popped into her head. *Baby, remember, a wise woman thinks twice before even speaking once.* The words her mother spoke finally made sense to her for once in her twenty-five years on this earth.

Bee stopped by D-Dawg's new apartment. They were about to go out and celebrate for moving the dope so quickly. Tonight they planned on hitting up Flexy, which was one of the hottest strip joints in Memphis. The quality of broads that they had in that joint was sisters who had ba-dunk-a-dunk.

When D-Dawg came outside, he was shocked to see Bee in a new ride, a Benz S-Class at that. Bee stood outside his ride and gently wiped it down on the door side.

"When you copped this joint, man?" D-Dawg asked in excitement as he walked around the ride checking it out.

"It ain't mines yet, but come tomorrow it will be," Bee stated.

"What you mean ain't yours yet? Either it is or it ain't," D-Dawg shot back.

"Get in, fool, and let's go," Bee said as he got in.

When D-Dawg got in, Bee handed him some papers that hipped him to what Bee was talkin' 'bout.

"All right! I get it now. You test driving this joint for today, and come tomorrow, you gotta buy the joint or they gonna have your black ass picked up for theft," D-Dawg cracked.

"Shut up, fool, and just roll the blunt," Bee told him as he tossed the bag of greenery into his boy's lap. D-Dawg smelled the bag and he could have sworn it was from Cali with the smell it had. He was used to smoking that kill-kill since he had moved out west, and he was tired of smoking the stress that they kept in M-City.

They hit the strip joint and sat in the ride in the parking lot until they finished the rest of the blunt. At this point, they were feeling good as fuck, but they were planning on feeling better than that once they got inside. Bee got out of his ride and hit the last of the roach, then tossed it into the grass. They walked up to the door and pressed the doorbell. Once inside, their eyes went to staring as they saw it was a packed house, with phat asses everywhere.

D-Dawg slapped his palms together and started rubbing them.

"Man, Bee! It's on and poppin' in this bitch," he said with a devilish grin.

"You can say that again. Check that bitch out in the green. I bet she got some bomb ass pussy."

"Damn, Nigga! You know who that is?" D-Dawg asked, looking hard.

"Who?" Bee asked.

"Man, that's Nikki from the 'Ville."

"Damn. You sure right. Now I know I gotta holla at her. Shit, she been gone just as long as your black ass," Bee joked.

They went and took seats at one of the few available tables in the place. It didn't take long for one of the honey brown-skinned females to come up to them and ask if they wanted a lap dance. She was all that and a bag of chips, standing six feet high and thick all over.

"How much?" D-Dawg asked, cockily.

"I'll give y'all two lap dances for sixty each," she stated, looking sexy with her g-string tucked deep in her ass crack.

"The hell you will! For that price, you give me some ass," D-Dawg shot back.

"Nigga, please! To get a shot of this ass it's gonna cost you three bills. Now, can you afford that?" She asked, looking straight at D-Dawg.

D-Dawg pulled out a knot and said, "Lead the way so I can blow your back out." She didn't hesitate to grab his hand when she saw he had a knot. "This may take a second, homie, so enjoy yourself cuz I'm fo' sho' about to," D-Dawg stated as he gave his boy some dap.

Bee watched his boy enter the VIP Room, aka the Fuck Spot. He was cracking up as he looked on. To him, he liked the way ole girl was straightforward and shit, 'cause he met so many broads that would just fuck a nigga and not even get anything out of it but some hurt feelings and a broken expectation of what it could have been. He sat there drinking his Henn-dawg, looking at all the females doing their hustling. He was glad that he had a good girl at the crib, 'cause to him, shaking your ass for money wasn't classy. Class to him was a female who was not involved in this type of business, who fucked a nigga at her crib where nobody was in her business, and who basically kept her shit on the down low.

Bee spotted Nikki going up on the stage and decided to go spend some of those dollars that he had on the table waiting to burn.

Nikki started off strong as she hit the pole. Bee took a seat at the front of the stage over to the right side. He was all eyes as she hit the headstand and started making all that jelly shake, crazy like. She was collecting dolla' after dolla', but she had yet to look Bee's way. He wasn't tripping 'cause ain't no way she could pass over the smoothest nigga in the joint. She was on all fours in the doggy style position making that ass clap. Finally, she looked his way while she was still in that same position, bleeding other niggas. She looked Bee up and down as he leaned back in his seat all cool and shit. She caught the platinum chain around his neck, the two-carat diamond stud earrings in his ears, the Cartier on his wrist, and the Enyce blue jean denim outfit he wore. Now she was all smiles as she kept looking at him while still performing. She stood up and hit the pole one last time before the song went off.

Bee pimped his game from start to finish, and when the song was over, it had worked to a tee. He got up and walked back to his table, and right behind him was Nikki. Bee sat down and chilled while he waited for his prey to make her way over.

"What's up, big baller?" Nikki asked with a stunning smile.

Bee looked her up and down through his Cartier lenses. Her caramel skin was like that to him, and her ass was even more like that with those thick ass legs she had. His eyes landed on her pussy, which was poking out of that g-string she had on.

"What's up with you, shorty?" Bee shot back as he looked into her hazel-brown eyes.

"I don't know. Why don't you tell me, playboy?"

They both looked at each other, basically sizing up one another in a sexual way.

"I ain't seen you here before," Bee stated.

She pulled out a chair and took a seat.

"That's because I ain't never been here before. Actually, it's my first day."

Bee looked at her with a cool persona. He knew that she was digging his style, so he just played along with it.

"So, do you do private lap dances with that extra twist?" Bee asked, wondering if she fucked for cash like the rest of them.

"Is that what you got on your mind?" She asked.

"Hold up, little momma! I asked my question first, so you can answer mines, then I'll answer yours. Cool?"

"It's whatever, baby."

"Then let's do this when you're ready," Bee suggested.

Nikki led the way to the back. He was walking behind her, and she was making that phat ass of hers bounce like a muthafucka. Bee was damn near hypnotized at the way she was stepping in those high heels.

She opened a door that led into a room that was completely red—red lights, red bed, red flowers, and because everything was red, the damn mirror was red when someone looked in it. She closed the door, then told Bee that the price was five strong. He was thrown for a loop, 'cause the other bitch told D-Dawg that it would cost three. He didn't front, though, 'cause when he thought about it, the broad that D-Dawg had damn sure wasn't no Nikki.

Bee peeled five big faces off his wad and handed them to her. Nikki didn't waste any time in taking off what little bit of clothing she had on. Bee had her come up to him while he sat in the red chair. She stood in front of him just the way he wanted her to. He eyed her whole sexy ass body, then started sliding his hand up and down her curvaceous frame. He slid his fingers in between her split. The heat and moistness was on point. Bee wasn't embarrassed to put his fingers up to his nose to see how the poo-nanny smelled.

"My shit is on point, ain't it?" Nikki asked as she smiled.

Bee didn't answer her and she didn't need an answer when he put his finger back inside of her. She leaned her head back and sighed as he fingered her pussy. He stopped what he was doing and took his pants down. She laid him on the bed and tore open a condom package. She then put the condom inside her mouth, and put his big daddy in her mouth. Like a magic trick, Bee had a condom pulled all the way down over his dick. He looked up to make sure it was all intact, no rips.

He had her mount him from the back. She was straddled across his legs with her ass facing him. Bee was looking at two phat ass cheeks and one nice ass-hole. She slid him inside and took care of her business. She wasn't fucking around when it came to trying to make a nigga bust a nut in two minutes. Bee was trying to slow her down, but just like a two-minute brother, he found himself outsmarted by her. Bee held on to her waist as he began to bust his nut inside the condom. Nikki could feel that she had succeeded in working yet another nigga with her bomb ass pussy skills, so she got up and got dressed.

"That's it?" Bee asked.

"Now come on, boy. You know I should be asking you that question."

Bee looked at her, then looked down at his dick with the used up condom on it, and thought that he couldn't go out like that.

"Yo, Nikki. How much to go at it again?" Bee asked, wanting another crack at her.

"What did you just call me?" She asked, stunned because he knew her name.

"Your name is Nikki, right?"

"Yeah, it is, but I don't know you."

"Baby, I know you. I'm Bret Davis. We grew up together.

She was beyond shocked, 'cause she just fucked a dude for cash that she knew. She couldn't run off and leave 'cause she was at work, and she needed the little job that she had. She already knew from back in the day that Bee was a hustler, and with him still looking the part, she decided to make a connection with him so he would stay wanting the ass for himself.

"Lay down," she ordered.

Bee did as she said, with his legs spread apart and dick back on hard. She began to dance seductively to help suck him in. She raised her legs up onto the bed and placed her feet on his dick. She looked at Bee and made all kinds of sexy fuck faces that had him going. Bee clasped his hands behind his head and kept his eyes on the prize. She slid her g-string down once again and gave him something to really look at. She took her hand and placed her fingers in between her pussy. What she was doing was so freaky that Bee couldn't help but to feel on his jones. She turned around and shook that ass for him.

Bee couldn't take it anymore, so he went to grab her, but Nikki wasn't having that just yet. She knew that in order to make a nigga do what she wanted, he would first have to understand that he had to play by her rules, or not play at all. Bee didn't like the way she pulled away. But Nikki had a way of fooling a nigga to where he thought she was doing something special for him. All she was doing was sucking Bee in deeper and deeper, to be the nigga that would take care of her by all means necessary, even if he did have a girl that he loved. The last trick she did was spread her ass cheeks with her hands and make her asshole breathe. She knew that would really suck him in, which it did, 'cause Bee was all eyes. Nikki finally got on the bed and lay down next to him.

She made Bee get on top of her so she could suck him in even further with a whole bunch of bullshit faces, which she knew men couldn't get enough of with their big egos. Bee climbed on top of her with a new rubber in place. He gripped hold of his jones and eased himself right inside of her. She flinched as he entered her canal. Her nails were on his back, but not scratching it up. She knew that only a dumb, lonely, messy bitch played a childish game like that to piss the nigga's girl off, but to her, she was looking at a long term thang, and she didn't need any problems with the missus.

Bee stroked her like he was making love, but he was able to tell that he wasn't from all the noise she was making. He had her legs pinned up on his shoulders, going as deep as his dick could go. He looked down at her and saw that he was doing way better than what he just did a little bit ago. He was trying to cause havoc on her pussy with all the bumping and grinding that he was doing, not to mention the digging and stroking.

"Baby, I'm cumming. Go deeper!" She instructed as she held him tightly. While she was cumming, she did something that sealed the deal, which was pulled his head in and kissed him passionately. Bee couldn't believe he just fucked the shit out of Nikki, and the good thing about it was that it felt damn good.

Bee got up while she still lay there, playing the roll of pussy got fucked real good. He finished putting on his clothes, then pulled out his wad of cash. He was about to give her another five bills, but she told him it was all good. Bee didn't get it, but it was all part of her plan to make him think that she wasn't all about the Benjamins. Bee stuck his money back in his pocket and looked at Nikki, who was all curled up in a cute, sexy way. He knew he had to see Nikki some more, so he asked her would she ever quit her job. Bee wanted that ass on standby for him at any time, and the only way he would be able to do that was to make her his own.

"That depends."

"Depends on what?" Bee asked.

"If I got a better way of taking care of myself," she stated, then put her finger in her mouth and sucked on it.

Bee didn't waste any time. He made her get dressed and told her to go home and call the number that he had just given.

"What's this?" She asked, looking over the paper.

"Just go home and start planning on having me over there on a constant." Bee peeled two thousand from his wad and gave it to her.

They walked out of the room and Nikki went to get her bag out of the dressing room. Bee waited at his table for her. Before she came out, D-Dawg came out smiling like a muthafucka.

"My nigga. What I tell you. That bitch won't be able to dance no more tonight. I promise you that, especially after I gave her some mean ass killa' dick," D-Dawg stated as he did the fucking motion with his body.

Nikki walked up right behind D-Dawg and tapped him on the shoulder. He turned around and saw her standing there, all smiles, just like he was a second ago.

"What's the dilly-o, girl?" D-Dawg greeted.

"Long time no see, Derrick," she replied, grinning and fully dressed in a gray and yellow New Balance sweat suit with shoes to match.

Bee told her they were rolling, and she followed right behind him like she was his woman. D-Dawg peeped the shit out, and wondered what was going on.

When they reached the exit door, the owner asked Nikki where she was going 'cause her shift wasn't over.

"Homie, she leaving with her nigga, so it would be wise to step aside," D-Dawg said as he approached them.

"So, you quitting, Nikki?" the owner asked, upset.

"Yeah, John. I guess I'm not cut out for this kind of work," she said, then walked out. Bee walked her over to a purple PT Cruiser, which he figured had to be hers.

"So you want me to call you tonight or in the morning?" she asked as she sat in her car with the door open.

Bee thought about it for a second, then opted that it would be better if she called tomorrow.

"Just go home and sleep real good tonight, and come tomorrow, give me a call." Bee closed her door as she started up the car. He bent down, leaned in, and gave her a kiss on the lips. D-Dawg just watched, thinking his boy done lost his fucking mind hooking up with a stripper broad, 'cause they were worse than gold diggers.

She put the car in drive and slowly drove off. She waved at D-Dawg, who was posted on the passenger side of Bee's new Benz. *He must got a lot of cash if that's the ride they're in*, she thought to herself. Bee walked over to his car, ready to roll out.

"Man, don't tell me that you're about to hook up with her like that."

"You gonna get in or ask me some stupid ass questions?" Bee shot back, not really wanting to discuss Nikki.

The night wasn't over yet, so they headed to Louie's Bar to shoot pool and get fucked up, and then they finally headed home.

Chapter Twelve

The dope shipment had come through once again, only this time, unlike the last time, the amount was bigger than what they had anticipated. Now they had four hundred bricks to move. Bee didn't like the idea that Tony was sending more than what they had agreed on, but there wasn't any way to deny the shipment when it had made its way all the way from Houston.

Bee and Jay were almost to Nashville. They had planned on paying their cousins, Rich and Lazy, a visit before the shipment got there, but time had slipped away from them. With the new bigger shipment, they were sure gonna need their family's help. They entered Washington Street and cruised all the way down until they hit their auntie's crib.

Bee stepped out of Jay's big, black Excursion and just looked around the neighborhood that they used to visit so much as teenagers, before their aunt had passed away. Bee knocked on the door and got no answer. He tried again, and still there was no answer. He walked around back to see if anybody was back there.

While Bee was in the back, a lady next door came outside and asked if they were looking for Rich and Lazy. Jay told her that they were his cousins and that they came all the way from Memphis to see them. When the lady told Jay that they got into a fight with some police for playing their music too loud in their car, Jay hurried up and called Bee so they could go downtown to bail them out.

When they got to the county jail, Jay found out that both of their bail was twenty thousand dollars for disturbing the peace and resisting arrest. Jay and Bee didn't have forty thousand on them right then, so they knew the only way to get their cousins out was to get a bail bondsman. Just when they were about to leave and seek out a bail bondsman, a black man in a suit stopped them. He told them that he heard that they might be in need of a bail bondsman. They filled out the paperwork and paid the older man four grand to do the job. Within moments, Lazy and Rich were walking out of the jail with their cousins, happier than a muthafucka.

"Man, what the hell brings y'all two muthafuckas up here?" Lazy asked with his hair in raggedy braids due to the rough conditions of the county jail.

"Shit! We ain't seen y'all in a minute so we came up," Bee stated. Bee and Lazy were the same age, and Jay and Rich were the same age, and with them having mothers who were sisters, one could tell that they were kin.

"Man, fuck all this talkin' shit. Just get me back to the crib so I can take a bath," Rich stated. Jay knew his cousin Rich always thought he was some kind of pimp or something. He always kept his hair permed and slicked back. Jay knew it had to be irking Rich the way his hair was all fucked up.

They all piled into the ride, and Jay drove back to his cousins' crib. While Rich took a bath, the other three sat in the living room sipping on some cold Budweiser longnecks, and chiefed on some kill-kill that Bee brought along. They talked about what they used to do as kids and how they used to cause havoc around the neighborhood.

When Rich came out of the shower, they all sat down and talked about the reason that Bee and Jay had driven up there. Lazy and Rich were all game to get their shit started, so Jay felt that it had to be done in the next few days.

"What's up with my little cuz, Dee Dee? Y'all still tripping on her living her life?" Lazy asked.

The look that Jay gave off told them the answer. Back in the days, Rich and Lazy had got dragged into a lot of fistfights 'cause their cousins were so overprotective of Dee Dee. Lazy still had a scar on his arm from when Jay started a fight with about nine older niggas who were trying to game on Dee Dee, but like real family, they all rolled together no matter who they had to roll on.

When Jay and Bee got back to Memphis later on, Jay was waiting for the phone to ring so he could give his cousins directions on how to get to the building. Just when he was about to get up and go piss, his cell started to ring. When he answered, he was glad to hear that it was them. Jay gave them the directions on how to get over there.

Rich and Lazy pulled up forty minutes later to the apartment complex and parked across the street.

They walked up to the apartment that Jay said to come to. Jay opened the door and they all greeted each other with dap and hugs. Jay liked the idea that they were all back together, doing the same thing. Jay led them to the bedroom, then flipped the sheet back on the bed revealing what they would now be taking back to Cashville to turn into cash.

There was no time for chitchat, so they all headed out to handle up. Jay saw them off as he watched them depart and head back. All Jay could hope for was that they made it back safe and cool with those fifty bricks he gave them. Jay knew that was a lot to be handling out on the front tip, but he had to take a chance with the niggas who were his blood.

He walked back inside to straighten things up. Once done, he drove back to his crib to spend some time with Miya and the kids. Miya was in the kitchen cooking up some tamales. Jay walked in and sniffed. The whole crib was smelling good. Miya's little kids heard Jay's voice from their room, ran out, and headed straight for him. Their smiles had Jay beaming with joy. He picked up Raphael and little Miya, and sat them on his lap. They both laughed loudly as Jay tickled them. Miya looked out at them and was all smiles as she saw the man that she loved playing with her kids who weren't even his.

Miya had finished with the meat, which was the last of what she needed to start serving. She sat all the bowls on the table and summoned Jay and the kids to come have a seat. Jay pulled Miya's chair out and took his seat. Before she could sit down, Jay's eyes gazing at her made her stand still and look at him. Miya's hair was down, just hanging and looking beautiful. Her apron was wrapped around her waist, so Jay untied it and tossed it on the kitchen counter. He took Miya in his arms, and since they were standing face to face, Jay gripped his hands on her ass.

"You see the kids is right there, Poppi," Miya whispered. Jay respected her words and released his grip, but not without telling her that they would continue what he had started later. Miya didn't have a problem with what he said 'cause that was her man and she would do whatever to please him.

Once they were done eating, Miya made sure the kids started their homework. Once she got them situated, she walked onto the balcony where Jay had gone. She handed him a beer, then took a seat in the chair next to him. The stars were in full effect in the night sky. Miya reached her hand out and Jay took it inside his.

"Jay, do you plan on being in business with my cousin long?" Miya asked with concern in her voice.

Jay looked at her and asked her why she would ask him something like that. She just told him that she didn't ever want anything bad to happen to him.

"Miya, baby, don't you worry your pretty little self about that cuz we gonna be all right," Jay stated.

After they were done chilling outside, Jay didn't go right to bed 'cause what Miya just asked him was on his mind. Jay replayed the shit that Don Valdez did to Chewy and thought that at any time, some shit like that could pop off involving him or Bee. When he first came home, he was ready to make love to his Spanish fly, but now all he wanted to do was lie down and fall asleep. He crawled into the bed and nestled up against Miya's warm, soft body and wrapped his arm around her waist in a tight clutch to show her that she was loved. He thought about his plans to leave the game, safely taking his whole family to a place where his connect couldn't find them.

Miya was ready to satisfy her man, but found that she would have to wait till tomorrow, as she heard snores coming from his direction. She just placed a kiss on his forehead and fell asleep herself.

Chapter Thirteen

$\mathcal{J}$ay had Dee Dee stay at the apartment so she could collect the money from the cats who were on their way. He and Bee were in the safe house watching everything on the security camera that Jay installed himself in a picture on the wall above the big screen TV.

The first knock hit the door. Dee Dee tucked the 9 mm Ruger underneath the newspaper that was on the table. She walked to the door and looked through the peephole. Terry Tee and Junior were on the other side waiting for someone to answer. Dee Dee opened the door and stood to the side until they came in, then closed it.

"What's up, sexy?" Junior said, greeting her with a wink.

"What's poppin', Junior," Dee Dee replied.

"Where's Jay and Bee?" Terry Tee asked.

"They had business to tend to," Dee Dee stated.

"So you handling shit then?" Junior asked smartly.

"It looks that way, don't it?" Dee Dee shot back strongly without even flinching.

Terry Tee dropped the bag on the table and told her it was all there. Dee Dee unzipped the bag and dumped the cash on the table. She slid stack after stack of cash into the counting machine. After all the counting was done, she took each ten thousand dollar stack and placed a rubber band around the money, then stuffed it back into the bag.

Bee and Jay looked at their sister handling up like a pro. Jay was pleased to see how she was handling herself. He couldn't hear what they were saying because he hadn't installed a mic, but he made a mental note to have that done as soon as possible.

"Dee Dee, when you gonna let a nigga take you out?" Junior asked slickly.

She just gave Junior a look that said, *With you? Never.* Before Junior could ask the question again, his brother ushered him out of the door 'cause he knew Jay and Bee acted straight fools when it came to her. Dee Dee closed the door behind them and tossed the bag of cash into the trash chute.

Jay grabbed the money out of the connecting chute on his side and tossed the bag to Bee so he could begin to store it.

Dee Dee stayed at the apartment doing the same thing with each one of the dudes who showed up. One after the other she tossed the bags full of cash into the chute.

Dee Dee sat on the plush green couch and rubbed her hands. She didn't know that counting money could put such a wear on someone's hands. The phone in the apartment rang, and when she answered it, she heard Jay's voice on the line telling her that she could go on home. She stood up and headed out, but before she opened the door, she remembered that the heater was still on the table. She walked back over and grabbed it from underneath the newspaper.

Dee Dee didn't understand, but a rush entered her as she held the gun. As she was acting like a cowboy from the old west with the gun, she had a flash of the night when she shot and killed Manny. The part where she pulled the trigger flashed before her eyes, scaring the shit out of her. Because Dee Dee couldn't take the vision that was haunting her, she dropped the gun, letting it hit the floor. She got herself together and picked the gun back up. Somehow she knew she was going to have to shake the nightmares.

Dee Dee stopped at the corner store and went in to get some ice cream. The niggas in front of the store were all trying to game, but Dee Dee just gave a smile and kept stepping.

Alastair was driving down the street about to pass the same corner store Dee Dee had entered. Spotting Dee Dee's ride he busted a U-turn and swooped his Escalade into the parking lot. When he stepped out, one of the cats outside the store recognized him.

"What's the dilly-o, Al?" One guy greeted.

Alastair looked over to the cat who just spoke and saw it was June, a cat he knew from back in the day.

"What's up with you, June?" Alastair asked as he gave him some pound.

"Man, I'm sorry about the death in your family, playa. I know when somebody passes, it's never easy. So just keep yo head up, huh!" June stated.

"It's all good, playa, but thanks for your sympathy," Alastair shot back.

"You know it's all love, baby." June extended his hand to give Alastair some handshake love. Alastair told him to get at him at the pool hall one day so they could chill and hang out before he left town. June was all game for that.

Dee Dee put a half-gallon of strawberry ice cream on the counter so she could pay for it.

"It's amazing how a girl as fine as you can eat ice cream and still keep her sexy figure."

Dee Dee turned around quickly to see just who had said that, but from the voice, she already knew.

"Are you stalking me, boy?" She asked sarcastically, but inside she was happy to see him.

"Come on, girl, do I look like a stalker to you?" He replied as he gave the clerk five dollars for the ice cream.

"And you think you don't cuz you look too good," she shot back with a black sister sassy stare.

"If I look like a stalker, then you do, too."

Dee Dee cracked a smile because what he had just said was funny to her. She headed out the door and walked to her car with Alastair right on her tail walking behind her.

"Damn, girl! You pass me up but you give my man some action. That's some cold shit, but I ain't gonna hate," June said, then puffed on his cigarette. Alastair waved, shooing June off with his hand.

"So, Miss Lady, what's on your mind for tonight?" Alastair asked, hoping nothing.

"I'm just going home to chill."

"Damn, that's too bad cuz I just went and rented some movies, including that old school shit, *Belly*."

Dee Dee really wasn't ready to go home, and since he mentioned the movie *Belly*, he got brownie points 'cause that was one of her favorite flicks. She had the pleasure of meeting DMX and the chick that played Kisha at the Celebrity All Star Game one year.

Alastair closed the driver's side door to her car, then had her follow him to his crib. As they were driving to Alastair's house, Dee Dee started to turn around 'cause where he was leading her looked like it was a setup. All she saw was the country, and to her that was the type of shit where a rapist took his victims. Alastair turned off the road and entered into his driveway. Dee Dee looked at the lit up estate, and was like "Whoa." The ranch style crib was hitting it. She couldn't believe that this was all his, like he had told her before.

Alastair parked his ride next to the rest of his cars and his blue and green Katana motorcycle. Dee Dee parked her car next to his and got out. She stood there looking in awe until Alastair asked her if she was coming in. When she walked in the door, a little Rottweiler came running up to her. She picked up the puppy and played with her, but then she saw the big Rottweiler standing in front of her looking like a straight killer. Dee Dee didn't move. All she could do was stand there scared as fuck.

Alastair grabbed his big dog and started to play with her. Dee Dee was relieved, 'cause for a moment there she thought that she was a goner.

"This is Sheba, and the puppy you're holding is her daughter, China." Alastair stated as he rubbed his dog playfully. Sheba rolled over on her back right in front of Dee Dee.

"She wants you to rub her stomach," he said as he waved her to go ahead.

Dee Dee lost all her fear when she saw the dog roll over like that. She gently rubbed the big furry dog like Alastair told her to, and right then Sheba took a liking to Dee Dee.

They walked into the living room with Sheba and China following. Dee Dee checked out Alastair's whole layout. The living room was connected to the dining room, which she liked. One was done in wood with green patio doors attached to it that led out into the back yard, where the lighted pool was located. She looked outside and thought how beautiful his place was.

Alastair went into the kitchen to store Dee Dee's ice cream in the freezer until it was time to eat it, but for right now, he had another idea of what they could eat. He took his apron off the hook and wrapped it around him. He opened the fridge and took out the T-bone steaks that he had been thawing since morning. They were already in a bowl soaking in seasoning. He placed the bowl on the island counter top, then took two pots and a pan from the rack hooks that hung above the center island.

He tossed six big potatoes in one of the pots and some spaghetti noodles in the other. Dee Dee looked over at Alastair wrapped in that apron and began to laugh.

"What's so funny?" Alastair asked with a grin.

"You in that apron is what's funny," she shot back, pointing.

"Well, let's see if you think my cooking is funny," he stated as he placed the steaks on the counter. Before Alastair got started tenderizing the meat, he walked over to the wine rack, grabbed a bottle of white wine, and poured two glasses until they were almost to the top. He walked over to her and handed her a glass. He planned on showing Dee Dee the smooth, suave side of kicking it.

"This toast is to me and you, cuz you can find love in the ghetto," Alastair said as he tapped his glass against hers.

Dee Dee looked Alastair in his eyes as she took a sip. The oil popping in the skillet brought his attention back to what he had to tend to.

"Make yourself at home, Deondra. There's a brand new pair of house slippers in that closet right there if you want to get your feet cozy."

Dee Dee watched Alastair do his thang with his cooking. He looked at her and gave a slight smile. He liked how she looked. That face of hers was overwhelming. Her hair was in a ponytail. She had jet-black hair that looked like silk when the light hit it.

He prepared the food on the plates and took them over to the table. He pulled two candles out of one of the drawers in the china cabinet, then set them into the holders.

He looked down at Dee Dee's feet and saw that she didn't accept his offer to switch footwear and put on the house shoes. He walked to the closet and grabbed them for her, then walked back over to where she was sitting at the table. She was eyeing the food in front of her. The smell was off the hook, and the sight of food was enticing to her mouth and stomach. She was pleased that the brother had skills like that in the kitchen.

Alastair sneaked up behind her, then eased down

to the floor. He grabbed her left leg and slid her shoe off. He couldn't believe that his baby had toes that looked that good. To him, if a female didn't have cute feet, then there wasn't a chance in hell that they could build a relationship, but Dee Dee had it going on from head to toe. He slid the house shoes over her feet, then got up and took his seat across from her.

The whole setting was beautiful to Dee Dee, and if her brothers weren't so crazy, she would have told them that she had met a really nice dude that they would approve of. They ate their food and sat there talking about different things as they sipped on glass after glass of fine wine.

Dee Dee felt herself becoming a little tipsy from the four glasses of wine she drank. She knew that Alastair had invited her to come over to watch movies, but she didn't feel like a movie anymore. What she did feel like was being held, 'cause since Prat, no one else has had the privilege to sample her goodies.

"Al, do you mind if I borrow one of your big T-shirts so I can get comfortable?" Dee Dee asked as she slipped the hair wrap off her ponytail.

He looked at her with her hair now down and rushed in his room to get her the biggest T-shirt that he could find. He laid the 3X T-shirt on the bed, then told her it was in there waiting for her.

As Dee Dee walked in, she took in the sight of Alastair's bedroom all done up. She grabbed the T-shirt, got undressed, and slid the shirt over her head. For a moment she thought she was going to pass out, but it all cleared up when she pulled the shirt down. The wine was playing tricks on her, but the biggest one it was playing was that she needed to be felt up.

She lay on his bed, rolling around like a little kid. The bed was king size, so it had plenty of room for her to move around. She was at peace, and the wine was just kicking in to where she had to move on her sexual instincts.

Alastair walked into the room and just stood there silently looking on. Dee Dee's shirt was scooted up on her back, so Alastair was able to see her ass cheeks poking out of the white panties she had on. He licked his lips with his tongue, but quickly changed his expression when Dee Dee turned around and spotted him standing there. She wasn't embarrassed at all, but she didn't know that he had gotten a free shot of her booty.

"I'm sorry I messed up your nice bed," she said seductively.

"Don't apologize for that. You just enjoy yourself."

"How will I be able to enjoy myself in a big ole bed like this by myself?" She replied as she patted the bed.

Alastair felt that the time had arrived to where he could be all up in those guts of hers. He eased on up to the bed and sat at the end of it. He took Dee Dee's foot in his hand and began to massage it. She lay back and enjoyed the whole foot thang he was doing. For Alastair, he was getting on in more than one way. He was able to look in between her legs and see a little something-something as he moved her leg into different positions. Also, he was able to see her feet up close as he gave her the massage. He took her foot and raised it to his mouth. One toe after another went inside his mouth, getting sucked on. Dee Dee was in bliss as the suck job felt better than the massage he had given her.

He didn't waste any time as he leaned in and grabbed hold of her panties and gently eased them down, hoping that she wouldn't stop the forward progress he was trying to make. When they were all the way off, he just looked at her nicely trimmed pussy hair. She was bushy where the entrance of her pussy was, but the sides were trimmed nicely. He leaned in then slid his tongue out. Once it made contact with her pussy lips, Dee Dee squirmed around the bed in ecstasy.

Once he ate her out good, he took off all his clothes and crept on top of her. Dee Dee looked into his eyes and was hoping that he knew what she wanted right then and there, which was nice and slow strokes with a lot of caressing. Alastair must have had the same thing on his mind, 'cause he caressed her body up and down with gentle strokes of his hands. He put one of his hands underneath her head and eased on inside of her. Dee Dee welcomed the way he was grooving her body. She moaned and squirmed around like it was her first time doing the nasty. Alastair pulled out 'cause he felt he was about to nut. So, to prolong the burst, he went back downtown for more foreplay.

He spread Dee Dee's legs far apart and ate like he never had before, burying his nose all the way inside her pussy hair. He liked the way she tasted in his mouth. There was no denying the way they were both feeling. The wait had paid off, and Dee Dee wanted more of this on a regular.

Prat, you don't know what you're missing out on, she thought to herself.

"You want this to be all yours, Al?" Dee Dee asked as she looked into his eyes.

Alastair wanted nothing more than to have Dee Dee as his lady.

"Dee Dee, I want your love morning, noon, and night if you will give it to me."

She smiled and told him to make love to her like he never did to any other woman before. Alastair went for broke, doing shit that he never did to another woman in his whole life. They made love till the sun came up. The whole love fest was done without a love glove, but what did they care 'cause neither one of them was a ho who slept around with just anyone.

Once Dee Dee woke up, she explained to Alastair just what the big problems in her life were, and went into explicit detail about her brothers. Alastair told her that he had heard of two brothers who were wild about their little sister. He respected that because some niggas he knew didn't even give a fuck about what happened to their own. She liked what he said, but she had to make sure that he really understood the seriousness if he was gonna be involved with her. Dee Dee told him that if he wanted her to move in with him she would. That way her brothers couldn't do shit that could jeopardize what they had just started.

Alastair was happy that she would even bring that up, 'cause he wanted her with him. He knew that she was the right one. Dee Dee didn't know if she spoke too soon or not, but she knew that she would have to play her game smooth, 'cause there was no telling what her two crazy ass brothers would do if they took this the wrong way, which she knew they certainly would.

Chapter Fourteen

*D*etective Perkins was on the phone with the cell phone carrier. He became upset when the lady informed him that she couldn't help him, and putting him on hold infuriated him beyond belief. Perkins didn't understand why she couldn't, since the damn phone number was from their service.

"Sir, the reason I can't help you is because the person who got the phone rigged their services."

Perkins still didn't understand what the fuck she was talking about, so he asked to speak to one of her managers.

"Hello. This is Mr. James," the man said in what appeared to be a black person's voice.

"Mr. James, I was just speaking to one of your employees about a certain phone number I am in possession of. I'm Detective Perkins with the Memphis Police Department, and I'm investigating a homicide. Now, your employee told me that she couldn't help me because the number I gave her was rigged or something like that," Perkins stated as he wiped the sweat from his forehead.

"I understand, Detective, but like she said, there is nothing we can do once these kids out here get these phones rigged," Mr. James said, trying to clear up the matter.

"What type of business are you running when you can't keep tabs on your own numbers?" Perkins asked in an upset tone. "That certainly can't be good for business."

"Let me put it like this, Detective. The number that you have in your possession goes to what people nowadays call a burnout phone. A burnout phone is when someone rigs a regular phone with a chip so they can get unlimited use of minutes. Or in other words, unlimited air time. Once they rig these phones, we lose track of everything, including how much free service that they are stealing from us. So, you can see you are not the only one who's in a bind."

Perkins was enlightened to what the man was trying to tell him, but all he could do was be pissed off 'cause he was now back at a dead end. He thanked the supervisor for his help, but before he hung up, he asked Mr. James where people who dealt in these items could be found. Mr. James explained to him that they were on every street corner being sold like drugs, and that Perkins should feel free to pick them all up and put them in jail. Perkins thanked him and hung up the phone, then leaned back in his wooden chair.

Gary walked in the door smiling and eating a cream-filled donut. His smile soon changed when everybody in the office spotted the box of donuts he was carrying and rushed him. Gary looked into his box to see that he only had one left, but soon he had none when Sarge looked in the box and spotted the last one.

"For me, Gary? Why, thank you. Now get back to work. Lunch was over ten minutes ago," he said as he walked away eating the last donut.

Gary crumbled the box up and slammed it in the trashcan next to another detective's desk, who was chowing down on one of his donuts.

"Hey there, Perkins," Gary said to his partner. "PERKINS, CAN YOU HEAR ME?" Gary shouted, snapping his partner out of a daze.

"Oh, hey there, Gary," Perkins shot back, still in a partial daze.

"Perkins, can you believe all of these guys have eaten our donuts up and didn't offer to pay for them?"

Perkins couldn't believe his partner had just said something as stupid as that, 'cause Gary was always at someone else's desk when he spotted them with a box of donuts.

"Can you believe we ran into another dead end with this phone number?" Perkins vented to his partner.

Gary opened his desk drawer and pulled out a piece of butterscotch candy. He was listening to Perkins, but he already knew that the case they were assigned to was going to lead nowhere.

The phone on Perkins's desk suddenly rang. Gary reacted quickly, reaching all the way across his own desk over to Perkins's desk to answer it.

"You don't say," Gary replied into the phone. "Just have someone deliver it to us in the next ten minutes, OK?" Gary hung up with a smirk on his face, so

Perkins asked him what that was all about. "Nothing really, except Brenda from the crime lab said to tell you that she pulled a fresh finger print from the window, and she believes it belongs to a female, from the size of the fingerprint. She's having it sent over right now so we can run a national check."

"I'll be God damned!" Perkins shouted in excitement as he leapt out of his chair.

The door to the Sergeant's office opened and Perkins quickly sat down so he wouldn't get spotted.

"Are you two assholes doing drugs or something? Cuz this shit is starting to become a regular routine," he shouted. Gary and Perkins looked at their coworkers who were all snickering at how the Sarge was getting on them.

"Sarge, you know we ain't on no drugs. It's just that we just found out that we were able to retrieve a good print from the hotel window," Gary spoke up once again, covering for his partner's outburst.

"Well, let's get the person who's responsible for that homicide behind bars, and I mean right now!" The Sergeant stated as he pointed his finger with a heated stare. As the Sarge walked away, Gary whispered to his partner that he had to get a hold of his outbursts because they were sure to get them both in hot water sooner or later.

At that moment, Brenda walked up personally to Gary and handed him a clear evidence bag containing the information they were waiting for. He pulled the paper out and cursed loudly.

"One fucking dead end after another," Perkins sighed as he read the paper saying that there was no information on the print. Perkins knew that whoever the Dee Dee person was never had a run in with the law, at least not yet, or else she was a pro, which he doubted, 'cause she had left a fingerprint, which is something a pro didn't do. Perkins was determined to solve this case if it was the last thing that he did as a cop. He stood up and grabbed his coat.

"You coming?" He asked Gary.

"To where?" Gary asked.

"To the streets. Someone out there has got to know who this Dee Dee girl is."

They headed out the door, one caring and the other not giving a fuck.

Chapter Fifteen

A new shipment of dope had come in, only this time it arrived before they were even finished with the other load. Jay and Bee were now looking at six hundred kilos of coke, plus what they already had. Jay didn't like the way business with Tony was happening. He grabbed his burned out cell phone to give him a call.

"Hello," Tony answered.

"Tony, man, what's going on? We just got another shipment and we haven't even finished pushing the other shit yet," Jay explained to him, upset.

Tony could sense the hostility in Jay's voice, so he cooled him down with some strong words.

"Listen, Jay. Don Valdez is a man of business. He's a serious man when it comes to taking care of business, so whatever he commands has to be carried out, no matter what."

Jay was like, fuck that, but he kept those words to himself. He was starting to feel the effects of someone owning him like a dog, and he wasn't gonna have that.

"Okay, Tony. Everything is cool. We'll take care of it."

Jay looked over at this brother and just shifted his eyes as he hung up the phone. They started putting the dope away behind the wall where it belonged. When they were done they just looked at all the dope and thought about how far they had come since the first four keys they had started off with. The wall was stacked with dope to where it looked like a medical lab.

"What you say we go and get some of those ribs downtown," Jay suggested to his brother. Bee was all game 'cause the place Jay spoke of had some of the best ribs that a black person could buy. They hopped in Jay's Excursion and rolled off.

Once they got their food they headed to the block to kick it with the fellas. Nasty spotted them pulling onto the street so he walked to the curb to meet them. Jay pulled right up to where Nasty was standing, and rolled down his window.

"What's popping, playboy?" Bee asked, then took a bite of one of the ribs.

"Man, y'all niggas gonna come on the block with ribs and not bring me none? That's some cold shit right there," Nasty stated as he looked at the ribs in both of their hands.

"Come on, playa. Your pockets ain't empty, and I'm sure your car ain't outta gas," Jay shot back with a grin. "So how's business?" Jay asked. Just when Nasty was about to speak on business, he caught sight of some funny shit across the street.

At the same time, Bee caught sight of some funny shit in back of Nasty. Bee was watching Lil Man slap-box with one of the older cats out there, and from what Bee could see, Lil Man was getting his off. Nasty couldn't make out just what he was looking at, but soon it was clear as day.

"FIVE-0! FIVE-0!" Nasty shouted as he saw cats in black jump out from behind damn near all the cribs. Everybody took off, hauling ass. Jay looked to his left and spotted them.

"Burn off, Jay," Bee shouted. Just when Jay was about to peel out, the jump out boys' van pulled in front of them and blocked them in. There was nowhere to go or run to as they saw nothing but black suits with "Task Force" written on them. Mad guns were pointing at them.

The cops kept yelling, "Put your fucking hands where I can see them." There was nothing they could do but do as they were told by the yelling cops. Two cops opened the doors and the next thing Jay and Bee knew, they were being yanked out of their ride roughly and slung to the ground.

While at the police station, Jay and Bee waited in a cell to be told what the hell they were arrested for. All Jay wanted to do was get himself a good lawyer and sue the shit out of the police's asses. A cop still in a black suit, looking like a straight gung-ho muthafucka, came walking up to them with papers in his hands.

"Look what we got here—the two brothers who've been flooding our city with dope. Yeah, we heard all about you two being the big boys in town. Now look at you," the cop said sarcastically.

"Fuck you, whitey! Wait till our lawyer gets a

crack of your sweet ass. He'll make this little city bankrupt for harassment and wrongful arrest," Jay said heatedly.

"I don't think so, Mr. Bad Ass Dope Man! You see, we got you two selling dope to one of our informants, so what you need to do is call that lawyer of yours and have him call the DA so he can get you the best plea bargain." He laughed, then handed Jay the papers.

Jay looked at the papers, which were indictments from the Grand Jury for selling half a brick to an undercover snitch.

"Damn!" Jay uttered. Bee grabbed the papers out of his brother's hand and was thrown for a loop also. Jay scanned his mind to see who it could have been. Jay and Bee didn't sell dope to people together, so Bee figured out who the snitch was.

"Bro, it was Shala's cousin! That's the only nigga that it could have been," Bee insinuated.

Jay knew Bee was right, so he made a collect call to her house. Shala accepted the phone call and Jay went right to work on grilling her. He was furious with rage as he went off, trying to find information on her cousin. Shala was pleading with Jay that she didn't know anything about what her cousin had done to them. She was in tears on the phone as Jay kept up the threats, which she knew he meant.

"You dead, bitch, and your punk ass cousin, too," Jay shouted, then slammed the phone onto the hook.

"Hey, you trying to fuck up the phone for the rest of us?" A tall nigga in the same holding area as Jay and Bee said. Jay was already looking for a way to relieve some tension, and dude opening his mouth was just the way. Bee already saw it coming when his brother whipped his body around to see who had said that.

"Nigga, fuck you and that phone!" Jay shot back.

"Nigga, ain't nothing in between us but air," the dude shot back.

Bee came from the blind side and hit dude with a straight right hook to his chin. Dude shook the lick off and rushed toward Bee. Jay made a move before he got to his brother. Jay grabbed dude from the back, locking his hands on his chin, then kicked dude in the back of his knees. Dude buckled to the ground on his knees. Before he had time to get up, Jay was working dude from the left to the right. Bee began beating dude senseless.

"Yo! The C.O.'s coming. Chill out, y'all," one of the other inmates said. Jay and Bee heeded his warning, since dude they just whooped was in no position to try to get revenge. He lay on the ground bleeding when the C.O.s came into the cell to see what all the commotion was about. They carted dude up on outta there and took him to medical.

For some reason, the same gung-ho cop in black looked at Jay and Bee and figured they had something to do with dude getting fucked up.

"Hey Marty!" the gung-ho cop called out.

"Yeah," another cop replied.

"Put these two in another cell by themselves, OK?"

"You got it."

Jay and Bee didn't give a fuck. Jay called Dee Dee when they got into the new holding cell. He told her to come down and bail them out. Once she was through talking to Jay, she hung up and called Miya and Ronshay. Not long after she spoke with Miya and Ronshay, they were at Dee Dee's door, knocking. Dee Dee came out and they piled into Miya's white Ford Explorer and headed to the police station.

When they got inside they went right up to the officer at the front desk, ready to pay whatever the bail amount was.

"I'm sorry, Miss, but those two do not have a bail yet. But they are scheduled for court in the morning," the desk officer stated.

Miya's heart sank, but she kept hope that everything was going to be all right. Ronshay started crying as soon as she heard that. She wanted her baby out, not tomorrow, but right then and there. Dee Dee wasn't used to her brothers not being around, at least not being able to come home when they wanted. They all headed out of the station and headed back to Dee Dee's house. Miya and Ronshay figured that they would just spend the night with Dee Dee so they could all be at the courthouse at the same time. They were discussing what the two brothers could have done to get locked up.

Jay and Bee couldn't understand what was taking Dee Dee so long to get down there and bail them out. Two hours had passed since Jay and spoken with his sister, so he decided to call her again. When Jay picked up the phone an automatic teller came on stating, "It is past phone time. Service will be back in use at seven a.m."

"What kind of shit is this?" Jay shouted.

"What up?" Bee asked.

"Man, the phone is cut off until the morning." It was all out of their hands, at least for the night, so they just tried to make the best of it until Dee Dee got her butt down there to bail them out, or at least that's what they were thinking.

Morning came, and all the girls were at the courthouse waiting to see Jay and Bee walk through the doors.

Jay couldn't get any sleep, and here it was morning. He kept dialing his house number, and kept getting nothing. He kept cursing so much that Bee was fully awake with a crook in his neck.

"Man, why all the yelling?" Bee asked.

"Boy, I'ma kill that sister of yours, watch and see," Jay shot back, mad as heck. Bee couldn't believe Dee Dee had left them for dead either.

"Hey, you two. It's time for court," a C.O. shouted. Jay and Bee were already hip to the being locked up shit routine, but they were hoping that they could have gone to court as free men if their sister would have come to bail them out like Jay told her to.

The van stopped in the garage of the courthouse. Jay and Bee were chained and handcuffed to about nine other cats who also had court that morning. The guard opened the van's back door so they could all climb out.

The guard called Jay and Bee's names first to go into the courtroom for a hearing. They walked through the courtroom doors with their hands cuffed in front of them. Ronshay screamed out Bee's name when she laid eyes on him. Bee turned his head in her direction and saw her, Miya, and Dee Dee all sitting by each other. Jay changed the way he was thinking about his sister when he saw her in the courtroom. Miya blew Jay a kiss and he returned one.

The judge entered the courtroom, and that's when

everyone stood up as the bailiff instructed them to do. The judge told them to sit back down. He addressed Bee and Jay by their real names, as he read off the charges they had incurred.

When he was done, it was their lawyer's chance to speak on their behalf. The judge listened closely to what the attorney had to say. Then it was the prosecutor's turn to speak.

"Your Honor, these two are known as two of the biggest drug dealers in Memphis."

"Objection, Your Honor!" Bee and Jay's attorney shouted.

"Let's be careful how we choose our words, counsel," the judge warned the prosecutor.

"Your Honor, the state is requesting that bail be denied because we have a suspicion that if the two defendants are released on bail, our witness's life will be in danger, and so will our case against the defendants. Our witness is an informant for the Memphis Narcotics Task Force.

The judge jotted down something that no one could see. Jay and Bee looked on with awe, waiting for the judge to make a ruling. Miya, Dee Dee, and Ronshay all held hands tightly, praying for them to get bail.

"Mr. Bret Davis and Mr. James Davis. As the judge presiding over this case, the court finds that the prosecution has made a valid point, and for that reason, bail is denied."

"Bullshit! What happened to innocent until proven guilty?" Jay shouted. Bee grabbed his lawyer by the arm and asked what the fuck was going on. Miya, Ronshay, and Dee Dee all cried, not knowing how long Jay and Bee would be in jail. Jay and Bee felt that they were being railroaded. The guards ushered them back out the door. Ronshay shouted out the words, "I love you, Bee," before the door closed.

Miya dropped everybody off at their cribs, 'cause they knew that Jay and Bee would be calling as soon as they were back at the county jail.

Dee Dee was chilling on the porch in deep thought when the phone started ringing. She ran back inside and snatched the phone off the base. The voice that spoke through it wasn't that of one of her brother's, but of Alastair.

"Hey, Al," she greeted sluggishly.

"Do I detect that someone is feeling down?" he asked. Dee Dee didn't know what to say at that moment.

"Dee Dee, are you there?" She was glad that he had called, but at that moment in time she wasn't up for conversation.

"Look, Al. My brothers are in jail for selling to a narc."

"Oh shit!" Now he understood what she was going through and why she was acting so down. "So, when are they getting out?" He asked.

"I don't really know cuz that faggot ass prosecutor asked the judge to deny their bail, talkin' about the muthafucka who set them up's life would be in danger." Dee Dee walked around the house talking to Alastair on the phone. She was already missing her brothers 'cause she knew they weren't coming right back, like they would when they ventured out of town.

Dee Dee was thinking about shacking up with

Alastair since her brothers were in jail. She wouldn't have any problems with moving in with him now.

"Look, Dee Dee, how about I come over there and chill with you?"

Dee Dee was game, but not at that particular moment. The thought of her and Al talking about moving in together entered her mind, and she figured he would ask her about that if she told him he could come over.

"Al, how about you call me back later on," Dee Dee suggested.

Alastair wasn't feeling that. Last time they were together they made mad ass love. Now she was acting distant. He knew she was taking that shit with her brothers hard, but then again, when they went out for the first time, she had burnt off in her ride without even saying goodbye. He didn't know if she had a split personality or another nigga. All he knew was that he wanted the girl who had won his heart.

The phone started clicking on the other end, so Dee Dee knew it had to be her brothers. She asked Alastair to hold up for a sec while she answered the other line.

"Hello!"

"Look, Dee Dee. Everything I been having you do has been for a time just like this," Jay said.

"So what you saying, Jay?"

"I need you to call everybody on the team and have them bring the money to you just like you been doing. The show is all you. Bee and me can't afford to lose this connect. I told Miya not to tell Tony about what happened to us, so you gotta handle up. All right?"

Dee Dee didn't know how to take the news her brother had just dropped on her. Yeah, he had groomed her to the game, but she didn't know if she could do it. She may have acted like her brothers, but the truth of it was she knew that she wasn't her brothers. But they needed her. That she did know.

Chapter Sixteen

*D*ee Dee needed some time to herself, so she went to the pool hall where her brothers and everybody from the hood frequented. When she walked in the door, niggas was throwing little hints out there like clockwork. Dee Dee wasn't in the mood for their shit or them trying to get comments out of her. She made her way over to the bar area and took a seat. Shit was running all through her mind. She was now in a predicament that she had to step up to. The niggas in the pool hall already heard about Jay and Bee getting swooped up in that raid, and Dee Dee could hear them talking about it. There was just too much gossiping going on in the pool hall for her, so she bounced.

Dee Dee walked into the building to chill out for a moment. She turned the thermostat, opened the wall, and looked at all the dope and money stacked on the shelves.

How the fuck am I gonna move all of this shit? she wondered. Dee Dee wasn't a female who ran from a challenge, especially when her brothers needed her help.

"So, I gotta move all of this shit, huh! OK then, let's play ball," she said out loud.

Dee Dee grabbed one of the kilos off the shelf and just looked at it. She walked over to the collection apartment, then pulled the list out with everybody's names and numbers on it. She gave everyone a call so they could bring the cash. She waited two hours before the first cat came through.

Lil Man knocked on the door. Dee Dee was happy someone had come when she told them it was time. Lil Man was all smiles as he handed her the money. Dee Dee had on a maroon shirt that revealed the upper part of her breasts. When she bent over to put the money in the count machine, Lil Man was looking hard as fuck, thinking nasty thoughts. When the money was counted, Dee Dee raised up and caught Lil Man staring hard.

"Lil Man! I advise you to keep your eyes to yourself, OK?

Lil Man wasn't really gonna listen to what she just said, but he did put his mind back on business.

"So, I'll get the same shit as last time, or more?" Lil Man asked, grinning.

"The same for now, Lil Man, but if you're my ears on the streets, I'll make something big happen for you." Dee Dee knew she had to have game to be able to handle business in a world where niggas were ruthless, thuggin' outlaws.

Lil Man liked what she had just said, so he was now Dee Dee's eyes and ears on the street.

"Don't forget, Lil Man. You're my ears."

"I got you, Dee Dee. Just don't forget me. Bet?"

"Bet, Lil Man," Dee Dee said as she closed the door.

Terry Tee and Junior both came by to drop off the loot, so she marked them off. Nasty shot through and dropped his off. She gave Rich and Lazy a call up in Nashville and told them the scoop on Jay and Bee. She also told them she needed them to come turn in the cash. Rich told her they would be down on Friday, like usual. Dee Dee was cool with that.

Rich and Lazy were doing it up. They hadn't seen so much money in their lives, and the quality of coke they had made them feel like they were in a dreamland. What Jay and Bee didn't know was that their two cousins were powder heads and alcoholics. Having all that dope fronted to them made it easier for them to take care of their habits and make money. Lazy loved his cousins, but when a person was hooked on drugs, all they could see was the dope, which meant trouble for Dee Dee since she was now running the show.

She did just like her brothers taught her, and slid the money down the trash chute and went to the other apartment.

When she walked outside, Junior was in the hallway waiting for her.

"What's up, sexy?" he greeted, scaring the shit out of her. If she would have peeped at the security monitor she would have scoped Junior out.

"Junior, have you lost your mind?"

"Nah, Shorty. But I did lose my heart to you."

"Well, since you feel like that, Junior, you can have it back free of charge," Dee Dee teased with a grin.

"Aw, that's some cold shit right there, Dee Dee," Junior said as he stood posted up against the wall.

"Junior, not to be rude seeing as how you're trying to get your game on and shit, but is there something you want?" Dee Dee had no idea what he really wanted.

Junior was there, trying to get what her brothers were always so protective over. His thang was to catch her when she opened the door and push her right inside, but he got caught slipping when he went downstairs to pee.

"Naw, Shorty. I was just making sure you was cool and all, but I can see you're doing just fine. Catch you later," Junior said as he walked away, meaning every word of the "catch you later" phrase.

Dee Dee could feel that it was something funny about the way Junior was in the hallway, so she told herself to always be strapped from now on.

She walked over to the safe house apartment to put the money away. The first thing she did when she got the door closed was to check the security cameras to see if Junior was out there waiting. She was glad to see that he was gone, but she still knew in her heart that the nigga was up to no good, and she wasn't trying to get beat up and raped by anybody.

Once the money was counted, Dee Dee went home slipped on her tan Azure mini-skirt and the halter top to match. She was down to loosen up, and what she had on said it all. She slipped on her brown Rockports and busted out the door. She looked at her brothers' rides in the driveway and decided she was going to rock one tonight. Bee's Benz was her choice, 'cause tomorrow Ronshay was coming over to get it.

Dee Dee whipped Bee's ride all the way to the club. She parked, then got out. Niggas was all up on her trying to holla. This wasn't a time to mingle, though. Dee Dee just wanted a chance to unwind.

She took a seat over by the dance floor so she could check out who was dancing and who was making a fool of themselves. Not long after Dee Dee took her seat, a nigga with braids in his head and wearing a Rocawear hookup, approached her.

"Do you mind if we dance?" Homeboy asked.

Dee Dee looked up and told him not right now. Dude took it upon himself to pull out a chair and take a seat. Dee Dee wasn't feeling dude, or his presence. For one, the nigga smelled straight like liquor. Two, he wasn't the nigga she had on her mind. And three, he was crowding her space.

"I'm not trying to be rude, but my friend is coming and you're sitting in his seat."

Dude got up and told Dee Dee he would catch her later. She watched dude walk off until he was out of sight. She cast her eyes back on the dance floor and caught what she was looking for, which was somebody who couldn't dance, and she cracked up.

"What's funny, little momma?" a female with a deep voice asked.

Dee Dee looked up and saw a chick who resembled Queen Latifah in the movie *Set It Off*.

"Nothing much. Just tripping."

"Well, you know a female like yourself shouldn't be tripping by yourself, right?"

Dee Dee could sense that ole girl was a dyke. Dee Dee didn't have any problems with it as long as she didn't bring it her way.

"Can I sit down with you?" Ole girl asked.

"It's not my chair," Dee Dee shot back.

"So why a fine young thang like yourself, chilling by yourself? Oh, don't tell me, that boyfriend of yours got caught cheating, huh?"

Dee Dee was cracking up on the inside 'cause ole girl was spitting like one of the niggas.

"Naw, just chilling. Feel me?"

"Well, you know we can go chill at my place, and I can make you feel good all over."

Dee Dee's eyes shot dead on ole girl.

"Look, I don't mind you sitting right there cuz like I said, that ain't my chair, but let's get this straight. I don't get down like that at all. Feel me?"

Ole girl just looked at Dee Dee, looking all good and shit, and licked her lips thinking how good it would be to sample what Dee Dee never gave a sister a chance to do.

"Look, I'm gonna play it cool and respect what you just said. So we cool?" Ole girl asked.

"We cool," Dee Dee shot back, staring ole girl in her eyes to see if she could detect some bullshit coming.

"By the way, people call me Chills," Ole girl said.

"What is that name short for?" Dee Dee asked, interested to know.

"My full name is Quanchilla Levona Mason."

"I'm Dee Dee."

Dee Dee thought her first name was cute for a female, but since she acted like a dude, the name Chills served her right. Chills kept looking at Dee

Dee with curiosity 'cause the name Dee Dee was suspect to her for some reason.

"Chills, I thought we understood each other about me not going that route," Dee Dee stated as she caught Chills staring at her with leering eyes.

"Aw, girl, it ain't nothing like that. It's just that I knew two homeboys of mines who had a sister named Dee Dee, and your name just made me think about my niggas. I sure miss those two crazy mutha-fuckas."

Dee Dee knew right then and there that she was talking about her brothers, but the question to Dee Dee was why hadn't she ever seen Chills around her brothers, or heard them talking about her if those were her niggas like she just stated.

"What's the two brothers' names?" Dee Dee asked.

"Jay and Bee. Why?" Chills asked.

"Jay and Bee are my brothers."

"No shit! Where those two niggas at right now?" Chills asked with a big smile on her face.

Dee Dee's heart sank when she told Chills where they were. Chills couldn't believe they were in jail, but then again, she knew that as crazy as they were growing up, they were bound for one of two things—jail or death.

"Chills, why haven't I ever seen you with my brothers or heard about you?" Dee Dee asked.

"Yo, shorty, it's like this. Eight years ago me and my two homegirls robbed a bank, and now we're just getting out."

Dee Dee was shocked to hear that Chills had done time, but what shocked her most was that she said that she and some other girls had the balls to hit a bank. Dee Dee never knew anyone that robbed a bank, so hearing that was ill.

"Did y'all get a lot of dough?" she asked, being nosey.

Just when Chills was about to answer, a nigga walked up and stood behind Dee Dee. She felt the presence of someone lurking behind her so she turned around and looked up. She saw that it was the same nigga who tried to push up on her earlier. He walked around her and stood in between Dee Dee and Chills. Chills just looked at the nigga like he was crazy. One thing she learned from doing time was never to allow a nigga to crowd your space, especially without permission.

"Damn, baby! This dyke muthafucka is the nigga you was waiting for? That's fucked up, cuz I would never guess you was down with bumping clits with a bull dagger. Damn! This nigga ain't got what I got. She ain't even a nigga. That's fucked up!" Dude said, looking crazy at Dee Dee with his ass in Chills's face.

Chills shot a killer stare at homeboy. She wanted to just floor dude right then and there, but she played her shit right.

"Homeboy, you don't even know me to be disrespecting me like that," Chills stated heatedly.

"Fuck you, bitch. You better take your manly ass on before you get smacked like a bitch!" Dude stated, looking Chills straight in her eyes.

"You got that, homie, and I'ma take your advice and speed on," Chills stated as she stood up and walked away.

Dee Dee couldn't believe that nigga just came back to her table and fronted like that.

"Now it's just me and you, baby girl." He took a seat in the chair Chills was just sitting in. Dee Dee was disgusted at having dude sitting at the table she was chilling at.

Chills walked straight over to where her home-girls were. Tricksy and Diamond were chilling at the pool table with two broads they had just met. Tricksy was a tall, high-yella chick, not really cute, but a nigga wouldn't have a problem laying wood to her if she were into dudes. Diamond was short and caramel skinned with short, thick, wavy hair. Thick, cute, sexy, and bisexual was the way to describe Diamond, but she also had a fucked up temper that could go off any time. That's why she liked pussy more than she liked dick.

Chills walked up to them, heated. They could see she was pissed off about something, so they broke the conversation with the two feminine females to see what was up. Chills pointed over to the table that Dee Dee was sitting at and pointed out dude.

"Let's get ill then," Diamond suggested right away.

They all followed Chills to check homeboy for his disrespect. Chills wanted to cause the nigga some serious havoc. She was used to checking peo-ple, and she had been battling dudes ever since she came out of the closet in seventh grade.

Dee Dee spotted Chills and the two females she spoke of earlier walking in her direction very quickly. She could tell from the look on Chills' face that shit was about to be on and poppin'.

Dee Dee slipped her hand inside her purse and eased her fingers onto the gat she was keeping in her purse to use on Junior's ass if he ever tripped.

She didn't know if Chills was going to trip on her or what, so she felt it was better to be safe than sorry.

Tricksy spotted an empty Moet bottle sitting on an unattended table. She yanked it up by the neck without stopping.

Dee Dee's hand now had a full grip around the handle of the gat inside her purse. She had it aimed in their direction to make sure she plugged somebody. Dude was still bumping his gums, talking shit that Dee Dee didn't care to hear about.

"What up, Chills?" Dee Dee asked as Chills got into hearing distance.

Dude turned his head around to see Chills standing there. As he stood up, Tricksy swung the bottle that she had in her hand and crashed it right on top of his head. He fell onto the top of the table Dee Dee was sitting at. The drinks spilled everywhere. Dee Dee jumped up out of her seat quick as a rabbit. She was stunned to see Chills and her two home-girls working ole boy over. Chills was stomping dude silly with the Timbs she had on. Diamond told them to move the fuck out of the way as she picked up a chair and threw it with force down on dude's head. Dee Dee couldn't believe these hoes were getting it on like some niggas in a gang fight. Dude was fucked up bad as fuck. Dee Dee thought to herself that the nigga had asked for it.

When dude wasn't moving anymore, Chills told Tricksy and Diamond to chill out. Tricksy chilled out, but Diamond's little cute, crazy, fiery tempered ass was another story. As she kept stomping dude, Chills had to grab her from behind just to restrain her from killing the nigga. Diamond kept kicking and tussling as Chills lifted her off the floor in a bear hug in the air, carrying her straight out the door.

Tricksy looked down at dude before she walked off and saw the nigga was still moving. She reached in her pocket and pulled out her butterfly knife she always kept on her. She worked the knife like a biker, flipping it back and forth until she had it open and ready to use. She bent down and grabbed dude by the head.

"Muthafucka! Next time you think about what you say before you open that big ass mouth of yours!" Tricksy spouted as she put the point of the knife at the right corner of his mouth. She jerked the blade, giving that nigga something to remember what she had just said.

Chapter Seventeen

*R*ich and Lazy were just entering Memphis's city limits, headed to their cousins' crib to drop off the money they owed.

Dee Dee was chilling on the couch talking to Chills about the work she had spoken about the night they whooped dude's ass at the club. Chills accepted Dee Dee's offer to be her strong arm. If a nigga didn't want to pay up, Chills was ready to show the nigga what was up.

Lazy grabbed the cell off the seat and called Dee Dee. She told Lazy to meet her at the apartment building. Dee Dee rolled on over to the spot and waited for them to arrive. It wasn't too long till they pulled up in a brand new, clean ass, red four door Caddie with gold Daytons on it.

Jay had told Dee Dee that Lazy and Rich owed seventy-five thousand, so that's what she was looking to receive in payment.

"What's up, cuz," Rich greeted with a hug.

"Nothing much," Dee Dee shot back with a

smile. Lazy stepped in and gave his little cousin a hug after his brother had let her go.

Dee Dee took them into the apartment where she collected the money. Rich gave her the bag and she started counting it right then and there, which is something her brothers would have never done, even with family like them around. Dee Dee wasn't to blame for that, 'cause that was something that Jay or Bee didn't explain to her, at least not on the topic of doing it around family. She put the last of the money in the count machine and wrapped it in a wrapper.

Since they were family, Dee Dee asked Rich to carry the money over to the other apartment so she could get what they needed to go back to Nashville to make that money. For some reason, Dee Dee only opened one side of the wall, the one that contained the dope. Rich and Lazy's eyes got big as fuck when they saw all those kilos sitting on the shelves. Dee Dee turned around and Rich and Lazy changed their eager expressions.

"Damn, little cuz! That's a lot of shit," Lazy stated with eyes still glued on the dope.

"Yeah, I know. Jay told me to give y'all the same thing as last time. Cool?"

Rich and Lazy said yeah so fast that if they would have said that to Jay or Bee, they would have picked up on some bullshit in the air. But because Dee Dee was still green behind the ears in some areas, she couldn't see that her cousins were up to something.

She watched her cousins roll off, headed back to Nashville to handle their business.

When she walked back into the safe house apartment to put the money away, she got a call on her cell phone from Lil Man. Lil Man told her that the new nigga Bee hired named Trey said he wasn't gonna pay the bitch shit. Dee Dee became mad as fuck when she heard that. She thanked Lil Man for the heads up on the information, and told him to keep her informed on anything new that came up.

She hung up the phone and called Trey's cell phone. He answered his phone, and when he heard Dee Dee's voice on the other end he hung up. She figured his battery was low or that it could have just been some type of interference, so she called back and got his voicemail on the first ring. Now Dee Dee suspected bullshit in the air. She called again, and still nothing, so she paged Trey four times straight with 911 after the number so he knew to get back at her right then. Dee Dee spent thirty minutes paging and waiting for the nigga to call back, but all she got was heated, and she knew the nigga was playing her.

She called Chills and told her about the nigga Trey who was jerking her around. Chills told her to find out where the nigga was at then call her back.

Dee Dee paged Lil Man and he called right back once he saw the code that he and Dee Dee used for when they needed each other, besides handling dope business. She asked Lil Man if he knew where Trey was right then. She was glad to hear Lil Man tell her that Trey was out there on the block with him and the rest of the niggas hustling. Dee Dee asked him what type of car he was rolling around in and he told her that Trey had a beige Grand Prix parked across the street. After she got the information, she told Lil Man that if Trey left he should try to tag along with him. But if not, for him to call her back before the nigga even made it to the car.

Dee Dee hung up with Lil Man and called Chills back. She ran all the information down to Chills that Lil Man had just told her.

Dee Dee chilled as she waited for Chills to arrive at the crib. It was already getting dark outside and Chills still hadn't shown up. Dee Dee looked at the clock and saw it was ten till eight, but the good thing was that she hadn't gotten a call from Lil Man yet, which meant that Trey must still be out there grinding.

Chills finally pulled up with Tricksy and Diamond in tow. They got out of the car and walked up to the door. Dee Dee let them inside and immediately Chills ran down the game plan. When Chills told her that they were going to use Diamond as the set up girl, Dee Dee looked at how ghetto-sexy-nasty Diamond looked. Diamond had on some tight ass, sexy Daisy Duke shorts that showed her ass cheeks clear as day, and the cut-off yellow T-shirt she had on wasn't holding anything back either, as one could see her nipples poking through the shirt. The plan was for Dee Dee to call Lil Man back and tell him to keep Trey there at all costs. She didn't give up much information 'cause there was no telling how far Chills and her girls would take the job. What little she or anybody else besides the R.B.M. Clique knew, the better.

They all hopped in the Tahoe that Chills was rolling and headed to the set. While they were around the corner, out of sight, Chills let Diamond out so she could do her thang and bait the nigga

Trey. As Diamond turned the corner, Chills pulled onto the block and parked far enough down so the car was out of sight, but still within viewing distance of Diamond.

Diamond walked nasty as fuck and caught everybody's eye that was on the block. She didn't know where Trey was at, but she spotted the beige Grand Prix and decided to use that as her way of finding out who exactly the nigga was. When she got up to the niggas, everybody crowded around her like flies.

"What's up, little momma?" one of the niggas asked.

"That blunt in your hand," she replied.

Dude didn't hesitate to extend his hand out so she could smoke. Diamond took the blunt, then leaned back on the wall. Niggas was trying to game on her hard, but she was biding time, smoking, and rapping with all the niggas until she could find out which one of them was Trey.

She asked the niggas whose car was parked over there, referring to the beige Grand Prix. Without thinking anything of it, Trey blurted out that the ride was his. She baited the nigga in by telling him how much she liked that type of ride.

"And what's your name?" Diamond asked. When he told her his name was Trey, she asked the nigga when was she gonna get to take a ride in the car. Trey was so geeked thinking about the pussy, that he told her now was as cool of a time as any. BINGO – GAME OVER!

Niggas was salty to see the fine bitch had picked Trey out of all of them. Trey copped a bag of kill-kill from TJ, who only sold weed.

"Hit that ass for all of us, nigga," TJ teased.

"You got that, my nigga, cuz I'm about to take that bitch to the telli and beat it up."

Trey blew out the smoke, making the front of the car cloudy. He passed Diamond the blunt and she began smoking, just waiting for her girls to pull up.

Chills pulled up and parked right next to Trey's Grand Prix on the driver's side. Diamond looked over nonchalantly and saw Chills smiling. Dee Dee saw Tricksy and Chills putting on black leather gloves. Right then, she knew how Chills got ready when they would hit a bank up. Dee Dee could see how calm they were acting when they were about to commit a crime, and even though she couldn't see Diamond, she had to assume that she had the same mindset, as she baited Trey like a fish to water.

"How you want us to handle this shit, boss?" Chills asked.

Dee Dee really didn't know what to say, besides that she only wanted the cash.

"I need the money, Chills. My brothers mess with some powerful people who can have Jay and Bee killed because one of these suckas not paying up, so I gotta get the cash," Dee Dee stated.

Chills saw the seriousness in Dee Dee's face, and from her knowing how Jay and Bee were, and how they got down, she knew that Dee Dee needed the cash.

"Let's do this, Tricksy," Chills said as she put her ski mask on. Tricksy put her mask on, then picked up her gat off the seat.

"I'm ready like Freddie, baby," Tricksy shot back.

Chills took the fuse out to the interior light so it wouldn't come on to reveal their sneak-up when they opened the door. Chills scooted her big ass into the back seat so she could get out on the oppo-site side, so their sneak-up would go even smoother.

Trey was giving Diamond a shotgun with the blunt and feeling all on her titties, when Chills opened his door quick as fuck. Trey turned around and was shocked as his door mysteriously opened. He saw Chills stick the chrome 9 mm dead in his face. Diamond just lay back, still puffing on the new blunt she had just fired up as she watched her girls do their thang.

Dee Dee watched on as Chills got the nigga out of the car at gunpoint. Tricksy couldn't help but do what she was about to do. With a nice swing, she whopped Trey upside his head with her gat, sending him crashing to the pavement. The blow was to show him what was to come if he didn't do what they wanted when they said.

Trey looked up while still on the ground and spotted Diamond smoking his shit while her hands were partly in the air, as if to say, "Oops! Look what you got yourself into."

Tricksy put the duct tape over his mouth and around his hands so he couldn't try any shit. She wanted to put duct tape over his eyes, but Chills stopped her from doing that, seeing as how that could probably fuck the nigga's eyes up and she didn't want that if Dee Dee didn't want the nigga dead. They threw Trey in the backseat and got set to take off. Noticing a bandanna that had been left in the car, Tricksey quickly tied it around his head. Diamond was to follow them in Trey's ride.

"Bitch, you think your funky ass is cool or some-thing, chilling in that buster shit like it's your ride, huh?" Chills hollered, smiling over at Diamond. All Diamond did was stick her middle finger up in the air and tell Chills to peel off.

Diamond followed Chills as she drove around, not really headed anywhere special, at least till she found out what her girl Dee Dee wanted to know.

Trey shrieked in pain when Tricksy reached over and pulled the duct tape off of his mouth in one quick pull, taking some of his skin off with it.

"Why y'all doing this?" Trey asked, sounding like a straight bitch.

Dee Dee couldn't hold back her words.

"Remember when you said this: 'I ain't paying that bitch shit. Fuck her.'?"

Trey not only recognized the words, but he also recognized the voice.

"Dee Dee, I was just playing. You know I wouldn't fuck around with your brothers or you like that."

Dee Dee just listened to the nigga tell her his lies so he could save his ass.

"Why you didn't call a bitch back? You was playing me like a Monopoly game, fool. But as you found out the hard way, Dee Dee always gets in touch with a person one way or the other. Now, where is my brothers' money, nigga?" Dee Dee asked, as she nudged him in the head with her gun. He didn't answer so Tricksy gave the nigga another whop upside the head.

"I'll get your money, Dee Dee. Just don't hit me like that again."

"Hold on, nigga! Whether we hit you again or not, you better believe my girl gonna get that cash from your ass. As a matter of fact, Tee, hand me that big ass dildo so I can show this nigga how I get down when I want something," Chills stated. Chills looked at Dee Dee and smiled at the little story she had just put into Trey's head.

"Look, Dee Dee! The money is behind my mom's crib in my pop's old broke down Nova, in the trunk."

"It better be there, nigga, or you gonna have a big problem going up in your dooky chute, BITCH!" Chills exclaimed.

"It's there! I promise, Dee Dee. Just go to my mom's new crib and you'll get your money. The key to the trunk is on my key ring in my ride."

When they got to Trey's mom's house, Chills turned into the alley and headed to the back. Dee Dee spotted the beat up, broke down Nova sitting on bricks, and pointed it out to Chills. Chills cut the lights off to her car so as not to attract any attention. Diamond was right behind them parked and waiting to see what was up.

Chills got out of her ride and walked up to Diamond to get the key. Once she had it, she made her way to the Nova's trunk. Just when she got up close to the trunk, she got the shock of her life when a Pit Bull lunged into the air at her. Chills dropped her gun onto the ground, startled by the dog's appearance. She instinctively covered her face and throat with her arms, thinking it was about to be over, but the thick link chain that held the Pit Bull could let the dog go only so far. The chain jerked the dog in midair, making it turn all the way around to land on its stomach. The dog kept on barking. It was now even more pissed off.

Dee Dee jumped out of the ride to go to Chills's aid.

"Girl, you cool?" Dee Dee asked in concern as she helped Chills up.

"Damn! I thought I was done for. Where the fuck did that mutt come from?" Chills asked as she picked up her gun and threatened to pop a cap in his ass. Dee Dee had an idea where it had come from, as she knew the dog was there to guard what was in the trunk.

"That nigga didn't mention that he had a fucking Pit guarding the money," Dee Dee said as she looked over at the Tahoe.

"That punk ass bitch! That's OK, though, cuz I got something for his bitch ass," Chills stated, now pissed off more than the dog.

Chills popped the trunk to the Nova and saw a blanket covering something. She flipped the blanket to the side and saw a brown paper bag. She leaned in and opened to bag to see that the money was in there.

"Bingo, Dee Dee," Chill said in excitement. Chills tossed the bag to Dee Dee, and they hopped back into the ride. Dee Dee was happy to have the cash in her hands.

"What about this bitch, Dee Dee? You want me to whack his ass?" Chills asked.

Dee Dee pondered on that idea for a minute, then the phrase that her mother used to say popped into her head: "A wise woman thinks twice before even speaking once." That phrase was starting to make sense to her more and more.

"Nah, I got something better for his ass. Pull over to that corner store for a sec," Dee Dee suggested. Chills pulled into the parking lot for the corner store and parked at the far end of the lot.

Dee Dee walked into the store and bought a disposable camera and a Bic Magic Marker. When she came out she spotted some cardboard boxes sitting on the ground in front of a big dumpster. She held her breath as she picked one of the boxes up, because the stench of the trash was unbelievable.

When she hopped back into the truck, Chills asked her what that was all about. Dee Dee just told her that she would see.

Trey was listening to everything they were talking about, not knowing what they were going to do to him. Dee Dee told Chills to pull over at the park they were coming up on, and instructed Chills to get close to the light. Chills wondered what Dee Dee was up to. But when she saw what Dee Dee wrote on the big piece of cardboard that she had just torn off the box, she knew right then and there that Dee Dee's brothers' style had rubbed off on her.

"Get his bitch ass out the car," Dee Dee ordered. Tricksy manhandled Trey's ass right up on out of the backseat. "Now, take his pants off," Dee Dee said. Trey wasn't trying to hear that, but another whop upside his fuckin' head got him right.

Diamond took his pants down for him, and when she saw the size of his dick, she couldn't help but to put her hands on it. Diamond liked pussy more than she liked dick, but she loved a nigga who had a horse dick, 'cause she felt that even if the nigga couldn't fuck, the size of his dick would do the job of getting her off.

Dee Dee got the dildo out of the truck and put everything into play. She had Chills get the nigga down on all fours. When she did, the nigga Trey was begging for them not to kill him. Dee Dee told the nigga if he moved, then he would surely meet his maker. She placed the cardboard with the writing on it by his foot, then she placed the big ass dildo up in front of the cardboard. Dee Dee stood back and looked at what she had created through the camera lens. It was all perfect.

"This bitch is ill thinking, Chills," Tricksy stated.

"I know," Chills shot back, glad to see that Dee Dee had an ill ass way of thinking.

Snap! Snap! Snap! Dee Dee then did the same thing in the front so she could see his face. *Snap! Snap! Snap!*

Chills put a blindfold over Trey's head so he couldn't see. She pulled Dee Dee over to the side and asked her what that was all about.

"Well, what did I write on the cardboard, Chills?" Dee Dee asked her.

"You wrote, 'Either Pay Up or Get Fucked Up! Up the Ass, That Is.' I got all of that and the dildo shit, but what were the photos for?" Chills asked, already knowing.

"Look, these niggas out here know I ain't my brothers, so they think I'm weak cuz I'm a female, right? But once they see these pictures of this fool, then they will think twice about fuckin' me over. I never knew how ill this game was, but if that's what I got to be like to handle up, then so be it. Feel me?" Dee Dee stated strongly.

"I'm with you, girl, if you can think like that. But what about this fool?" Chills asked as she looked over at Trey's ass bent over like a bitch about to get fucked doggy style.

"Do what you want, but don't kill him, cuz niggas gonna rag on his stupid ass and know I mean business when they see the flicks."

Chills gave Dee Dee some pound, then walked back over to Trey. She picked up the dildo and held it in her hand.

Diamond told Chills to hold up for a sec so she could see something. Diamond hadn't seen a big, black dick like that in a while, so she wanted to sample it. Diamond made the nigga get on his back. She took her pants off and slapped a magnum rubber on his dick. After she mounted Trey, she went right to work trying to get hers off. Dee Dee looked at Diamond fucking this nigga, and even Chills and Tricksy were watching, and thought that she was straight up gone. Diamond wasn't holding anything back as she fucked that nigga like it was nothing. She finally came all over his dick. As quickly as it had started, she was finished, up, and dressed.

Trey seemed relieved that nothing bad had happened to him. He didn't know that the party was still going on until Diamond told him that she wanted to lick his asshole. He got back on all fours like she said. Diamond spread the nigga's ass cheeks wide open, and with one motion, Chills aimed and thrust that dildo in his asshole and rushed him to the ground face down so quickly that he didn't know what had just hit him. He tried tussling and squirming, but Chills rode his ass until she had control to do what she wanted.

"Nigga, that's for not telling me about the dog. This is for trying to play my girl. And this is for GP cuz I think you like this shit," she stated as she kept jamming the dildo in his ass with no lubrication. No scream could match the sound that was coming out of Trey's mouth.

Damn! The nigga got fucked twice in less than ten minutes. Ain't that about a bitch, Dee Dee thought. Dee Dee blew the horn as they all looked at Trey on the ground with the dildo sticking out of his ass. Chills cut the duct tape off his hands and tossed his keys on the ground by him.

"Baby, you got some good dick, but I think my girl likes your ass better," Diamond joked as she gave her girls some dap, and they were off.

Chapter Eighteen

$\mathcal{D}$ee Dee was inside chilling on the couch when she heard Ronshay's voice yell her name through the screen door. Dee Dee didn't bother getting up 'cause *All My Children* was on. Ronshay wanted Dee Dee to come chill on the porch with her, but when Dee Dee didn't come see what was up, she walked on inside.

"You and those damn soap operas. I tell you!" Ronshay said as she stared at Dee Dee.

"Sh-h-h-h-h-h! It's about to go down," Dee Dee stated.

Ronshay just threw her hands in the air in frustration, then headed for the kitchen. She opened the fridge and spotted some cherry ice cream. Even though it was now getting cooler as the month of September was coming to an end, Ronshay could see that Dee Dee still loved her ice cream.

"Damn! They always gotta continue the good shit the next day," Dee Dee shouted in disgust.

"Somebody's mad cuz their little soaps have gone off," Ronshay teased.

Dee Dee just stuck her middle finger up in the air.

"You went and saw Bee already?"

"Yeah. That boy is gaining weight. I told him he better start going on a diet, cuz ain't no way my man gonna have a gut when he gets out, and he didn't have one when he went in," Ronshay said while eating.

"I miss my brothers, Ronshay. Even though they was cock blockers and shit, I still miss their funky asses," Dee Dee said as she stuck a spoon into Ronshay's bowl.

"Dee Dee, I been hearing shit on the streets." Dee Dee looked at Ronshay.

"You gonna tell me, or am I supposed to guess?" Dee Dee asked.

"They say you teamed up with the R.B.M. Clique, Dee Dee. I know all of them, and what I know about them is all bad."

Dee Dee didn't look at Ronshay at all as she spoke. Jay and Bee had been locked up for four months now, and if it wasn't for the Real Bitches Murder Clique being on her team, niggas would have been done took her for a sucka, and not paid what they owed.

"Your name is also ringing almost harder than Jay and Bee's was. All I'm saying, Dee Dee, is this: sometimes a person should play the back instead of being in the front."

"Ronshay, you my girl, right?" Ronshay told her that she knew that she was. "Well, contrary to what people are saying and thinking about me in the dope game, and me hanging with the R.B.M. Clique, it's all good cuz I'm handling up for my brothers," Dee Dee stated with heartfelt feeling.

Ronshay could see that the game was taking Dee Dee to another zone. She knew too many people who had been sucked into the game and found no way to get back to reality. Ronshay knew that Chills and her crew liked to fuck around with girls, and she could only imagine what Dee Dee was doing.

There was a knock at the door, so Ronshay told Dee Dee that she would get it. When Ronshay made it to the door, she saw Alastair standing in front of it with a dozen long-stemmed roses in his hand.

"For me, Al? How sweet," Ronshay teased.

"Not exactly, Ronny. Is Dee Dee here?" He asked.

"Yeah, she's inside. Dee Dee," she yelled out.

"What's up," she shot back.

"I'm about to break out, but you got company at the door," Ronshay said, then walked out the door and headed for her car.

Dee Dee walked to the door and saw Alastair standing there in a clean ass brown suit that matched his skin color to the tee. She opened the door and saw Ronshay driving off with a smile on her face.

"This is unexpected," Dee Dee said to Alastair.

"What was unexpected was me falling in love with you," he exclaimed as he handed her the roses. Dee Dee raised the flowers to her nose and took a whiff of the sweet scent they had.

"What you mean it was unexpected? You know you was in love with me the day you stopped by this house."

Alastair knew she was right, but by him being in

love with her, shit seemed to be going all bad. He had come over to ask Dee Dee one last time about her decision to move in with him.

"Listen, Dee Dee, I don't know what's going on, but I need you. I asked you ten times already about you coming to stay with me and ten times you told me that you needed time to think about it. Now, the first day we made love, you was game. Now this is the last time I can do this to myself. If your answer is no, then I won't bother you ever again."

Dee Dee thought about what Alastair had just said, but the only reason she didn't pack her shit and move in with him already was because her brothers needed her right now. When they were out, it seemed like the perfect plan to get away, but now shit had changed, but not to where her feelings had changed for him. It was just the game she was in was a real task to deal with, especially by being a shot caller. She sat Alastair down on the porch, then sat between his open legs.

"Al, I really care for you, and I do love you, but right now is not a good time for us."

Alastair stood up at the sound of those words. His heart was on fire, burning straight up in flames. Dee Dee was trying to explain the rest of what she had to say, but his aching heart had forced him to head for his car. Dee Dee stood there, but when he got into his car and started it up, she felt the need to stop him and make him hear the rest, although it was too late. Alastair burned rubber as soon as she made it to the back passenger door. Dee Dee screamed Alastair's name loud as hell, over and over again. She even went as far as to scream his real first name out, but to no avail.

"Got man problems, huh?" A voice said behind her.

Dee Dee turned around to see Mikey sitting on a little kid's bike.

"What you want, Mikey?" Dee Dee asked sluggishly.

"I don't want nothing but my life back like it used to be, remember?"

"Mikey, you did that to yourself. Nobody told you to start smoking crack. And the tripped out thing about you is my brothers never fucked with you. For some reason they liked you being my boyfriend, and I did too, but then you had to go fuck shit up with the drugs."

Mikey's heart slumped inside of him. Dee Dee was his everything, but because his punk ass uncle asked him to try a joint, which his uncle had laced, Mikey got hooked on the first try.

Down the line, Dee Dee started noticing shit was different with him. His dress code started getting tacky. Then he just stopped having money, but she just thought he was going through some shit 'cause he lost his moms and his job at the same time. What really brought the shit to life about his problem was when she found his antenna missing off his car, and then when he took her shopping later on, she found it underneath his car seat all charred up from being smoked on. She had seen antennas used as crack pipes many times before, so there was no denying that he was smoking crack. Dee Dee still cared for Mikey 'cause he was always around reminding her of the time she gave her virginity to him.

"Mikey, you need to get off that shit so you can live again. I believe you can do it." She took Mikey's hand in her hand. "It's crazy, but all this time you been smoking, I still see the nigga that I gave my virginity to. If you want some help, Mikey, all you gotta do is be man enough to say it. I gave my virginity to you cuz I knew you was man enough to respect me and not brag about it. Now be man enough to leave that dope alone."

Dee Dee spoke so compassionately that Mikey believed everything she had said. When his eyes teared up, Dee Dee knew he had heard her.

"Look, Dee Dee, I gotta run. I got this job to do, but it was good rappin' and shit. Later!" Mikey lied and took off before he started to cry.

"Remember, Mikey, all you gotta do is man up and ask for help, cuz you know I'm there for you," Dee Dee shouted before he was out of hearing range. Mikey threw his hand up in the air to signal her that he heard what she had shouted. Now he was completely out of her sight.

Dee Dee headed to the building to collect from the people on the list. Lil Man was the last one to show up. She now trusted him enough to give him something to really work with.

"Can you handle this?" Dee Dee asked as she tossed him a kilo.

"Damn, Dee Dee! You bet I can. You know I'll come correct with the cash too," Lil Man stated.

"You better or you'll get what that punk ass nigga Trey got."

"That was some cold shit y'all did to him. Hell, he would have been better off just taking one to the dome instead of getting fucked up the ass by a female," Lil Man explained.

"That's nice looking out on the info and passing those photos out."

"That nigga ain't showed his face since those pictures hit the block. Niggas know you ain't playing about your cash, but you still got niggas hating on you so watch your back," Lil Man warned.

"You just watch yourself out there so we can keep doing business." Lil Man left, ready to hit the block and make a killing.

Dee Dee sat by the counter and poured herself a shot of Henny. The taste was something else, but she still managed to hold it down and drink it all. Her cell phone started ringing so she reached her hand out and picked it up from the other end of the counter.

"Hello," Dee Dee answered with her throat still on fire from the Henny.

"Miss Davis?" the white voice asked.

"Yeah, this is her."

"This is David from Tailor's Auto. Those cars you wanted just came in."

Dee Dee was glad to hear that, 'cause now she could show Chills n' them just how much she appreciated them.

"David, I'll be down in a minute."

"I'll be here," David shot back, happy that he was going to make a nice commission off the sale.

Dee Dee hung up with David and called Chills and told her to pick her up. She also told her to bring Tricksy and Diamond, so they could all be surprised.

When Dee Dee had Chills pull into the parking lot of the car lot, she could see that David did exactly what she had asked him to do. Chills parked the ride and cut the engine off. She didn't know what was going on, but she could feel something was up.

Dee Dee got out of the ride and walked up to David, the salesman, who was coming toward her.

"Glad you could make it," David greeted with a handshake. He liked how Dee Dee looked. As a white dude, he always dreamed of being with a sistah to see what was really behind all that thickness.

"Everything ready like I asked?" David pointed to the back so she could see for herself. Dee Dee motioned for Chills n' em to hold up for a sec as she went to the back of the car lot to check on things.

When she and David reached the back, her eyes got big. Four Hummer H2s in four different colors sat next to each other with big matching bows on them. He handed Dee Dee the keys to all four rides. She had hers done in a special color. The metallic champagne-pinkish color was off the chain, and the chrome had all the rides sparkling.

Dee Dee went to the edge of the building so Chills could see her, and Chills leaned her head out of the car window 'cause she couldn't hear shit Dee Dee was shouting.

"Come on back," Dee Dee shouted louder. Chills started up the ride and started to drive to the back, but Dee Dee was shouting and waving her hands for her to leave the ride where it was and walk. Chills, Tricksy, and Diamond all walked to where Dee Dee was at, and when they got to the corner, their eyes damn near busted out of their heads. All their names were blowing on banners that were attached on each antenna. Tricksy and Diamond ran like banshees to go check out their new rides. Chills just looked on in awe at what she was seeing.

"You gonna just look, or go check out what's yours?" Dee Dee asked with a smile. Chills looked at Dee Dee, then wrapped her arms around her body, arms and all, and swung her around.

"I should kiss you, but then you might think I like you, so I'm gonna just go check out my new ride. Thanks, Dee Dee. I mean that from the bottom of my heart."

Chills meant that 'cause ever since she was born, nobody gave her shit but ass beatings and plenty of rape sessions. Dee Dee was the first person who gave her a gift, and an expensive one at that. Chills hopped in her ride, and the first thing that she saw were the initials, R.B.M., embroidered in the seats and on the steering wheel.

"This is dope," Chills said.

Dee Dee was talking to David inside the auto showroom, as he counted the cash. He was the same cat Jay and Bee fucked with when they wanted to buy a new ride. David could find any type of ride there was, and paying cash was no problem with him, even if the price exceeded $9,999.99. He could shake the IRS like it was nothing.

"Everything is all good. If you need me again, just holla. Tell your brother thanks for the referral," he stated, not knowing that Jay and Bee were locked up.

Dee Dee gave David the address to her crib so he could have Chills's mom's Tahoe dropped off, then she shook his hand. As she walked out, he just looked at all the jelly shaking as she walked away.

Like follow the leader, Dee Dee led the way in her champagne-pink H2. Chills was behind her in her canary yellow version. Tricksy was next, smoking already in her new all black, chromed out H2. And finally, Diamond brought up the rear in her navy blue and purplish tinted vehicle. Diamond leaned back, chilling and listening to "Oops, Oh My" by Tweet. That was her jam, and Tweet was her baby, at least in her mind.

Chills got to thinking to herself that now was as good a time as any to make Dee Dee down with them, so she sped up and pulled in front of Dee Dee, so Dee Dee could follow her.

Dee Dee pulled behind Chills into a tattoo parlor parking lot. She didn't know why Chills was parking, but she knew she would soon find out. Dee Dee stepped out of her ride and looked around. A police car drove past, then made a U-turn and drove by again, only this time he drove real slow to get a good look at the four brand new H2s parked side-by-side.

"Fuck him, girl. He just mad cuz us bitches riding better than his funky ass," Chills stated. Chills then told Dee Dee to just play along with what she was about to do to throw the cop off, 'cause she knew how Dee Dee got spooked. Chills swung Dee Dee around and laid a big kiss on her lips. Tricksy and Diamond did the same to each other. Once the cop saw four bitches kissing each other, he burnt off. Dee Dee broke the hold that Chills had on her and started spitting like crazy to get that taste out of her mouth.

"If the muthafucka was mad at us for having new rides, then he shouldn't be mad about females kissing females. But you know I only did that to throw him off, right?" Chills explained to Dee Dee.

After that display for the cop, they all went into the tattoo parlor.

Dee Dee watched Tricksy get the R.B.M. initials tattooed on her upper right breast, just above her nipple. She wanted the tattoo to be seen when she wore her shirts that showed off her cleavage.

Now it was Dee Dee's turn, and pain wasn't what she was trying to feel.

"Come on, girl. It's your time," Tricksy said as she tugged on Dee Dee's arm.

Dee Dee was honored that they would even want to put her down like that, but a tattoo was pain, and she didn't know about all that. Finally, after a pep talk from the tattoo artist, she finally agreed to go ahead and have it done. She lay down on her stomach and had him put it on her tailbone, just above her ass. Dude felt that Dee Dee was too cute just to have some initials on her, so he hooked it up with some sprouting flower stems going around the initials. When he was done, Dee Dee felt pain like she had never felt before, but she was happy how the tattoo had come out.

"Now you're a full-fledged member of the Real Bitches Murder Clique," Chills stated.

Chapter Nineteen

"Jay, I got this," Dee Dee told Jay over the phone.

"Just make sure you do, cuz without him it's on and poppin'," Jay reiterated.

Dee Dee reassured Jay that she would have Chills n'em get on it. Jay felt a lot better now that he had gotten Dee Dee to handle the matter that he'd been pondering on for a moment now. He asked her in code about the dope shipment. Dee Dee didn't have a problem with the shipment, even though she was up to receiving two thousand bricks every two weeks now.

"Listen, Dee Dee, I want you to buy something real nice for Miya. Preferably some bling-bling with ice," Jay told her.

Dee Dee knew that she had taste, so the gift that she was going to pick out was going to blow Miya's head off.

Jay heard the beep, which told him that he had

thirty seconds to finish what he had to say before the phone would be cut off.

"Dee Dee, I love you, sis. Stay safe!" Jay said before the phone went dead.

Dee Dee was left with the words of what her brother had just said to her. She and Jay had never been close, but the love was always there. Jay never said the words I love you to her before, which left her in deep thought.

Later Dee Dee, Miya, and Ronshay decided to hit the mall. Dee Dee parked in the mall parking lot. Miya got out of the H2 first and began stretching her arms. Ronshay was looking in the visor mirror as she put on her lip gloss to make those lips of hers cute. Dee Dee got out of the ride and walked around to where Miya was standing.

"I'm glad you called, Dee Dee, cuz I needed to get out of that house for a while or I would have lost my mind with those two kids of mine. Jay was so good with them. I think they just acting out cuz they miss Jay's presence," Miya expressed sincerely.

Dee Dee took Miya in her arms and gave her the biggest hug that one could receive.

"Everything's gonna be all right. You hear me?" Dee Dee assured her.

"I'm ready!" Ronshay shouted as she stepped out of the ride.

"It's about time," Miya and Dee Dee teased in unison.

They all walked into the mall and headed straight for Kaufmanns. Dee Dee hit the perfume counter right off the bat. She was spraying every last one of the bottles until she couldn't stand the smell of all those different scents floating in the air.

Ronshay walked over to where Dee Dee was, and when she got up close to Dee Dee she started gagging from the too strong smell in the air.

"Dee Dee, you got this place all smelling like shit," she said with her shirt over her nose.

"It do, don't it? Let's get from over here before one of us passes out," Dee Dee suggested with a smirk on her face.

Miya was over at the clothes section picking out some outfits for Jay. She always bought Jay clothes when she went shopping, and now that he was locked up, it was no different. Her love for Jay extended beyond him being present in the physical form. To her, her love for Jay was unconditional no matter whether he was in jail for one day or in there for twenty years.

Dee Dee and Ronshay spotted Miya at the service counter with a shit load of clothes in front of her.

"Damn! Miya, you trying to buy the store up, or what?" Ronshay asked. Dee Dee just nodded her head in acknowledgement when Miya looked her way.

"Look, Dee Dee, I got to do some shopping myself, so I'll see you in a little bit, all right?" Ronshay said.

Dee Dee told her that it was cool 'cause she had some shopping to do herself and then they all went their own ways, but before they left they decided to meet at the pay phone section when they were done.

Dee Dee walked out of Kaufmanns and headed to the jewelry stores. She spotted Richard's Jewelers down the aisle, so she hit that one up first.

"May I help you?" The tall, white man in a schoolteacher type suit asked her.

"Just browsing," Dee Dee answered back.

"If you need any help just holler," he said with a smile. Dee Dee thought that if she hollered like he said to, she knew the police would come.

She looked through the glass display cases checking out all the nice jewelry. There were rings that caught her eye, but not enough to purchase any one of them. She then spotted a gold necklace that was just calling her name. Dee Dee called the white man over and told him that she wanted to see it. He pulled the case holding the necklace out of the display case. Dee Dee's eyes got big when she saw it up close. It was sparkling out of control. He took it off the velvet pad and placed it around her neck so she could see just how it looked on her. She walked up to the full-length mirror and checked it out. She pulled her hair back to the left side and twisted her neck to get an all around look.

"I'll take it," she said. The white man looked at her in awe as he knew that Dee Dee didn't know how much the necklace cost.

"Ma'am, that piece is eight thousand dollars."

"Did I ask how much it was? I don't think I did, did I?" Dee Dee stated strongly.

"I'm sorry, ma'am, it's just that most people ask about the price first. Please forgive me if I sounded rude," he said apologetically. He went to the back and got the same necklace and the registration papers that went with it out of the safe.

When he was about to close the vault, he remembered the matching two-carat diamond earrings that were wrapped up, and he figured that if she could afford the necklace without asking the price, then she probably could buy the earrings also. He took the jewelry out to where Dee Dee was, hoping that another sale was in the making.

"Ma'am, I just thought I would show you the matching two-carat earrings that go with the necklace."

He saw in her eyes that it was a go, so he quickly unrolled the black silk cloth containing the earrings. Dee Dee loved them and paid for them both separately to keep from going over ten grand and alerting the IRS.

"Where can I find a nice engagement ring?" Dee Dee asked.

The white man held up his finger in a "just one moment" gesture. He returned from the back with a long case about the length of his arm. He sat Dee Dee down at a private desk so she could see what he had to offer. He opened the case and there were diamonds taking up half of the case on one side, and different types of rings on the other side of the case for the diamonds to be set in.

He took the time out to educate Dee Dee on how a person who was buying a diamond ring should always go about purchasing a diamond separately, so the person will always be able to tell how much their ring is worth and how much the diamond is worth. Dee Dee was happy to be given the game on the diamond side of things.

He showed her the clarity levels and how to detect any flaws by looking through a special magnifying glass that jewelers used called a loupe. Dee Dee tripped out like a little kid when she noticed by looking through the loupe that a diamond had rainbow colors in it. That is something she never knew. She picked a diamond and requested it to be set into a ring. It would be ready in twenty minutes.

She also had the white man, who she now called Carl, hook a card up on his computer to say, "Baby, will you marry me?" She then told Carl that when she came back later with two other females, he should call both of them over and tell them that he had a delivery from James Davis and Bret Davis for both of them. Dee Dee knew that would have them going and tickle their fancies.

Chapter Twenty

$\mathcal{D}$-Dawg was just entering the glass booth where Bee was sitting down on the other side. When D-Dawg sat down on the steel stool, he and Bee picked up the black phone at the same time.

"How you holding up, playboy?" D-Dawg asked.

"Shit! The best I can, you know?"

"Yeah, I know exactly what you mean. Ronshay said that you was gaining weight and I see she was right," D-Dawg teased.

"Shit! I gotta gain something outta this bitch, seeing as how they don't wanna let a nigga regain his freedom," Bee stated as he blinked.

D-Dawg could tell that Bee wanted out, but he was stuck like chuck for right now. They talked about that night they went to the strip joint. D-Dawg was looking out for Nikki like Bee had asked him to, but in more ways than one. D-Dawg tried to warn his boy not to get mixed up with a stripper broad who fucks for cash, but Bee wasn't trying to hear him. Bee asked D-Dawg how she was doing, and as much as he wanted to tell his boy that he was fucking the broad, he kept the truth hidden and just told him that she was cool.

The time they spent looking through a fucking glass wall between them, talking to each other and kicking it was so good that they didn't know that their time was up until the guard screamed it out. They both stood up and placed their right fists on their chests to show that they had mad love for each other.

"Peace, my nigga," D-Dawg said.

"Peace to you, too, and stay focused out there," Bee shot back, then hung up the phone as the guard on his side ushered all the inmates out the door.

D-Dawg had just parked his ride at his crib when he spotted Nikki in his rearview mirror pulling up behind him. He stepped out and saw a look on her face that said something was wrong.

"Why the fuck is you looking like that?" D-Dawg asked with a mean look on his face.

"Nigga, I'm pregnant!"

"Pregnant by who?"

"Come on now. Bee been locked up almost eight months now, so how the fuck can it be his and I'm only seven weeks so far?" she asked with her hands on her hips.

"It ain't mines, bitch, so I advise you to go find the nigga who knocked your stupid ass up."

"Okay, nigga, it's like that, huh?"

"You knew what it was when we started this shit," D-Dawg reminded her.

"We'll see if Bee knows exactly what it is when he finds out that his boy been fucking his pussy," Nikki stated coldly.

"Bitch, my nigga ain't worried about your tramp ass. All you was to him was a piece of ass. He got a woman at the crib, or have you forgotten?"

D-Dawg's words stung, but Nikki wasn't gonna let that fuck shit up. She'd been fucking this other nigga more than she was fucking D-Dawg. The other nigga had a lady, too. Nikki hooked up with him after Bee went to jail. He told her he would never let her want for shit, but on one condition, which was he never wanted to hear the words "I'm pregnant" for anything in the world, or else she was cut off.

D-Dawg was just a nigga who fucked her like she wanted, rough and tough and didn't give a fuck. The reason she told D-Dawg that she was pregnant by him was because she needed money for an abortion. She couldn't get the money from the nigga who she was really pregnant by 'cause everything she would buy showed up on the credit card he gave her. And if he saw the card was swiped at a doctor's office, he would surely call up there and find out what it was for.

D-Dawg walked away with his hands in the air as she kept running off at the mouth.

Nikki was heated beyond belief when D-Dawg threw that bullshit in her face about Bee's girl. If that's how she was being handled, even though she had her own game playing, then she might as well blow everybody's spot up so they could be fucked up like she was. If she had to have the baby, and had no help to take care of it, then niggas was gonna hate her for what she was set to do. She decided to pay Bee a visit.

Bee had no idea who the person was who was

there to see him. He had already spoken to Ron-shay, who told him she was coming at her regular time, which was at six.

When he walked into the visiting room where the phone booths were and took a seat, he saw Nikki walking up. His heart started thumping 'cause he told her not ever to come up there for fear of her running into Ronshay. He picked up the phone quick as fuck to say what he had to.

"What the fuck is you doing here?" he asked, pissed off.

"I came to see you," she shot back.

"I talk to you every day on the telly. You fucking up, Nikki."

"Well, I needed to tell you something about what your boy said," she stated, looking straight at Bee.

"What boy?" Bee asked, unsure.

"Your boy, Derrick."

The first thing that came to Bee's mind was that his main man had gotten killed.

"Is he all right?" he asked with concern in his voice.

"Ain't nothing wrong with that nigga, except that he's talking bad."

"What you mean?"

"He said that I ain't nothing but a fuck thang to you. I know we started off like that, but you did tell me that you love me, right?" she asked, looking at him hard for an answer.

Bee couldn't help but to crack a smile. When she saw it, she didn't like it at all.

"Well, I bet he didn't tell you that we been fuck-ing ever since you been locked up, and that he got me pregnant, huh?"

Bee jumped out of his seat with a fucked up look on his mug, staring down at her.

"You dirty bitch! Fuck you, you stankin' ho! I shouldn't have ever started with your stank ass in the first place," Bee shouted, then slammed the phone down on the hook.

Nikki banged on the window to get his attention as Bee walked away. He looked back to see her laughing and pointing at him like the joke was on him. Bee stuck his middle finger up at her and kept on stepping.

Bee was furious to think that his boy D-Dawg would cross him like that. He knew there wasn't anything he could do about it while locked up, but he damn sure was gonna check D-Dawg when he got out.

"I'm here to see Bret Davis," Ronshay told the guard. He looked down at the visiting book.

"Ma'am, inmate Bret Davis has a visitor right now," he told her.

Ronshay told Bee never to have anyone come visit him at this time because this was the only time that she could make it, seeing as how she worked full-time and went to school.

"Can you tell me who it is that's visiting him, sir?" she asked.

"A Ms. Nikkole Jackson." Ronshay knew Nikki, but she hadn't seen her in years. She didn't know why Nikki was here seeing her man. She took a seat in one of the chairs in the visiting room. While she waited, everything was running through her head about why the fuck Nikki was up here. Every thought was negative 'cause she couldn't see why Bee would have another bitch coming to visit him.

Nikki stepped out of the elevator and walked to the guard's booth to get her I.D. When she and Ronshay caught each other's eye, that's when the heat started to rise. Ronshay shot out of her seat, not to set it off, but more so to ask Nikki why the fuck she was visiting her man. Nikki was receiving her I.D. when Ronshay walked outside. As soon as Nikki stepped out of the door, Ronshay stepped up to her.

"Nikkole!" Ronshay yelled to get Nikki's attention.

Nikki turned around and saw Ronshay standing there. Nikki didn't know that Ronshay was Bee's girl, but she was sure about to find out.

"Oh! Hey, girl. It's been a long time," Nikki greeted.

"Look, I'm gonna get straight down to it. Why the fuck was you in there visiting my man?" Ronshay asked, not holding back her distress.

"Why you coming at me all crazy and shit? And who's your man?" Nikki shot back with an attitude of her own.

"The muthafucka that you just got through visiting. The guard told me that you was Bee's visitor."

"If that's your man, then you need to get a better leash on his dick cuz he ain't trained enough to let him go walking by himself."

Ronshay didn't need another word to be said. She let her open hand fly and smacked the shit out of the right side of Nikki's face. After that, Nikki swung back and now both had each other's hair trying to yank it out. The police rushed from everywhere to stop the sudden fight that had erupted. They finally broke the two apart, but they were still trying to get at one another.

"That's cool, bitch! But I'ma get that ass later," Ronshay shouted.

"That's why your man loved eating my pussy! By the way, did you taste my shit on his lips? Cuz the nigga loved cleaning my asshole out with his tongue."

Ronshay was heated and wished that the police would somehow release her so she could get to the bitch.

Both of them were handcuffed and charged with disorderly conduct. As the police took them inside, Nikki shouted, putting the nail in the coffin.

"Oh yeah, Ronshay, I forgot to tell you that I'm pregnant, and guess who the daddy is."

Ronshay was crushed to hear some shit like that. *It can't be true. Bee wouldn't have a baby by another woman when I just got off the pill so we could make a baby. He wouldn't!* Ronshay thought to herself as tears started to roll down her face.

"Hey, Davis," one of the guards shouted. Bee walked up to the intercom so he could see what the guard wanted.

"Yeah!"

"You know a Nikkole Jackson and a Ronshay White?"

"Yeah. Ronshay's my girl."

"Well, they just got booked for fighting downstairs. Nice going, Romeo."

Bee punched the wall in front of him. He knew if Ronshay saw Nikki downstairs somewhere that it was gonna be on and poppin'. He wanted to punish

Nikki, if he could just get his hands on her. He couldn't tell Jay 'cause they were separated long ago for taking their frustrations out on one of the niggas who thought he was 'bout it.

Dee Dee woke up from another bad dream about when she killed Manny. She couldn't shake the dreams. Lately they had been occurring more and more frequently.

The house phone started to ring and she reached her arm out and picked it up off its base.

"Hello," Dee Dee answered.

Bee's voice was so loud that Dee Dee had to move the phone away from her ear. When she put it back, the first thing she did was shout into the receiver for him to quit yelling. Bee heard her yell and he got his composure together and started talking calmly.

"Dee Dee, I need you to come down here and bail Ronshay outta jail before her people do."

"Why is she in jail?" Dee Dee asked.

"Look, this bitch I was fucking around with showed up here when Ronshay did and they got into it."

"Damn! She gonna be mad at you for a while," Dee Dee taunted.

"Just get her out and get her to somehow stay at the crib so you can talk some sense into her head."

"Who was the broad?" Dee Dee asked.

"This bitch named Nikki Jackson. The bitch came up here to tell me she was pregnant by D-Dawg. I ain't tripping on that 'cause that wasn't my woman. Ronshay is, and I can't lose her, sis," Bee stated.

"I got it covered. Don't call tonight, just wait till

morning. I should be able to work something out with her."

Dee Dee went down to the jail and waited for Ronshay to come out from the back. When she came out, her hair was all fucked up and her clothes were ripped.

"You cool, girl?" Dee Dee asked as she put her arm around her shoulders.

"I can't believe your brother, Dee Dee. He had that stank bitch up here visiting him. You know what the bitch told me, Dee Dee? She said that Bee got her pregnant." Ronshay started crying so badly that Dee Dee had to sit her down on the brick steps outside of the jail.

"She said she's pregnant, right? But let me ask you this." Ronshay didn't raise her head up so Dee Dee raised it for her with the tip of her fingers. "How big was her stomach?" Dee Dee asked.

Ronshay got to thinking about Nikki's stomach. A smile lit her face up as she recalled that Nikki didn't have a stomach.

"Bee been locked up for eight months and that bitch ain't even got one inch of fat on her ass," Ronshay answered with a smile.

"See? Anyways, Bee called me and told me that the bitch wanted him to lend her some money for an abortion 'cause D-Dawg wouldn't help her out, and he told her that he ain't the daddy," Dee Dee said, making up lies to try to keep them together.

"So Derrick is the one who got her pregnant. That serves that bitch right. I just knew that Bee wouldn't do me like that. I love your brother so much, Dee Dee."

"I know girl. I know."

Dee Dee drove, headed for the house. When she turned onto her street and got close, they saw thick smoke clouds in the air and a whole lot of police lights up ahead. Dee Dee couldn't pull onto her block 'cause it was blocked off by two police cars parked sideways in the middle of the street. She parked around the corner on another block. They got out of the car and walked onto the block to see which house was on fire. Dee Dee broke through the barricades and ran as fast as she could when she saw that her own crib was the one smoking. She jumped up and down, holding her mouth as her house was engulfed in flames. The firemen were spraying water all over the house, trying to put the fire out.

Ronshay caught up with Dee Dee and wrapped her arms around her as Dee Dee cried hysterically.

"Oh my God, Ronshay! How did this happen?" Dee Dee asked in tears.

"I don't know, Dee Dee."

"Oh, there you go, girl. I was so scared that you were in that house when that nigga was dousing it with gasoline," Janelle told her with tears in her eyes.

"What nigga, Janelle?" Dee Dee asked, surprised.

"I don't know who it was cuz it was dark, but I seen him pouring that gas everywhere. I shouted at him, but he didn't stop, so I went and grabbed the phone and called the police. When I came back outside, the nigga done set fire to the porch and ran down the street."

"You didn't see how he looked, Janelle?" Dee Dee asked with her hands on Janelle's shoulders.

"Naw. I couldn't see shit except for him doing what he was doing."

"Ma'am, are you the owner of this house?" the fire chief interrupted.

"My brothers are, but they are outta town right now."

"Do you know who would want to do this to your brothers' house?" he asked.

"Not really," Dee Dee stressed.

"OK. If you think of anyone, please give us a call. Here's my card and the card for the detective who will be investigating this case." Dee Dee took the cards.

Janelle offered to let Dee Dee come stay with her, but Ronshay cut Janelle off by telling Dee Dee that she would be staying with her at her and Bee's apartment.

They looked around and saw that nothing could be done as the fire had been out of control, destroying everything there was to be destroyed. They left and headed to Ronshay's apartment. When they got there, Dee Dee just sat on the couch fucked up, stressing badly, and trying to think who could have done that to her home.

Dee Dee put the word out that whoever knew anything about the nigga who set fire to her and her brothers' crib would get a reward for pointing the nigga out.

It didn't take Lil Man long to give Dee Dee a call when he got word that Trey was that nigga. Dee Dee had suspected the nigga, but didn't know for sure. When she spoke to Jay and Bee on the phone and told them what had happened to their house, they were the ones who told her to put the reward out and just wait. Lil Man didn't have a clue as to where Trey was laying low, but he told Dee Dee that the nigga Trey was out to put her and those R.B.M. broads six feet under. Dee Dee was ready for whatever, 'cause the game had changed her to where she was beyond just being street smart, book smart, and a pretty face with a dope body. Dee Dee was getting schooled in all areas that her brothers didn't have the time to take her to school on.

By waking up night after night with the same killer back and neckaches, Dee Dee felt she couldn't see herself sleeping on Ronshay's couch any longer. She thought of calling Alastair and talking to him about what he had been trying so hard to get her to do. When Ronshay left for class, Dee Dee called Alastair on his cell phone.

"Hey, fella," she said sweetly.

"Oh, hey," Alastair answered, not really happy.

"You don't sound happy to hear from me."

"Deondra, you done caused me enough pain. All I was doing was trying to get you off my mind since you been so fucking busy now'days."

"Alastair, just hold up a minute."

Alastair was shocked to hear her speak his real name.

"What did you just call me?" he asked excitedly.

"Your name is Alastair, ain't it?"

"It sure the fuck is." Alastair was dancing all around the bedroom floor like he was on a dance floor at a club somewhere 'cause he was so happy. What he always wanted a female to call him had just happened.

"Alastair, are you there?" Dee Dee asked 'cause he was taking too long to respond.

"Yeah, I'm here. So what's up?" he asked, listening closely.

"Look, somebody set our house on fire."

"WHAT? Are you OK? Did you get hurt?" he asked in serious concern.

"I'm OK, but I lost everything. We have insurance, though, so everything will be covered," she explained.

"So, where are you staying now?"

"I'm at Ronshay's crib now, but I'm gonna go to my mom's house 'cause Ronshay only has one bedroom and me and her couch ain't working out."

"Dee Dee, you know I would love for you to come and stay with me. That offer still stands."

Dee Dee didn't answer right then, which had Alastair worried that she was gonna stall him out again like she'd been doing. The main reason she called Alastair was so she could go stay with him, but she knew a girl never came like she was desperate for shit from any nigga. That was just a golden rule between the women of the world. She had milked Alastair to where he had asked her to stay.

"Dee Dee, is everything OK?" he asked, waiting for an answer.

"You know I ain't got no clothes or anything, huh?"

Alastair didn't give a fuck about no fucking clothes. Hell, he had enough cash to buy out a fucking mall, and so did Dee Dee.

"You know, as fine as you are, you don't have to wear anything," he teased.

"I'm being serious, Alastair, and you wanna crack jokes."

"I was just trying to make you smile, you know,"

he said, trying to smooth shit out and not blow his chance to be with the girl of his dreams.

What he said did put a smile on Dee Dee's face, she just didn't want to admit it to him.

"So, can you come and get me right now?" she asked.

"I sure can, but what are you gonna tell Ronshay?" he asked.

"I'm gonna tell her that I'm going to stay with my man."

Alastair's heart instantly filled with joy when he heard that.

"HELL YEAH! THAT'S WHAT I'M TALKIN' 'bout!" he shouted as loud as he could in pure happiness. Dee Dee smiled on the other end of the phone 'cause his words also filled her heart with joy.

Chapter Twenty-One

In the meantime, the Robinson boys had beaten their case on a technicality, and they were now being released from jail in Cincinnati, Ohio. As they made their way back into M-City, they decided to hit the bar to celebrate happy hour. They ran into one of the niggas who used to work for them. He told them all about Bee, Jay, and their sister Dee Dee taking over the dope trade in M-City. He even told them that D-Dawg was back in town and teamed up with his boy, Bee, and how D-Dawg has been pushing a lot of dope around town too. That was enough to set them off to go look for D-Dawg. They told dude not to tell anyone that they were back in town and their man agreed, so they gave him some dap and bounced in search of D-Dawg.

D-Dawg was just getting into the shower before Nikki was to come over. He missed fucking her pussy. To him, if a bitch liked to be talked to crazy, and liked to be fucked every way possible she could be fucked, then she was the type of chick he liked having around.

D-Dawg told Nikki he would loan her the money to get what she needed done by the doctor. Bee never bothered to call D-Dawg and tell him that the bitch came up to visit, 'cause Bee wasn't gonna let her come between him and his man's childhood friendship. But if D-Dawg knew that Nikki visited Bee and told him what she said she was gonna tell him, then he wouldn't have considered giving the bitch shit but a thug-ass whoopin'.

Nikki made it to D-Dawg's crib and knocked on the door. There was no answer because D-Dawg was still in the shower. D-Dawg's ride was in the driveway so she knew he was there. She tried the door, and to her surprise it was unlocked, so before entering, she looked around to see if anybody was being nosey, thinking she was trying to break in.

She heard the shower going so she walked into the bathroom and saw D-Dawg's body through the shower curtain. D-Dawg didn't know she was there, but he would. Nikki took off all her clothes to give him some of her nookie, just to make sure he kept his word about the money. She pulled the curtain back and stepped in. She placed her arms around his body, which startled the shit out of him.

When he turned around and saw who it was, he released his tight grip on her arm and eased her naked body up against the wall. He thug kissed her all over her body, making it rough. He had one of her breasts in one hand manhandling it and the other in his mouth sucking away, enough to make her tingle all over. D-Dawg turned Nikki around, placing her hands up above her on the wall, then slid his dick inside her from the back. He had her bend down slightly to where he could ram his dick in her as far as he could. He pulled her hair tightly in a downward way to make her feel what he was delivering. She moaned and talked dirty as hell to him. D-Dawg was tired of losing his footing because of the water that was steadily hitting their bodies. He led her out of the shower, headed for the bedroom, with his manhood still inside of her. He gently sat her down on the bed on all fours so he could pump his dick in her doggystyle.

Ronshay had just made it home, and for some reason, what Nikki had told her was still on her mind. She needed to talk to D-Dawg to bring closure to the pain she still felt from Nikki's words. She picked up the phone and dialed D-Dawg's number.

D-Dawg was all up in Nikki's gut when the phone started to ring. He wasn't studying that phone or the caller, whoever it was. He was punishing Nikki, taking out all his frustrations on her. He didn't forget what the bitch had said the day that she told him she was pregnant. He felt this was his way to fuck her back. He planned on pulling his dick out and nutting all over her face, which was his way of showing a bitch she wasn't shit to him but a slut who gave up the pussy.

The phone was still ringing, which got on his nerves. He reached over and answered it despite Nikki telling him not to.

"Yeah," he shouted into the phone.

"D-Dawg, this is Ronshay. Why you shouting at somebody?" she asked.

"My bad, girl. What's up?" he asked, still fucking. When she told him all about what had happened at the county jail, D-Dawg looked down at the back of Nikki's head and swung the phone at it, knocking her right down to the floor. Ronshay heard Nikki screaming. She didn't know that she was over there, but it did tell her that Bee wasn't the one fucking her. Ronshay now felt that had gotten closure to the Nikki situation, so she hung up the phone and laughed, 'cause from what she heard over the phone, she knew that Nikki was getting that ass whooped.

The Robinson boys were told where D-Dawg had his crib, so they drove over there to kill the nigga who had shot one of their brothers so long ago.

D-Dawg was beating Nikki's ass all through his crib, not letting up until he told her she was gonna learn to quit being messy. He went to the closet to get a wire clothes hanger, and that's when Nikki got up off the floor and made a dash for the door. She stumbled over a rug and fell onto the couch. D-Dawg saw she was trying to make a dash for the door. While on the floor, he walked slowly toward her, thinking he had time to get to her. He untwisted the hanger to where it was straight, ready to give Nikki that lesson he had told her about.

The Robinson boys had just pulled up to D-Dawg's crib and saw that the car described to them as belonging to D-Dawg was parked in the driveway. They were hoping the nigga was at home 'cause they were ready for the payback. They sat in the car, just checking shit out before they got out of their car.

Nikki got the front door open, but D-Dawg grabbed her by her hair and yanked her back in. She received two licks before she was able to block his arm from hitting her again. As D-Dawg tussled with her, Nikki raised her hand and scratched D-Dawg across the face. He couldn't see shit except for a blur 'cause she had raked her nail across his eye. Nikki opened the door all the way. D-Dawg couldn't see, but he knew the door was right in front of him and so was Nikki. He reached his arms out and grabbed hold of her butt naked body by her waist. Nikki was screaming, but not from what D-Dawg was doing, but because she was looking at four niggas in a silver Buick Park Avenue pointing guns in their direction. She tried to tell D-Dawg, but all he was doing was shouting, telling her how he was gonna beat her ass real good.

The loud explosions from the heaters started popping off, and Nikki's body took about four bullets in the chest before she went limp. D-Dawg could feel all of the bullets impact into her body by the way she was moving. When D-Dawg's vision started to clear, and he could now see his enemy, he used Nikki's lifeless body as a shield to get him back inside. As he was moving, a bullet caught him in his exposed shin. D-Dawg dropped Nikki's dead body to the ground and fell back into the wall outside the house by the door. Before he could again make a move for the door, bullet after bullet sank into his naked body. D-Dawg's body moved as if he was being electrocuted by a major high voltage wire.

After every bullet was fired, D-Dawg's body finally stopped convulsing. His eyes were wide open as he slid down the wall of the house with blood trails smearing up the white wall.

"That's all for that fake ass West Coast Crip, sucka," one of the brothers stated. Then the car peeled off, leaving only a smokescreen behind.

News traveled quickly on the streets about D-Dawg and Nikki getting gunned down like they did. It also made its way all the way to Bee's ears. Bee couldn't believe it when one of the dudes in his pod told him.

The six o'clock news was about to come on, but three other cats were watching the pre-game NFL talk show. Bee walked up to the TV and changed the channel without permission. He didn't care about what they were looking at 'cause this was his boy everybody was talking about.

"Man, didn't you see us watching TV?" one of the dudes stood up and asked.

Bee just looked at dude with a look on his face that said, *Nigga, if you want some, then come and get it.* Dude waved his hand at Bee in a way that said, *You ain't worth it*, but he knew the real deal. Bee had that killer look on his mug that said, *I will whoop your muthafuckin' ass, nigga!*

Bee stood in front of the TV with his ear close to the speaker so he could catch everything. The news came on and started with the words showing up on the whole screen.

"BREAKING NEWS!" The reporter showed D-Dawg's crib and the blood smeared on the wall, but there was no D-Dawg, as he and Nikki had already been taken to the morgue.

"Not my nigga!" Bee shouted, then put his hands on his forehead. "Muthafucka! Why, Lord, why?" Bee shouted as he walked to his room with his eyes full of tears. Every thought of him and D-Dawg together flashed through his mind, until finally he got down on his knees and started to pray.

Chapter Twenty-Two

Alastair kissed Dee Dee's lips as he lay on top of her naked body. The looks they were giving each other told them both that they could have been making love like that a long time ago if they had stayed together.

Alastair wanted to go again, but Dee Dee was too sore and exhausted after going three times already. He respected his lady's body and let her nestle into his own.

Dee Dee was having the bad dream again. She was seeing it over and over again in her sleep, and once she got to the part where the blood started flowing, she woke up screaming and drenched in sweat.

Alastair jumped up, thinking that someone was breaking in. Once he saw Dee Dee sitting up with her hands on her head and her elbows on her knees, he knew something was wrong.

"Baby, you all right?" he asked with concern. He wrapped his arm around her shoulder to give her comfort, and that's when he felt the sweat. "Dee Dee, you're soaking wet. What's going on? Did you have a bad dream?" Dee Dee just kept rocking back and forth, disoriented.

Alastair got out of the bed and went into the kitchen to make some hot cocoa to relax her. When he came back, she was in the shower. The shower was doing the job. She had been dealing with the dreams, but they were haunting her in a horrible way.

"What my brothers get me into, please, Lord, forgive me!" she said quietly to herself. Because the bathroom door was cracked open, Alastair heard her words, but he just didn't know what they meant.

Once Dee Dee was out of the shower and dried off, Alastair gave her the cocoa, which she gladly accepted and began sipping on slowly. He asked her what her dream was about, but she couldn't and wouldn't disclose the truth, not about that, and not to him, even though she wanted to badly. She took one of the sleeping pills prescribed by her doctor and sipped on the cocoa until it was all gone and tucked away in her stomach. She grabbed Alastair's hand and led him back into bed, where she nestled up against his body like before.

When Alastair heard light snoring coming from Dee Dee, he leaned over, planted a kiss on her forehead, and whispered, "I'm here for you, baby."

The next day Dee Dee walked down the stairs, leaving the safe house. She had collected from everybody, and even put Lil Man on better than what she had given him last time. Lil Man had proven that he could move a kilo with no problem, and his information was always helpful, so she felt he could now work with three bricks instead of one.

Dee Dee hopped into her H2 and settled in. She took the gun and placed it underneath her seat in its strap. She wanted to check out what was left of her house since she hadn't been there since the fire. She knew it was fucked up, but she needed to see for herself. She wished she would have gone by there earlier in the day when it was lighter outside.

She pulled up onto her street and drove around back. Mikey had seen her SUV coming, so he ducked out of sight. He couldn't face her when he just got through getting high. The conversation they had last time they saw each other was too deep. He realized through her words that he was tearing up his life, but he figured what the fuck could he do about it. The dope had him.

Dee Dee didn't know she had been followed ever since she left the apartment building. She pulled into the alley and parked her ride at an angle so the headlights would allow her to see what used to be her crib. She stepped out of her ride and just stood there staring at the rubble. The smell of burnt wood was just as strong as it was when the house was engulfed in flames.

Just when Dee Dee was about to turn around to get back in her ride, a hand clasped around her mouth and an arm wrapped around her throat. She was scared as fuck. She made as much noise as she could, but the grip of her attacker was tight. She could feel herself about to pass out 'cause the grip was cutting off her oxygen. Dee Dee tussled herself right into submission as she finally passed out. While she was out, he tilted her head back and forced a small pill into her mouth.

Junior laid Dee Dee's limp body on the seat of Dee Dee's car, and then scooted her back so she was stretched out along both of the front seats on her back. He unfastened her belt and her pants and slid her shoes off. He then slid her pants off and stood there massaging his already hard dick as he stared at her thick hips sticking out of her white panties. He slid his pants down to his knees, then he slid Dee Dee's panties off. He raised her panties to his nose and sniffed hard, taking in her essence. He couldn't wait to go up inside of her. As he looked on, he only wished that she was awake for what he was about to do, but how she was now was just fine.

He rubbed his hand around her pubic hair, then slid his finger over her pussy lip. He got so excited that he felt himself building up a load of nut to shoot. He didn't want to waste it, so he began to scoot on top of her to get it poppin'. Just as he leaned his body into Dee Dee's ride, he felt something hard and powerful crash against his leg.

"Muthafucka! You trying to rape Dee Dee! I'll kill ya punk ass!" Mikey shouted as he landed another blow. Mikey had been watching Dee Dee in secret ever since he spotted her drive up.

Junior slid right out of the ride and off of Dee Dee as Mikey pulled him out. While he was on the ground, Mikey's eyes glanced into the ride and saw Dee Dee's naked bottom half. He became so heated that he swung the bat at Junior, trying to tear his head off. Junior was helpless as Mikey kept up his swinging motions. Crack after crack, swing after swing, scream of pain after scream of pain came out of Junior's mouth until he wasn't making any noise at all.

Mikey stopped when he heard Dee Dee ask what had happened. Mikey grabbed her panties and slid them back on her body. He slid one foot after the other back into her pants, then scooted them all the way back to where they belonged. Dee Dee was groggy as he held her head up.

"What happened, Mikey?" She asked as she tried to focus on his face. Mikey didn't really know how to tell her what had just happened, but he knew he had to.

"Junior tried to rape you, but I stopped him just in time. Whatever made you park in a fuckin' alley anyways, Dee Dee?" He asked with tears forming in his eyes.

Dee Dee raised up and saw Junior on the ground fucked up beyond belief. Blood was everywhere, but that didn't stop her from getting out of her ride and picking up the same bat that Mikey just used to beat the shit out of Junior. She swung that bat as many times as she could before she collapsed to her knees.

"Dee Dee, you OK?" Mikey asked as he helped her back up.

"Yeah, I'm OK. Mikey, if you wouldn't have been here, this piece of shit would have had his way with me. Thank you, Mikey. Thank you," she said as she wrapped her arms around his neck and gave him a tight hug.

Dee Dee didn't see a crack head when she looked at Mikey. No, all she saw was the guy to whom she had given her virginity, the guy she trusted, and the guy she hoped would one day return to normal.

"I got to get you outta town before Junior and his

brother try to hurt you," Dee Dee exclaimed as she held his hands.

Mikey knew she was right, but he couldn't leave her with this nigga still around.

"But what about you, Dee Dee? I can't leave you here with this nigga," he stated, still holding her hand.

"Look, I'ma have my brothers take care of his ass, so don't worry about me. He's just lucky I didn't have this in my hand." Dee Dee reached under the driver's seat of her car and retrieved the gun. "As a matter of fact, I should plug his rapist-ass right now," Dee Dee said as she pointed the gun at Junior's dick.

"No, Dee Dee! He ain't worth it. Besides, the nigga gonna be fucked up long after your brothers and 'em beat that case and come home."

Dee Dee just looked at Mikey and knew she needed to find the nigga who set her brothers up, 'cause she was really gonna need their help when Junior was healthy.

"Get in," Dee Dee told Mikey.

"Where we going?" he asked.

"I told you I gotta get you outta town. I couldn't stand myself if Junior and his brother tried to hurt or kill you. You gotta leave town," she said with her hand over her heart.

"Dee Dee."

"Yeah, Mikey?"

"Remember you said to just man up and ask for help and you would help me?"

"Yeah, I remember. What about it?" She asked him.

"Well, I need help now. I don't need to leave

town. I need to go into rehab. Besides, by the time I get outta there, your brothers will be home and already done took care of that punk. I just wanna get cleaned up. I want my old life back, Dee Dee."

Dee Dee leaned over and gave Mikey a big hug and a kiss to go with it.

"All right then. Let's go get you signed up into one of the best rehabs that money can buy," she said as she put her truck into gear and rolled out, rolling right over Junior's leg. Mikey asked her what that bump was, but Dee Dee just gave a smirk. She knew it was part of Junior's body she had run over.

Dee Dee had Mikey stay at the collection apartment for the night, and if he was still there in the morning, she knew he was serious about getting clean.

Morning came, and Dee Dee was right at the apartment, going up the stairs. When she got to the door she saw it cracked open. She put her hand on her heater, not knowing what to expect. She put her hand to the door to open it, but Mikey opened it all the way. They both looked spooked as they held their hands over their hearts.

"Boy, you . . ."

"Girl . . ."

The words came outta their mouths at the same time and they laughed.

"I'm not gonna even talk about how your face just looked," Mikey teased.

"What you mean, my face? You should have seen yours," Dee Dee shot back with a smile. She was happy to see he was still there, but she didn't know that Mikey was about to leave just before she arrived. "So, are you ready?" Dee Dee asked as she put her hand on his shoulder.

"I'm as ready as I'll ever be, I guess."

"Mikey, you can't second-guess yourself about getting your life back on track. It's either you're a man and ready, or you're a mouse and you're cool with settling for scraps." The words she spoke sounded like the Dee Dee Mikey had grown up with. She didn't hold her tongue for anybody.

"Let's do this," Mikey stated.

"I made accommodations for you at the Greenland Health Center. They're supposed to have one of the best facilities in the state for helping people recover off shit. You just make sure you get right in there and come back looking like the Mikey I gave my virginity to, you hear me?"

They arrived two hours later at Greenland Health Center in Greenland, Tennessee. Mikey looked at the whole complex and saw that they had horses and other farm animals. It was a beautiful place, a place he believed could help him change.

"Now you're on your own. When you're ready, just give me a call and I'll be here. The tears couldn't stop flowing out of both of their eyes. An old school song from Shai started playing on the radio. "Remember that?" Dee Dee asked him.

"And if I ever fall in love again, I'll make sure that the lady is my friend," Mikey sang.

"I promise I will never leave you lonely," Dee Dee sang back.

Mikey heard enough because to him that was their song, and for a minute he believed he could have Dee Dee back in his corner one day.

Mikey waved goodbye from the top of the steps of the center. He could still see the love in Dee Dee's eyes that would give him the strength to get himself together.

Chapter Twenty-Three

Chills got the word that Trey was chilling at a Motel 6, Room 32. This was something she wanted to handle on her own, so she didn't bother telling Dee Dee, Tricksy, or Diamond. Dee Dee had come through for her, and Jay and Bee were her homeboys, so she was ready to put in work just for GP.

Chills pulled up into the Motel 6 parking lot and smoked the last little bit of the blunt she was chiefing on. Once done, she checked her Tech-9 to make sure it had one in the chamber. She pulled her skullcap down to her forehead, making sure it would partially block her identity, but not make her look suspicious to anybody.

When she stepped out of the black, old school Oldsmobile Ninety-Eight, a cool breeze crossed her body. The temperature was falling into the low 50s now that it was October, and approaching Spook Night, aka Halloween. Chills had her coat open, but after she felt the chill of the wind she zipped it up.

She walked down the sidewalk, scanning the room numbers on the door, and came upon 30 and 31, and then she was standing in front of the jackpot room, the room that had Trey's bitch ass inside it. Chills listened at the door and could hear that the TV was on, which told her that Trey was in there.

Her plan was to knock on the door and wait till he looked out the window or asked who it was, which would tell her how close or how far he was from the door, then she would let him have it, either through the door or the window.

Chills first looked in both directions to see if everything was cool, then she raised her hand and knocked on the door three times. Her ears were open wide. Nothing! So she knocked again and still she heard nothing but the sound of the TV blasting. Her hand was on her weapon inside her coat pocket just waiting for its chance to make some noise.

Just when Chills was about to knock again, she was startled as she caught a glimpse of someone coming up the sidewalk. She played it off by acting like she was freezing.

"Hurry up and open the door," she said loudly, pretending that she was waiting for someone to open the door for her. When she got up enough heart to look at the person coming toward her, that's when she recognized just who it was, and the person also recognized just who she was.

Trey released the case of Budweiser he was carrying, and dropped it when he saw Chills pull out her gat. He turned around and tried to haul ass. Bullets were firing out of Chills's gat and making a hell of a noise. Plenty of sparks came from the barrel as every bullet was trying to hit Trey's ass. He slipped trying to turn the corner of the building, but luckily no bullets hit him before he was able to make it around the corner of the motel. With heart pounding and damn near busting out of his chest, Trey ran non-stop, headed straight for the safest place he could think of.

Chills made it to the corner and saw the nigga was out, moving quicker than Carl Lewis in his prime. She cussed at herself for not having the girls with her because she knew if she would have just stuck to the plan and picked them up, they would have had Trey's trick ass wrapped up tight right now.

She hopped back into the ride and burned rubber, intending to ditch the boosted, beat up ride and jump back into her own shit.

Trey stood across the street from the police station watching all the cops going in and out. He was contemplating whether this was the right thing to do or not, but reason set in and he weighed his odds. He either had to stay out here and deal with Dee Dee and the R.B.M. Clique, not to mention the brothers, or put the heat on Dee Dee and fuck everybody up. There was nothing more to think about. What they did to him that day they set him up was enough to make a grown man cry, so he walked across the street and went inside.

"Yo, man! I need to rap with a detective," Trey said.

"What for?" The white cop asked with suspicion.

"Look, man, just tell ole boy that I got something hot. Something that will make his dick stand up hard as a brick."

The white cop looked Trey over for any bullshit. He could sense bullshit, but all he saw was a nigga who wanted to talk for some reason or another.

"Wait right here," the cop instructed Trey.

Officer Charlie escorted Trey into the detectives' room and brought him to the first detective they saw. One of them saw Officer Charlie and the black dude walking in, so he greeted Trey.

"What's up. They call me Mason, Detective Mason," he said with his hand extended, ready to shake.

At that same moment, Detectives Perkins and Gary walked into the office. Gary was smiling, but Perkins looked upset. It was the opening day for his son's play for the drama club, and all he got to see was a tad bit of it 'cause the case that Sarge had stuck them on was taking up all his time.

"I'm telling you, man, those bitches tried to kill me! The bitch got a reward out for me. A year ago, that bitch wasn't shit, but now that she's pushing all of that dope, she thinks she's Queen Fucking Dee Dee now!" Trey yelled heatedly. Perkins looked at Gary as if to say "Did you hear that?"

"Excuse me, Mason, but did this guy just say the name, Dee Dee?" Perkins asked.

"Did you just say the name, Dee Dee?" Mason asked Trey with his arms crossed over his chest.

"Nah, man, I said Queen Fucking Dee Dee," Trey shot back, trying to be funny.

"Yeah, I know, but would this Dee Dee chick just happen to live here in town?"

"Man, what's this cat's problem? You on dope, man? Of course she lives here."

"Tell me something, do you recognize this phone number at all?" Perkins asked as he fiddled in his pocket to get the phone number he found in the hotel room with the name Dee Dee on it.

"Yeah! That's her old number. I think she lost it or something.

"Hot Damn! We're moving now, Gary," Perkins shouted as he did a dance in the middle of the floor.

"Perkins! Gary! I told you two about that loudness . . ."

"Slow your roll, Sarge. We got a big lead on 'you know what,' " Perkins said, signaling the Sarge with a wink so as not to spook Trey.

"All right, but no more of that shit," the Sarge said, then walked off.

They talked with Trey for about four hours, finding out everything he knew about Dee Dee, except the part about her brothers being in jail. How that part ever slipped Trey's mind was beyond belief, but Gary and Perkins were cool with what they had, or soon would have—Dee Dee.

At about that same time Chills picked up Diamond and Tricksy. She told them how she lit Motel 6 up like the Fourth of July. Now she had to tell Dee Dee. She told Diamond, who was in the passenger seat, to call Dee Dee. When the phone started ringing, Diamond passed the cell to Chills. The phone rang ten times and there was no answer. Chills felt that it was kind of crazy seeing as how Dee Dee worked and lived by her phone. Chills just hung up and headed to the apartment building where she was supposed to meet Dee Dee anyway.

Lazy and Rich were with Dee Dee. They felt bad for doing what they were doing, but it was too late for an apology, as Dee Dee was already tied up. All she could do was look at her flesh and blood as they cleaned off the last shelf. Three hundred twenty bricks filled nine black Hefty trash bags. They took two bags at a time down to their car.

As they were coming and going, Dee Dee was desperately trying to get her hands free. She was twisting and bending her hands in every way possible in an attempt to loosen the ropes. She was happy as hell that she had never showed her fake-ass cousins the other side of the wall where the money was hidden. If she had, then she and her brothers would surely have problems when they were not able to come up with the $20 million to pay Tony and Don Valdez.

Chills and 'em had just pulled up to the apartment building and parked. Chills spotted Dee Dee's H2 parked across the street, so she knew she was inside. They were smoking a blunt so they were in no rush to go up just yet.

"Listen, little cuz," Rich was telling Dee Dee, "I'm sorry about this, but what's done is done. This is just a tip, so take it how you wanna, but I'ma tell you anyways. Get out of this business, cuz it's not for you," he finished, then headed out the door.

Dee Dee felt the rope around her hands getting looser, so she struggled hard to free herself. The door opened back up, which made her stop her struggle.

"Oh yeah, little cuz, don't bother to look for us, cuz we ain't going back to Cashville. Be good!"

Dee Dee was heated as he said those words. She wanted their asses more than ever, but it looked like she had got jacked, and there wasn't a damn thing she could do about it.

Rich walked down the steps headed for the Caddie where Lazy was already waiting with the engine running.

Chills spotted Rich coming down the steps. She had only seen him one time before, so she rolled down the window and asked him whether Dee Dee was upstairs, and the answer he gave her threw her for a loop.

"Nah, she ain't up there. I don't know where she's at, but tell her we gone back to Cashville."

Chills looked at the car Rich was getting into, and she got some real fucked up vibes. She couldn't put her finger on it, but something wasn't right. She looked over at Dee Dee's H2, then at the building.

"Y'all, something ain't right with this. I can feel it in my bones," she said to her girls.

"You think something done happened to Dee Dee or what?" Diamond asked.

"I don't know. I just got a funny feeling."

Dee Dee finally got her hands free of the ropes. If her cousins were smart they would have used duct tape. That would have kept Dee Dee from ever getting loose on her own.

She stood up and rubbed her wrists where the rope had left bruises. She then ran to the window and saw Rich and Lazy driving off, but got happy as hell when she saw Chills's H2 downstairs. Dee Dee grabbed her phone and dialed Chills's cell number.

Chills looked at her screen and saw it was Dee Dee. "This is her, right here," she told Tricksy and Diamond. "What's up, girl? . . ."

Dee Dee cut Chills off so she could hip her to what had just happened.

"Chills, those niggas in that Caddie just jacked me!" she told Chills as she looked out the window.

"What? Your cousins?"

Dee Dee didn't need to say more, as Chills had already started her ride up and now had her own H2 floored. Chills knew that they had to hit the expressway to get away, so she headed that way also. She spotted Rich and 'em's car by the Caddie's broken brake light in the back window. Chills knew that her gut feeling had never lied to her before, and she was glad that it didn't let her down now. She saw the car turn off on one of the side roads. Since they had all that dope in the ride, they wanted to get back safe. If Chills had been ten seconds later taking off, she would have missed her chance at spotting Dee Dee's slick-ass cousins. Chills turned off on the same road Rich was now on, following him and gaining speed as she rolled her new ride into the 4x4 gear.

Rich looked back and saw somebody gaining on them fast. He knew the way that the ride was coming that it had to be somebody who knew about the lick that they had just put down. Rich put the pedal to the floor and had that Caddie moving out, but Chills had already made up the ground to play catch up. All she wanted to do was get close enough to shove her gat in both of their mouths.

Lazy leaned out of the window with his gat in his hand. He didn't care if the people in the ride chasing them were after them or not, the problem was that the other vehicle was getting too close at a fast rate.

Shot after shot spit out of Lazy's gat, and one of the bullets crashed through Chills' window, not hitting anybody, but making Chills drive off the road. Since she had the ride in 4x4 mode already, she decided to just stay off-road and let her ride show her what it had.

Tricksy leaned out of her window and fired back, but the bumpy off-road ride that Chills was maneuvering caused the shots to go in some other direction from where she was aiming.

Chills spotted a semi truck coming from the opposite direction in which Lazy and Rich were heading. She figured if she could bump them or scare them, they would roll off the road with them, which would cause the Caddie major problems, including getting stuck.

Chills got parallel to Rich's ride. Tricksy spotted Lazy aiming his gun out of the window, so she let off a round before he had a chance to. Lazy ducked back in the window, but Tricksy missed anyway because of the off-road driving. But when Chills hit a bump, Tricksy's aim finally paid off, as one of her bullets popped Rich in his arm.

Rich swerved side to side before losing control. Whatever they were seeing as their car was spinning around in circles was all they would ever see from here on out, 'cause the semi truck wasn't stopping for anything. The driver was blowing his loud horn, but it was so close that he couldn't stop, and if he did, he would surely jackknife his trailer and kill himself.

"Blawwwhhhh," was the sound the semi made when it slammed into the Caddie. The Caddie blew right up into a ball of fire. Chills and 'em looked on at the explosion and the huge flames. Chills felt bad that Dee Dee's dope was gone, but she was happy that Dee Dee's fake-ass cousins got what the fuck they deserved. Chills called Dee Dee and told her the lowdown on what had happened. Dee Dee was sick to her stomach. She didn't know what to do about the dope she had lost.

Then the knock came. The new shipment had come early, just like it had been doing. Dude unloaded a shit load in the basement—five thousand kilos. Tony knew how much the wall could hold, so he sent it. He knew he was sending more than they could push at once, but they proved to him and Don Valdez that they were loyal and could eventually push whatever they were given. He wasn't worried about the money because Jay always made sure to call the collector to come pick up the cash when it was time. Dee Dee couldn't believe her luck. Now she wouldn't have to tell her brothers about what their sucka ass cousins did because of her stupidity.

In Texas Don Valdez was chilling at the pool with five Spanish flies swimming butt naked in the clear pool water. He turned over and lay on his back as some of the girls got out of the pool to give him his daily massage. He had all his bodyguards standing at point.

Tony had just arrived at the compound. He got out of his car, but was suddenly taken by surprise, as one of Don Angelo Ruiz's assassins shot him in the back three times with a high powered rifle with a silencer attached to it.

About fifty men dressed all in black came storm-

ing out of the woods headed for the compound.
They spread all around the house, but not without
being spotted by one of the maids. She ran to the
back and yelled in Spanish that they were being at-
tacked.

Don Valdez hopped up off the lawn chair and
headed for the back door. Don Angelo Ruiz had had
enough of dealing with Don Valdez and the way he
was handling things.

Three of Don Valdez's bodyguards quickly escorted him back into the house so they could get
him into the secret getaway tunnel he had built for
just such a situation as this one. The rest of his bodyguards spread out, but were shot down by a hail of
bullets. Don Valdez was shaking as he heard all of the
gunfire. He wanted to get into that tunnel and live
to see Angelo's head resting on a platter. He knew
Angelo had ordered this, and not the heads. He only
wished he could have been better prepared for it.

They made it to the secret door and one of Don
Valdez's men opened the door so Valdez could enter.
The assassins made their way into the house, gun-
ning down everyone in sight with automatic weapons,
including the women. They made it into the room
where Don Valdez was just entering the secret door
to the tunnel. Don Valdez's bodyguards let off plenty
of bullets, taking out many of Angelo's men, but that
wasn't enough, 'cause the bullets from Angelo's men
blazed through the corridor, striking the three armed
men who were protecting Don Valdez, and killing
them. Don Valdez quickly shut the door and began
making his way to safety.

Angelo walked into the room. One of his men
pointed to the door and explained to him that Don

Valdez had gone in there. Angelo snapped his finger, and one of his men with grenades strapped to his body walked up. Angelo ordered him to blow everything up, starting with the tunnel. The assassin busted open the tunnel door and dropped the whole belt into the hole, except for one of the grenades.

"Let's see if you live through this," the assassin stated.

Angelo ordered the other men to put explosives around the whole house, and when he gave the order, they set a timer for ten minutes. Everyone was out of the house, clear and safe, so the assassin pulled the pin on the one grenade, tossed it into the secret passageway, and took off running.

"Ka-BOOOOOOOMMMMM!"

Don Valdez didn't have a chance with all the grenades going off at once in the close confines of the tunnel. The fire rushed through the tunnel like water going through a pipe and burned his body to ashes, melting all skin, hair and organs.

And then Don Angelo Ruiz watched the whole compound, except for the barn, all go up in blazing flames when the timer hit zero.

Chapter Twenty-Four

Dee Dee couldn't get control of her dreams at all. They were happening more frequently than ever. Alastair would just sit with Dee Dee in the bed holding her tightly until she was able to fall back to sleep. He wanted to know what was making her have those dreams. Because she never disclosed what the dreams were about, he kept asking and asking. He knew whatever it was had to be scary. Alastair could remember how scared he was when he would have a recurring bad dream as a child about zombies chasing him down and trying to eat him. Only when they cornered him in an alley would he give up and let them eat him, but they never made it to him. Alastair would scream at the top of his lungs in his sleep when they were about to take a bite of him. Then he would wake up in a drenched sweat, still screaming. Alastair could relate to whatever Dee Dee was going through. He just wished she would open up and talk to him about it.

Dee Dee got out the shower and got dressed. Alastair had already taken off to go handle some business of his own. Out of all this time they had been kicking it, Dee Dee never told him that she was pumping dope. She did, however, tell him that she had to keep collecting her brother's cash until they came home. Alastair had left the TV on, which was on channel eleven. Dee Dee walked by the TV headed for the fridge. When she got through pouring herself a glass of orange juice, she heard the news lady say, "The man who was shot in the head last night has now been identified as one Jimmy Tolen, aka Baby J."

Dee Dee sat in front of the TV and listened to the rest of what the news lady had to say about the nigga who had set her brothers up. Dee Dee couldn't wait to call Chills and tell her thanks, but when she got Chills on the line, Chills swore to her that it wasn't her or the girls' handiwork. Dee Dee didn't bother to ponder on the situation 'cause the bottom line was that the state wouldn't have enough evidence to prosecute her brothers anymore.

Jay and Bee were in the attorney/client room. The lawyers told them that they had already filed a motion to dismiss the brothers' case, but the judge said that they could only be released on their up and coming court date. Jay was upset, going off, but Bee spoke some wise words to him, which got him to calm down. The attorneys reminded them before leaving that they just had to hold out for two more weeks and it would all be over.

* * *

Alastair took Dee Dee to Sapphire, an elegant, upscale restaurant. As they waited for their food, they got deep into some high profile discussions. Alastair took a sip of his wine as he listened closely to Dee Dee's view of Bush having top power and fuck'n shit up. He was surprised to hear his baby speak like this. Alastair clasped his hands together and rested his chin on top of them. He liked looking at Dee Dee in that black silk Donna Karan body-hugging dress with spaghetti straps. It made him like looking at her even more, because her sexiness was unreal.

Alastair decided to bring up a new topic, so he started with what he went through as a child. Dee Dee listened and knew that Alastair was trying to get her to open up about her nightmares that she'd been having. She wanted to tell Alastair badly, but she wasn't sure how she could share something as bad as what she had done. Alastair put Dee Dee's hands into his own and spoke some real sweet and kind words to her. Dee Dee started crying. She knew Alastair would understand 'cause he had been the best thing that had happened to her in years. She figured if she went on ahead and told him, then maybe her dreams would stop. Alastair took a napkin and wiped away her tears. Dee Dee grabbed Alastair's hand and let everything go.

"I wish I would have never pulled that trigger, baby. I can't stand myself for what I've done. I wish I could bring him back. I really do, baby!"

Alastair was in shock 'cause what she had just told

him was that she had killed his own flesh and blood. Dee Dee couldn't tell that the look he was giving her was a look that said *Bitch killed my fucking cousin*. Dee Dee just thought that the look was from her revealing the story.

Alastair got up from the table and walked to the men's room. He stood in front of the mirror staring at the hurt revealed on his face. What was once a mystery to him and his family was now known. Alastair turned around and kicked the door to one of the toilet stalls. The door swung open slamming against the other part of the stall's wall.

"I can't believe this shit," he shouted in anger and confusion. "The muthafucka who I'm in love with killed my people. I knew this shit was too good to be true!"

Alastair walked out of the restroom and back to the table.

"Come on. We bouncing," he told her with a fucked up attitude. They got in the car and rode silently all the way back to the crib. Alastair didn't say anything to Dee Dee the whole night, which got her worrying about what she had done wrong.

Dee Dee slept with worry on her mind, but she slept in peace without the bad nightmares that had haunted her for so long. Alastair got off the couch and walked into the bedroom. He stared at Dee Dee all curled up with the blanket and the pillow wrapped up tight in her hand. He didn't know what to do. She had become his everything and now she had become his worst nightmare. He walked over to the bed and looked down at her beautiful face. He could see the drool line shining as it made its way outta her mouth and down the side of her cheek. He normally kissed it clean when he saw it, but now he didn't want to touch her. He knew if Dee Dee was anybody other than the lady he was in love with, then he wouldn't have hesitated to put one in her head, but he couldn't, nor could he go on with the life of love they were sharing.

Dee Dee woke up from her sleep as the sun beamed it rays on her face. She got out of bed and walked into the living room. She saw no signs of Alastair. She then looked out the living room window and saw that his car was gone. Dee Dee wanted to talk and now she would have to wait till later. She walked into the kitchen and saw a letter fastened to the door of the fridge. Dee Dee slid it from underneath the watermelon magnet and opened it up. She was happy to have the letter in her hand, thinking that her baby had come to his senses and was apologizing for his rudeness. She sat down on the couch and opened the envelope.

Deondra,

What I'm about to say is not what someone should be saying to the woman who has won his heart over. You have become my everything and more since the first day I became brave enough to stop in front of your crib. I know I will never be able to forget about you for two reasons and now you shall find out what those reasons are.

What you told me last night was honorable. I know that's something that people don't go around broadcasting to just anyone. Remember I told you about my cousin who got killed? But what I didn't

*tell you was how he got killed. Well the police said
that they found him butt naked in a Howard Johnson Inn with a bullet in his head.*

Dee Dee's hands started to tremble when she
read that part of the letter. All of a sudden she felt
her stomach turn upside down. There was still more
to the letter, so she kept on reading.

*That was my flesh and blood, my first cousin,
and now he's gone. I know the game he was in is a
cutthroat business and had no rules to it, but he was
family. I knew your dreams were eating you up
from the inside out, but never would I have guessed
that you could pull a trigger. We as humans kill at
will and I too have done dirt and felt remorse, so
don't think any less about yourself than what you
have already put yourself through. When you told
me the story last night I got put between a rock and
hard spot. That man that you killed was my cousin,
Manny.*

There it was. The man Dee Dee killed was his
family. She couldn't believe her luck. Dee Dee didn't
wait another second, nor did she finish reading the
letter. She let it fall straight to the floor. She new
that Alastair couldn't stand to look her in the face
anymore, so she packed what she could and
bounced. If she would have read the rest of the letter she would have seen that the letter was telling
her it was over and to be out by the tine he got back.
When Alastair would return home he would see the
letter on the floor and know that his message was
conveyed.

Dee Dee cried her heart out all the way to Ronshay's crib. The nigga she was in love with was now gone, and she knew there was no way to make things right.

"Fuck the game," she shouted as a nice slow jam came on the radio. Dee Dee hurried up and cut the radio off for fear that if she turned it to another station it would just have another slow jam waiting to cause more hurt to the pain already deep inside her soul and heart.

Alastair came home and saw that Dee Dee's car was gone. He figured that she had gotten the message loud and clear. His heart was in his stomach, and already his world was crumbling down. Love was what he wanted, and the price he had to pay was severe. The choice he had to make was the right one, or else Dee Dee would have probably met the same horrible fate as Manny.

A few days had passed and Ronshay was talking on the phone to Bee, telling him about what his sister was going through. Dee Dee was sleeping in Ronshay's bed as Ronshay told Bee that she had been staying with her ever since the house had burned down. Bee told Ronshay that Dee Dee should have known better than to give her heart to some nigga. Ronshay stopped Bee right in his tracks.

"Then I guess I shouldn't have gave you my love and all then, 'cause I'm a female just like your sister. Dee Dee is in love and she was happy. I know that because I saw her smiling all day long. The boy treated her good just like she should have always been treated. And maybe if you and Jay wouldn't have been so overprotective of her, then just maybe Dee Dee could have found love a long time ago and experienced what hurt really felt like when the nigga that a female falls in love with leaves you!"

Bee didn't have any words in his mouth. He always thought of niggas as muthafuckas who just saw a fine female and tried everything in their power to fuck, including play the nice guy role. Bee didn't want Dee Dee to become what he and his brother Jay had made so many other black sistahs become— a piece of meat and nothing more. Bee knew a man had to fuck his way to the top in order to find that special someone. In the process of traveling that road, a lot of females got fucked over and nutted in, when all females wanted was someone to call their own.

"You right, baby. How she feeling?" Bee asked.

"Like I said, she's sleep and hurt, but whatever happened between her and Alastair got something to do with you and Jay!"

"What! How the fuck you figure that?" Bee asked in curiosity.

"Because all she kept saying is fuck my brothers. I shouldn't have never did what they asked me to do at that motel."

Bee asked Ronshay to go and wake Dee Dee up so he could holla at her about what happened. When Ronshay walked into the room she had the phone away from her ear as she woke Dee Dee. As a result, Ronshay couldn't hear the recorded voice when it interrupted Bee's call to say that the caller only had thirty seconds left to talk, nor could she hear Bee yelling for her to get back on the phone before it went dead. Dee Dee woke up and after a second she took the phone outta Ronshay's hand. When she put the phone to her ear all she heard was the busy tone where the caller on the other end had hung up a while ago.

"Here, Ronshay," Dee Dee said quietly as she handed the phone back to Ronshay.

"He wanna talk to you, not me, Dee Dee," Ronshay stated.

"Ain't nobody on the phone," Dee Dee told her, then laid back down.

Ronshay held the phone to her ear and heard the busy tone for herself. "He must've ran outta time before I woke you up."

Dee Dee's cell phone started ringing, but she didn't want to get up and get it outta her purse. Ronshay asked her if she was gonna get it and Dee Dee told her no. Ronshay walked over to the dresser and grabbed Dee Dee's purse, thinking that it could be Alastair calling to make up.

"Here, girl! Go on and answer it," Ronshay told her.

Dee Dee looked at the screen and saw it was a number that she didn't recognize. She was hoping that it was Alastair, but then again she figured that it probably wouldn't be him, 'cause after all, she did kill his cousin.

"Hello!" Dee Dee greeted.

"This is a collect call from a federal facility. The caller's name is Chills. Press five to accept or seven seven to block this number for good," the automated operator voice instructed. Dee Dee couldn't believe what she was hearing. She quickly pushed five and she heard Chills's voice say, "Hello."

"Chills, what the hell is you doing in there?" Dee Dee asked, waiting to hear the answer.

"Dee Dee, it's all bad."

"What's all bad? How much is your bond? I'll be there in a second."

"Dee Dee, slow your roll. There is no bond, and I ain't getting out for a long time, and neither is Tricksy or Diamond."

"What the fuck do you mean by that, Chills?"

Dee Dee listened very closely as Chills told her about what they had done. It was in their blood to rob banks, so they had hit another one up in Nashville. Dee Dee couldn't believe how Chills and the girls could be so stupid as to rob a fucking bank when they had it made. What Dee Dee didn't know or understand was the criminal mind. Criminals like the crimes they commit, so they get a rush when they commit that same crime again. It was in the girls' blood to want to see the muthafuckas who they was robbing scared ass faces when they showed those pistols.

"Listen, Dee Dee, you're a real down ass home-girl. As soon as your brothers get out, leave the game alone. It's not for you. There's nothing but rough roads and plenty of heartaches in the game. You're my nigga, Dee Dee! You're an R.B.M. chick for life, but now just be Dee Dee," Chills stated, then began to cry like the real female that she was.

Dee Dee could hear Chills letting the tears come down, but there was nothing she could do to console her home girl.

"Chills, you need anything?" Dee Dee asked.

"I'm not gonna say I need something, but if

you're ever thinking about me, just send me and the girls some flicks on a regular, some books, and some cash here and there so we can make it. Other than that, I'm gonna say goodbye."

"Wait, Chills! How am I gonna send you that stuff if I don't even know your address?"

"Just hook up with my moms. She'll hook it all up. Be cool, little sis. I love you." After those words Dee Dee didn't hear anything but a click, then silence.

Dee Dee explained to Ronshay what had just been told to her. She felt like everything was getting torn apart as fast as things were put together.

Eventually Dee Dee got back to doing her thang, and after she collected, she went over to her house so she could meet with the insurance man. She looked at what used to be her brothers' crib. The smell of burnt wood was still in the air. She looked around and saw that people in the neighborhood were still chilling like usual when she was there. She wondered why she hadn't seen Mikey on that little kid's bike yet, but then she remembered that she had taken him to rehab. She started to wonder about how he was doing, then she told herself that she wouldn't wonder anymore 'cause she was gonna get up there and see him this weekend.

As Dee Dee was looking around the rubble of debris, she noticed four cop cars and one plain, unmarked car pull onto the street in front of what used to be her crib. Dee Dee didn't know what was going on. She looked at the police coming her way. The plainclothes cops, who just so happened to be Perkins and Gary, led the way. Dee Dee walked toward them just to see what was up.

"Ma'am, is your name Deondra Davis, also known as Dee Dee?" Perkins asked.

"Yeah, that's me. Why? Did I do something wrong?" Dee Dee asked with her heart pumping fast.

"Ma'am, we need you to come down to the station with us so we can ask you some questions about a Manuel Stevens."

"Who? I don't know nobody by that name," Dee Dee said.

"Ma'am, can you please just come down to the station with us, and we can get this all straightened out," Gary said in a harsh tone.

As Dee Dee was being hauled down to the station, Jay and Bee were getting released from jail. The judge had finally dismissed their case.

Dee Dee sat in the interrogation room, looking at the two-way mirror. She still didn't know what the hell was going on.

Gary and Perkins walked through the door, and then closed it behind them. Gary had a brown folder in his hand, browsing through the contents inside. Perkins leaned back against the wall, with his arms folded and his eyes staring. It was hard for Perkins to imagine how a girl as cute as Dee Dee could be able to commit as heinous a crime as putting a bullet in a man's head.

"Ma'am, do you recognize this piece of paper and the handwriting on it?" Gary asked as he slid the piece of paper closer to her. Dee Dee stared at the paper with her old cell phone number on it. She was now starting to figure out that something was dreadfully wrong.

"Yeah. That's my handwriting and my old celly phone number," she stated.

"Well, would you mind telling us why this piece of paper was in the window of a room at a Howard Johnson Inn with the dead body of this man?" Gary asked as he placed the crime scene photo of Manny on the table in front of her.

Dee Dee was shocked to see the photo, but she knew she couldn't let them see her sweat, 'cause she now knew they were trying to hook her up with that shit in some form, shape, or fashion.

"I don't know. I've been to that motel before. You know, just getting my booty call on."

"Booty call? What's that?" Perkins asked with his hands now resting palms down on the table.

"Perkins, that's a street phrase for getting laid," Gary explained, being semi-fluent with ghetto slang.

"Ohhhh. I see. So you don't deny that you have been to that motel before."

"No, I don't. I just told you that I have," Dee Dee stated smartly.

"Ma'am, I find it kind of strange that we found your fingerprints on the window of the room that this man was found murdered in, along with this piece of paper with your name and number, written by you," Perkins interjected.

Dee Dee's mother's words hit her again before she opened her mouth and stuck her foot in it. "A wise woman thinks twice before even speaking once." Dee Dee looked at the two detectives and thought for a second. Her mother's words were coming in handy more and more as a reminder on how to be a wise, black female.

"Look, I don't mind y'all asking me questions about this poor man, but this stuff sounds serious enough that I think I should have an attorney present."

"So you want a lawyer here just to answer some of our questions?" Gary asked, trying to get her to keep talking without counsel present.

"Bingo!" Dee Dee shot back with a smile.

"If that's the way you wanna play, then let's play! You're under arrest for the murder of one Manuel Stevens. Now you gonna need that lawyer," Gary said in a raw dawg tone.

Dee Dee was pressed to use the phone. The heavy-set black chick that was on the phone was steady dialing the same fucking number and not getting in touch with anybody. The chick finally got tried of trying and hung up the phone angrily, slamming it on the hook. Dee Dee moved quickly to place a call to Ronshay.

"They charged you for what?!" Ronshay asked in a shocked voice.

"Yeah. This shit is crazy. I don't know what to do."

Dee Dee didn't know that her brothers were out of jail already, nor did she know that they were at Ronshay's house.

"Hold up for a sec, Dee Dee."

Jay took the phone from Ronshay. "Dee Dee!" Jay said.

"Jay! That's you? How the heck is y'all outta jail?" Dee Dee asked, shocked.

"Don't worry about all of that right now. Bee is on the other line right now talking to a hard hitter attorney. That shit ain't gonna stick at all."

"But Jay, I'm scared!" Dee Dee said.

"I know, little sis, but as soon as they set bail on Monday, you'll be out and we'll deal with this shit head up, all right?"

When Dee Dee heard the word bail, she felt better, but she would have to wait the weekend out in the nasty, overcrowded jail.

Bee grabbed the phone in excitement. He couldn't wait to tell his sister the good news about who was coming to see her.

"That's right, sis. He had a case load, so when I told him money wasn't a thang, he said, 'If that's no problem, then you should hire Mr. Johnny Cochran.' I was like, 'I would, if I could get in touch with him.' So the cat called J.C.'s secretary and plugged me in with the man. So don't worry, little sis. Those honkies ain't got shit on you, especially with big bad ass J.C. on the job," Bee exclaimed.

Dee Dee felt ten times better knowing "The Man, J.C." would plead her case. She knew that it would cost a lot for him to be retained, but she knew how much money was in the wall. She also had five thousand kilos in the wall, which was worth millions. Jay and Bee would have no problem taking care of business for a long time, but the business at hand was to get their sister free and outta jail.

Jay was told by Miya that Tony and everybody on the ranch, including Don Valdez, had been killed. Jay felt bad for Miya, but knowing what he did about Don Valdez and the rest being dead, and him and Bee having all that money and that dope with no one to pay back, they now had a straight jackpot goldmine.

Dee Dee was told she had a visitor. She got as cute as she could with what little she had to work with. The guard escorted her to the visiting room. Female inmates were allowed contact visits, which meant they didn't have to talk between a glass and use a germ infested telephone. She thought it was Ronshay who had come, but when she saw the familiar face, she was stunned. Mikey was smiling and looking good in his Rocawear blue denim suit.

"It's good to see you, Mikey," Dee Dee greeted with a warm hug. She still had her hands on him as she stepped back and looked him up and down. She liked his nice new, high fade haircut. He had also gotten four new piercings, so now he had three earrings in both ears.

"How you holding up?" Micky asked as they took their seats.

"I'm OK. How about you?"

"You tell me. If it wasn't for me getting cleaned up, I would still be doing bad as fuck."

Dee Dee couldn't believe that Mikey was looking as good as he was. She felt a feeling inside of her that made her just want to keep her hands on him. His appearance was hitting it, and even though she was in a fucked up predicament, it still felt good to look at her first love.

Mikey wanted to cry as he looked at the vulnerable Dee Dee, but he couldn't let her see him weak when she was being too strong with the mess she was in.

"Mikey, I shouldn't have ever got in the game. This shit fucked everything up. Nothing is going right," Dee Dee stated with her head now looking down.

"Dee Dee, it's not over. This is just the beginning. All this is doing is making you be able to see what you can really do, not what others want you to do," Mikey exclaimed.

"But I lost everything. My homegirls is locked up. Me and Alastair ain't together no more. I lost everything I love," Dee Dee stated with tears streaming down her face.

"You haven't lost me, girl. Matter of fact, you helped me find my old self. Dee Dee, maybe you don't want to hear this, but I love you. I always have and I always will till the day I die. The niggas that you been with didn't recognize your worth. I always knew your worth, that's why I'm in love with you," Mikey stated as he looked into her teary eyes.

Dee Dee was overwhelmed with joy from Mikey's heartfelt words. She had also always stayed deeply in love with Mikey.

"Dee Dee, I will go through this shit with you if you want me to. All you gotta do is be woman enough to just ask me to."

Dee Dee tightened her grip on Mikey's hands. She felt a strong vibe floating through their connected hands. She knew that what Mikey had just told her was true to the bond.

"Mikey, I would love for you to stand by my side if you will. If you can stay straight."

"Straight! Girl, don't you worry about me. Ain't nobody got time to be fucking around with that bullshit. You need me, and I gotta say I always needed you."

Dee Dee smiled and pulled Mikey in for a kiss. They kissed until the guard told them that visitation was over. Dee Dee left that room feeling loved by the only person she ever truly trusted.

Bee and Jay stood on the block rapping to the fellas. Everything was going smooth as they handled business around the clock. They saw some familiar fellas shooting dice down on the next block, so both thought they would give the niggas a chance to win some real cash if they were lucky enough. In Jay's mind, he always knew that if a nigga's cash flow wasn't long enough in the dice game, then he would be bankrupt in no time, 'cause the rule of shooting dice was that the big bank always took the little bank.

As Jay picked the dice up off the ground, a black Blazer rolled by. One of the two guys in the Blazer looked over at the cats kneeled down shooting craps. What really caught the driver's eye was the sight of Jay and Bee, the two muthafuckas with whom his homeboy had conflict. Jay and Bee weren't the most liked muthafuckas around.

The driver pulled his gat outta the glove compartment and laid it in his lap. He drove around the block and parked around the corner. His boy had told him a while ago that "the streets would be where his disrespect would take place," and here was the moment, as he had the two brothers in sight. He took a winter skullcap he used for making moves, and cut two eyeholes in it with his pocketknife. His heart was beating fast as his homeboy told him to handle up, but he didn't need any geeking up, 'cause he knew this was something he had to do.

The driver got out of the Blazer and peeked around the corner. He saw everybody was all into the dice game, so he made his move. Up close and undetected, he raised his gun and aimed. Two shots rang out, which made everybody on the block run and scurry for cover, except for the two bodies that lay on the ground with blood draining out of them.

Mail call came and Dee Dee received two letters. One was from Mikey, and one was from her mom, whom she hadn't spoken to or heard from in a while. Dee Dee read Mikey's letter first, hoping to receive some lovey dovey stuff inside like he'd been writing lately. Just like she thought, it was all good. Dee Dee knew that she would be happy with Mikey. For some reason she always knew that. She opened the other letter and began to read.

To My Daughter Deondra,
*   You are my only girl and now you are my only*
child!

Dee Dee didn't get that part, so she kept on reading to find out what her moms meant.

*   I tried to give you and your brothers a good life*
but y'all seem to have wanted what I worked so
hard to keep y'all protected from—the streets. My
eyes are filled with sorrow and my heart is filled

with pain. I cannot come see you while you are in there, just like I couldn't bring myself to visit your brothers while they was in there. Life is a strange thing. One minute we are here and the next thing you know, poof, we're gone. I know you probably don't know this, but my boys are no longer with us. Someone shot and killed them yesterday.

"Lord, no! Please don't let this be happening. Please, Lord. Please!" Dee Dee pleaded loudly. She didn't want to believe what her mother had written, but deep down inside she knew it had to be the truth.

"Deondra Davis, your lawyer is here to see you. I see all that dope money paid off if J.C., the big dawg of Tennessee lawyers, is asking to see his client, and that client is you," the guard said.

"Fuck some dope and fuck you, too. Fuck everybody. I hate this place. I hate my life," Dee Dee shouted as she cried. The guard just looked at Dee Dee as she remained kneeled down and continued to cry her heart out.

"If these muthafuckas want the real me to come out, then let's see if they can handle the baddest bitch to come and shake shit up in Memphis, 'cause now it's really on and poppin'."

About the Author

$\mathscr{A}$lastair J. Hatter, author of *It's On and Poppin'* and its sequel, The Baddest Chick, was born in Galveston, Texas. Back in the days growing up on Galveston Island, Alastair could not have foreseen how being an island boy would play an important role in his life. Dealing with many difficult lessons in life, the worst being his mom passing away in 1985, he found some serenity in going to the piers on the beach late at night and listening to the sea crash into the walls of the rock piers. Still feeling lost and like no one understood—or could understand—what he was going through, Alastair took to writing letters to his mom while seated on the pier. He would seal the letters in bottles and send them out to sea in hopes that his mother would reach down from heaven and retrieve them.

Alastair didn't really find out that he could write stories until he was completely down and out and searching for a new way to live his life. After writing a few novels and reading books that told him how he could get published, he submitted to several publishers. Rejections didn't deter him because he knew in his heart and soul that creating stories was his calling. For some reason seeing the book My Woman His Wife gave Alastair a good feeling. He felt that Anna J.'s publisher, Q-Boro Books, would be the perfect place to send his work. He then submitted some of his novels to the very talented Mark Anthony at Q-Boro and the rest is history. Alastair has turned his life around and found something that he absolutely loved to do as a career.

Alastair believes in never giving up on your dreams and always giving 110% till the end, the end being when you are in heaven with God.

Acknowledgements

*F*irst I give thanks and praise to My Father above for granting me this talent many shall be able to read. Lord, I praise you in the name of your son, Jesus.

A big thanks to my father, Herbert 'Big Duke' Hatter, & my mother, Bertha 'Tot' Hatter, for giving me life and raising me to be the man that I am today. Pop, mommy really loved you and so do we, your children and grandbabies. Mommy, we miss you! I miss you!

Now to a man who I no doubt know will break boundaries that others have not even seen or conquered yet. MARK ANTHONY, man! man! man! After talking to you on the phone, I knew that I was in good hands. I prayed to God to send me to a company that I could build with, and look where home is at. God knows both our hearts and that's why he put that idea in your head (you know what I'm talking bout) then guided me to submit to you. It is written and anytime it is written it's all good. I'm so glad that you started Q-Boro Books, my friend, cuz now you can receive all that is due to you. You made your own dream come true and you gave me a chance to make mines happen. I owe you brother, so for now I will start off by saying I loved *Paper Chasers*, *Dogism*, and your latest bonafide work of art, *Ladies Night*. Oh yeah, that measurement shit in *Dogism* is some real ass playa stuff. Men should be hip on the Measurement Game now. We needed that knowledge. Thanks To My Publisher, Mark. Word Up I'm indebted to you. Thanks! One hundred, cat Daddy!

To My Peeps (Q-Boro Family). Mannn . . . Y'all know what I felt when I got signed by Mark. The feeling is on real when someone believes in you and your work and they haven't seen anything but the work you sent in the mail. I read all y'all books and I must say that I am proud to say that y'all are ARTISTS, real storytellers. Its crazy how it takes us months to create a book but it takes a reader a couple of days to flow through one of our page turner. What's I'm saying is keep blazing the market so Mark can keep our pockets fat as his dream of becoming the dominant force in this game come to pass. I Got Mad Love 4 Y'all.

To my 'Super Mom' Linda Williams. Girrrlll . . . You are so crazy. You are the realest. You don't hold anything back. But what I like the most besides your humor and you keeping it krunk is your ability to tell what story is banging and what story ain't. I love your honesty and hard work ethic. When you tell me something whether constructive or destructive I will listen. For here on out just remember that you are my Super Mom so keep holding it down and thanks for opening your home to me. Much Love or shall I say I Love You Super Mom.

To Dolly Lopez, thanks or your comments on my books. That means a lot knowing that you loved the story. You are a real good lady. May God Bless You.

To the ladies who gave birth and raised my children, Enadina, thank you for Anthony. Christina, thank you for Aubrianna. Jada, thank you for Cedes, Lexy, and Atl. Kia, thank you for Alil. Tiffany, thank you for Ashley. Y'all deserve more said but I got y'all next go around, God Bless!

To my family: Marvin Willie Jobe, Rutha 'Rudy' Jobe, Bobby Jobe, Danny Jobe, Christina Hatter, Marcella Sally Ann Jobe, Albert Jobe, Herbert Len Hatter, Evette Jobe, Tina Jobe, Diane Jobe, Karen Jobe, Greg Dickerson, Samatha Hatter, Jada Hatter, Linda Hatter, and all of our kids. Nephews and Nieces: there's too many of y'all to name get on the next run, okay. Uncle Al loves y'all. Hatters and Jobes are running sh#t! and so is the Caffeys in Sandtown.

To Dianna 'Dreamy' Hatter. Yo, Dreamy I gave you that name cuz you was the girl that I always dreamed of having. You brightened my days to where I didn't need any light. You showed me that it was okay for a brother to let a female love me. You showed me that you wasn't a woman that was all about the Benjamin's. You made me realize the worth in you to where I cut all the other females loose. I love you with all my heart. I don't dwell on the past on what happen between us cuz the past is the past, feel me.

Christian Hatter. What is a brother to say? When I met you at the club that night you won me completely over. You rode with a brother before this deal popp'd off. I mean what I said and I will hold you dear to my heart. True love is to be recognized and respected. Love my aggressiveness and cherish my heart that I give to you, for that shall be the reason that we grow old together and stay happy as SOUL MATES. I love you dearly to where words can't describe, but I will always show you just how much each and everyday. You got me PRETTY BROWN. GOD BLESS.

To my Home-Girls. Dee Dee (G-Town), Shanay McCoy (Cleveland, OH), Liz Strausbaugh (Fremont, OH), Lenna Sabriana & Sparkles Banks (Toledo, OH), Michelle 'Me Me' Pleasant (G-Town), Leslie N. Smith (Fruit City, TX), Tosha Lockett (Texas City, TX), Angela Davis (G-Town), Bobby-Dale (Fremont, Oh), Tammy Mathews (Sandtown, OH), Nikki & Tiffany Chaney (Detroit), Stephanie Brown, Marie-Cathey-Maxine-Nikkie-Causwella Dickerson. Oopps and Shalisa Conway (Sandtown, OH), and LaDonna Shorter (Toledo, OH). Nikkie Watson (Sand-Town where are you, girl), Simona aka Mona, April, and the other sis (Texas City by way of G-Town), Alquetta (G-Town), Christana Hall aka Chip and your sister and that cute lil' girl of hers. Ms. Fontenote, take care of her (G-Town). Laquetta LaFleur (Beaumont, Tx), Cynthia Tarr, thanks for being there for me like a real friend Mardie Gras 06' is on me (G-Town). Felicia Johnson what can I say. You held me down and for that I will always love you along with what I always told you. You are dear to my heart, baby girl. I don't need to say no more (G-Town), Ronnette Wingate (G-Town), Margaret Ali, Lady I cannot begin to express my gratitude towards you. Sometimes people can be blind to the fact and sometimes we can have our eyes wide open and still not see what's good for us. I never stopped caring, but know that I wish you much happiness in life (Fremont, OH), Crystal Walker-What's up shorty. Hold it down, okay (Fremont, OH)

To all the fellas: Taj Wood, my brother of another color, Elih Abad, my brother who's true. Derrick Arrington, my road dawg since 5th grade. Derrick 'Sincere' Patterson, you was always there through the ruff time. Devin Young, my OG and friend, thanks for being there/for listening to me on all subjects. M. Avery Johnson, author of *Politics-Population-Prison-Plantations*. You, homie, gave me game on the book world. It's my pleasure to call you a friend. Gaylin 'Gator' Johnson, author of *Deepa Than Tha Beepa*. You know what it is. We shared stories, so blaze the market with me. Melvin "Big Flava Adams, man look at the book now. Thanks for the RBM Clique and the support. Alex Walker, no more struggling. Thanks brah. Terrance Allwood, you my dawg. Darrell Rhett, thanks for the encouraging talks. Jermain Ward, what's up big boy? Stephen 'Big Show' Sutton, homie I got this and that dime piece we joke about. James "Big Red" Wedgeworth, the nicest white man or any man that I ever met. Thanks big guy. We are friends. Lamont Washington outta Elyria, Ohio. Perry Perry Cherry, God is going to unite you and your kids. Keep the Christian Glow going.

To Ms. Ethel Mueller you are God sent. You did so much for me and the tripped-out thing is that you never met me once which is the overwhelming part. Jim Mueller, I can see where you get your kind heart from. Like mother like son, huh?

To all the struggling artists out there that's trying to get your work recognized: I know your struggle cuz before I was discovered I was where you are. One thing to say. Keep your head up. Stay focus. And never give up. One day your name will be called to showcase your work, and you know you gotta be ready to step up to the plate. Keep submitting and submitting, cuz I did. Stay up. God Bless.

To all the black bookstores across the US. Thank you for the support. To all the book vendors holding it down on the corners across the US. I owe y'all for pushing my books. And last but not least, thanks a million to my readers and fans. Y'all made this happen and know that I started this without cash so cash ain't gonna make me get brand new on my writing and turn y'all off. I'm gonna keep dropping hot sh#t for y'all for years to come, cuz I'm here to stay to blaze the market. Once again know that I am humble to y'all so peace and love be unto y'all and y'all families. ONE in the name of Jesus!

PREVIEW

The Baddest Chick
The Sequel to It's On and Poppin'
Coming in July 2007 from Urban Books

The day was gloomy and the clouds in the sky were dark and gray. All who were present at Jay and Bee's funeral were crying and holding onto each other for comfort.

Dee Dee sat next to her mother outside in the front row seats in front of her brothers' open caskets. Assorted flower arrangements and different sized wreaths decorated the gravesite. Miya and Ronshay sat on the opposite side of Dee Dee, both crying away. Today was truly a sad day for all who were connected to the two brothers who lay in their caskets ready to be buried six feet deep.

Pastor Troy went on with his sermon, stressing that Jay and Bee had been called back home to the sky above to be with God. As he preached, the ten-person choir sang softly. The whole service was beautiful, but it was all too much for Dee Dee to bear.

Memories of her brothers started bombarding her mind, taking her into serious thought of how she got mad at the overprotective ways her brothers would dish out on any guy that said something to her; who tried to touch her; who got caught looking at her wrong. She wished that she had her brothers here now to do the things that used to piss her off so much back then.

Dee Dee stood up with tears falling from her eyes. The black dress she had on with her cashmere trench coat was lightly swaying from the autumn wind that was blowing. Her hair was laid down straight. She walked over to Jay's oak wood casket, which was draped inside with red silk. Jay looked like he wasn't dead at all, but more like he was asleep. The mortuary had done a lovely job on their faces to make them look that way. After all, they were shot at point-blank range in the head, sending their brain and skull fragments here and there.

Dee Dee leaned over and kissed Jay on his forehead, and then told him that she would see him again. She promised him that before she met back up with him and Bee, she would get the bitch ass muthafucka that got them, no matter what.

After that, she laid three of the roses on his chest, then patted them, telling him to look out for her when she couldn't.

Next, she went to Bee's oak casket. The black Gucci suits that she had picked out for them to be buried in did both true justice, as they looked like they were ready to step out on the town.

Dee Dee looked back as she heard Ronshay cry out loud. It was truly obvious she was taking it hard. Since the incident, Ronshay had changed. She was no longer the happy-go-lucky female that Dee Dee knew. Now all she did was mope around as if she were dying. She had big dreams for her and Bee, but now she couldn't see anything without him being around. What she had for Bee, was true love—love that couldn't die. Ronshay wasn't in her right state of mind anymore, but no one was able to see the trouble that would soon come around.

Dee Dee took the last three roses and placed them in the same place on Bee as she did with Jay. She leaned her head into the casket and gave him a kiss, telling him that whoever did this to them would pay with their life, and that she meant it.

As Dee Dee walked away crying while the service was still going on, her mother looked at her, wondering what fate lay in wait for her only child left. She wanted to go after the daughter she had birthed, but she remained stern like she always had since her Dee Dee chose to be a grown woman and move out. She just closed her eyes and let her tears fall with the sheer black veil hanging down in front of her face so no one would notice. She then gave a silent prayer for all of her children to be kept safe in Almighty God's hands.

After the funeral, Dee Dee drove around on the expressway in her H-2, zoned out and not knowing where she was headed. For a moment her tears had taken a break, and by then, God knows her eyes needed it. They were too bloodshot already, not to mention that the bags under her eyes were starting to look bad. As she was driving, the blaring sirens on the police car that just flew past her broke her sad thoughts and made her think about what she was going to do with the dope she had, 'cause it was plenty.

Before Jay and Bee were killed, they told Dee

Dee all about Tony and Don Valdez getting killed.
Since she now had no one to pay back, she was a
rich muthafucka, even though she didn't feel like it.
But the bottom line was she was the sole beneficiary
of her brothers' estate and belongings.

Dee whipped her Hummer H-2 around in the
middle of traffic as she busted a U-turn. The action
behind her driving recklessly like she did was to
head back to the safe house and check things out
since she hadn't been there since she got released.
She figured if she was gonna find out who killed her
brothers, she was gonna have to become one with
the streets again.

Her mission was to get back in the game, shake
shit up, and pump the dope. While she was doing
that, she would seek out her brothers' killer or
killers involved. She knew that she had to step her
game up and take it to the next level, which was the
only way that she could become the baddest bitch
that ever hit the streets of Memphis.

More titles from Q-Boro Books

Talk to the Hand by Darrien Lee—October 2006
$14.95
ISBN 0977624765

Nedra Harris, a twenty-three year old business executive, has experienced her share of heartache in her quest to find a soul mate. Just when she's about to give up on love, she runs into Simeon Mathews, a gentleman she met in college years earlier. She remembers his warm smile and charming nature, but soon finds out that Simeon possesses a dark side that will eventually make her life a living hell.

Someone Else's Puddin' by Samuel L. Hair—December 2006
$14.95
ISBN 0977624706

While hairstylist Melody Pullman has no problem keeping clients in her chair, she can't keep her bills paid once her crack-addicted husband Big Steve steps through a revolving door leading in and out of prison. She soon finds what seems to be a sexual and financial solution when she becomes involved with her long-time client's husband, Larry.

Poison Ivy by Travis Vp. Fox—November 2006
$14.95
ISBN 0977733521

Ivy Davidson's life has been filled with sorrow. Her father was brutally murdered and she was forced to watch, she faced years of abuse at the hands of those she trusted, and was forced to live apart from the only source of love that she has ever known. Now Ivy stands alone at the crossroads of life staring into the eyes of the man that holds her final choice of life or death in his hands.

Nympho by Andrea Blackstone—May 2007
$14.95
ISBN 1933967102

How will signing up to live a promiscuous double-life destroy everything that's at stake in the lives of two close couples? Take a journey into Leslie's secret world and prepare for a twisted, erotic experience.

Get Money Chicks by Anna J.—September 2007
$14.95
ISBN 1-933967-17-X

For Mina, Shanna, and Karen, using what they had to get what they wanted was always an option. Best friends since day one, they always had a thing for the hottest gear, luxurious lifestyles, and the ballers who made it all possible. All of this changes for Mina when a tragedy makes her open her eyes to the way she's living. Peer pressure and loyalty to her girls collide with her own morality, sending Mina into a no-win situation.

Freak in the Sheets by Madame K—September 2007
$14.95
ISBN 1933967196

Librarian Raquelle decides to put her knowledge of sexuality to use and open up a "freak" school, teaching men and women how to please their lovers beyond belief while enjoying themselves in the process. But trouble brews when a surprise pupil shows up and everything Raquelle has worked for comes under fire.

Attention Writers:

Writers looking to get their books published can view our submission guidelines by visiting our website at:
www.QBOROBOOKS.com

What we're looking for: Contemporary fiction in the tradition of Darrien Lee, Carl Weber, Anna J., Zane, Mary B. Morrison, Noire, Lolita Files, etc; groundbreaking mainstream contemporary fiction.

We prefer email submissions to: candace@qborobooks.com in MS Word, PDF, or rtf format only. However, if you wish to send the submission via snail mail, you can send it to:

Q-BORO BOOKS Acquisitions Department
165-41A Baisley Blvd., Suite 4. Mall #1
Jamaica, New York 11434

*** By submitting your work to Q-Boro Books, you agree to hold Q-Boro books harmless and not liable for publishing similar works as yours that we may already be considering or may consider in the future. ***

1. Submissions will not be returned.
2. Do not contact us for status updates. If we are interested in receiving your full manuscript, we will contact you via email or telephone.
3. Do not submit if the entire manuscript is not complete.

Due to the heavy volume of submissions, if these requirements are not followed, we will not be able to process your submission.